Rustler's Bride

Anne Manning

Hard Shell Word Factory

Dedicated...
To Kathy Faleris, my first reader, my dear friend, for her support, encouragement, thoughtful comments, not only on ***Rustler's Bride***, but on all my work. You are the best boss anyone could have, Katya.
To "Jake." For the inspiration.

Heartfelt thanks...
To Kathryne Overton, my friend, critique partner, fount of information and insight. To the EPICureans, a circle of support unparalleled. To Christine Gee, a superb editor whose careful eye has made this book better than I ever hoped.
To Mary Wolf, a wise, wonderful woman and publisher.
To my children for their patience.
To my husband, David,
as always. I couldn't have done this without you.

ISBN: 0-7599-0268-2
Trade Paperback
Published November 2002
© 1998 Anne Manning
Ebook ISBN: 1-58200-055-7
Published November 1998

Hard Shell Word Factory
PO Box 161
Amherst Jct. WI 54407
books@hardshell.com
http://www.hardshell.com
All electronic rights reserved.

All characters in this book have no existence outside the imagination of the author, and have no relation whatsoever to anyone bearing the same name or names. These characters are not even distantly inspired by any individual known or unknown to the author, and all incidents are pure invention.

Prologue

July 1871 - The Indian Territory

JAKE BOWMAN came to, face down in a puddle of coppery-smelling mud. His head throbbed as if a smith were banging him into shape on an anvil. When he moved, the fire in his right shoulder stopped him.

Two figures lay near him, still. Too still. He struggled to focus his eyes, then wished he hadn't woken up.

Cold, like a wave of freezing water, washed over him. The nearer of the two was the owner of this property, his former employer. Randall Tall Trees lay in a pool of her own blood in her dusty front yard, her brand-new Winchester rifle by her side.

It all came back then....

They had ridden up and Randall, when she saw Jake and Sam with the men, lowered her rifle.

Wil had drawn and shot her dead.

Jake had sat like a fool while Randall's daughter, Nancy, ran out to weep over her mother's body.

He squeezed his eyes shut. He'd sat there on his tall palomino, hearing, but not really understanding the scene playing around him. All he could see was Randall's accusing stare as she lay there in the dirt.

The charge was as loud as if she were shouting it.

You brought these men here, Jake? Why would you?

He was guilty. Jake reached the verdict with little deliberation. He'd come along, knowing what Wil had wanted. Even the fact that he and Sam had come to try to prevent this didn't make his guilt any less damning.

"We'll relieve them Injun squaws of the responsibility of all those cattle," Wil had said.

When the boys had seen Nancy, the cattle were no longer enough.

"Shall we have a little bit of fun, boys?" Wil had asked.

Jake's Colt Navy revolver nuzzled the back of Wil's head before Jake even realized he'd been thinking about it.

"No, Wil," he said.

"You won't kill me, Jake."

"No?" Jake pulled back the hammer on the piece.

Wil's eyes cut to the left, toward Jake, and he chuckled softly.

"No. You're a lawman deep down inside. You wouldn't kill me like this."

"I won't let you hurt her anymore, Wil."

Wil leaned away from the muzzle of Jake's gun and looked around.

"Jake, observe," he said with a sweep of his hand.

Five guns were trained on Jake's head. These old boys weren't especially good shots, but a couple of them had new double-action revolvers and could put six bullets somewhere in his carcass in a matter of seconds.

"I won't let you hurt her anymore, Wil," he repeated, his voice low.

"Then shoot, Jake. Because I'm getting down off this horse right now and I aim to ride that squaw until she spits blood."

Nancy turned pale under her smooth, copper-brown skin and fell to the ground.

Jake didn't know, wouldn't ever find out, if Wil had simply moved at a convenient moment or if he'd made a signal to the boys on his right, and it didn't matter, either, as the report of the rifle shot echoed across the yard.

Pain slammed into his shoulder. The Navy revolver went flying as he fell from his horse. Beau skittered. His ears flat against his head. Jake rolled away from the iron-shod hooves, teeth clenched against the pain in his useless arm.

"Run, Nancy," he croaked.

Sam put himself between her and the gang, raising the revolver in his left hand and picking off two of the riders. An instant later, another crackling report sent Sam to the ground, blood pouring from his left arm, just above the elbow. One man kicked his horse and took off after Nancy. He scooped her up and tossed her across his saddle. She kicked and screamed, but he held her until he'd returned to Wil, now dismounted, where he threw her on the ground.

Jake crawled toward Randall's body, toward her rifle.

"Don't let him get that rifle," Wil shouted in warning.

Bullets flew like bluebottle flies around his head.

Damn, I hadn't wanted to die like this. Even Point Lookout would have been better, he thought, remembering for an instant the horror of two years at that Yankee prison camp.

At least then I still had my honor.

He froze at the sudden silence. The shooting had stopped. The screaming and yelling had stopped.

Jake raised his head from the dirt and focused on Sam struggling, face distorted with pain, to escape the grip of two remaining members of the gang. The one on his left side twisted his injured arm behind him. His face turned a pasty gray, but not a sound escaped Sam's lips.

Jesus, not his shooting arm, Jake begged.

"Sammy, you killed your partners," Wil said as he approached. "Tie him to that tree over there. Let him watch, since he doesn't seem willing to participate."

The men laughed and dragged Sam between them toward the tree. He was making a powerful lot of noise and Jake realized through his haziness that he was creating a diversion so Jake could do something.

Randall's rifle was just out of his reach.

Jake stretched his healthy arm.

"No, no, Jake," Wil said, sweeping the weapon away with a quick kick. "Can't have you interfering with the party." Laughing, he swung Nancy around in front of him, his big hand wrapped around her thin wrist.

"Please," she begged, her sweet voice nearly inaudible over Sam's yelling and cursing as Wil's men tied him, "you're hurting me."

Derisive laughter answered her plea.

"Sweetpea, whether I hurt you more is very much your choice." Wil stroked her cheek with tenderness that turned Jake's stomach.

"Take your hands off her, Wil," Sam shouted, getting a backhand in reply. "I'll kill you, Wil. I swear, I'll kill you."

"Sure, Sam. Sure." Wil guided Nancy's hand to his fly. "Do a good job, Sweetpea, and maybe I'll keep you for myself."

Tears filled the brown eyes that first sought out Sam, then Jake.

The tears, big, round, heavy tears, spilled over her eyelids and plopped into the dirt in front of him, defying him to look away. But Jake couldn't face her and, cursing himself for his weakness, he rested his head on his arm. A pointy-toed boot shoved against his shoulder, turning him over onto his back. He stifled a moan. The pain had dulled to a throb, but he still couldn't move his arm.

"See, Jake. I told you. You can't kill me. I'm a better man than you. No matter what my daddy said." Wil fondled the girl's budding body. "Daddy always tried to make you out such a big man. Jake did this and Jake did that. He wouldn't think much of you now, would he, Jake?"

Jake didn't reply. What could he say? He wasn't exactly a model citizen anymore. Nope, he'd pretty much ruined his entire life and right this instant he didn't give a good goddamn if Wil put a bullet in his brainpan.

"So, Wil," he taunted, hoping to God he wouldn't have to see what was going to happen. He couldn't stop them. He was helpless now, unable to even raise a gun. "Stop blowing like a bull at green corn time and get the hell on with it." Jake locked his gaze with his cousin's, because he couldn't bear to look into Nancy's. "Come on, Wil. If you have the guts."

Wil's face blossomed a deep red. "Why waste a bullet on you?"

Stars exploded in Jake's head as the toe of Wil's boot cut across his head. His blood, warm and thick, trickled across his brow. An instant later, a second blow sent him to the blessed land of unconsciousness....

Mind clearing, he struggled to raise up so he could see.

"Oh, God," he muttered, his eyes clouding with tears of anger and self-hatred. "You should have stopped him, Jake. You could have stopped him." He crawled over to Randall. "I'm sorry, ma'am." He closed her eyes, partly out of respect for her, partly because he couldn't bear to see the accusation in them. He glanced over at Nancy, then turned quickly away. She was sprawled, dress up around her waist, just like she'd been when the last man had gotten off her. She'd died under him, like a used-up whore.

Somehow, sometime, Wil is going to pay for this night's work.

Jake let his aching eyes move across the yard. His brother was still tied to the tree, head hanging onto his breast. He feared the worst, until he heard Sam's muffled sobs.

Jake wanted to cut Sam down, but he was spent. He couldn't do anything to help anybody. He rolled onto his back. He hurt all over and could feel his lifeblood seeping from his body. Wil had wasted that extra bullet on him after all. Somewhere in his middle. He was gut-shot.

Well, then, that's that. He accepted it. He had earned it.

Opening his eyes, he looked up to the starry, early morning sky, up where the preachers said God was. The sky lightened as he lay there, just looking, wondering how his soul would be carried away. Mama had told him about the angels coming to get him to carry him to Jesus. He chuckled weakly. Jesus wouldn't want him, now.

Then as his eyes closed for the last time, he felt gentle hands lift him. Maybe Jesus did still want him. His soul took comfort from the thought.

"I'm coming, Mama," he whispered.

Chapter One

Travis City, Texas
February 1872

Martha MacLannon pulled her shawl tighter around her shoulders and stared at the heavy doors of Butler's Mercantile, wishing she had somewhere else to go.

"Don't be a coward, Martha. Get it over with." Drawing a deep breath, she straightened her shoulders and walked in.

While her eyes adjusted to the dimmer light inside, she wrinkled her nose at the stifling mustiness inside the store, an atmosphere Martha couldn't recall from her childhood memories. It had been her favorite place in Travis City, and the smells had especially delighted her. Now, the store no longer breathed with the fragrance of fancy French toilet water or fresh apples or new leather. The mercantile wasn't the only thing that had changed in the last twelve years.

Two old men sat by the front window, playing a game of checkers that had gone on uninterrupted for thirty years. They nodded and tipped their battered hats as she passed them. At least some things haven't changed. She smiled at the grizzled sportsmen and congratulated them silently for holding on to what they loved.

Halfway down the middle aisle, her sister was already touching and examining everything she saw. Martha smiled and wished she could get as excited about shopping as Mary did, but the fun of it disappeared when there was no money.

She followed Mary down the too-narrow aisle, formed by long tables bowing under the mountains of blue denim pants and cotton shirts in a rainbow of colors and bolts of fabric from the mills in the north. There was an absurdity -- no, she corrected herself, an obscenity -- about it all. So many men dead, and here we are going on just like before, like it never even happened.

Well, almost like before. Things could never be like they were before the war.

"I guess we'd better get on with our business," Martha whispered as she stopped beside her sister, anxious to go home.

Mary sighed. "I sure wish we had some extra money. I need a new dress. Do you suppose Clarissa will extend our credit?"

Martha had worried all night how much further her credit would stretch. Glancing toward the front of the store, she caught the proprietor's buxom wife watching her.

"I don't know, but I'll bet that woman is just waiting to tell everyone how bad off we are. I can't believe my luck in running into her at the tax office last week." She sighed heavily. "Let's look around some more. Maybe she'll leave soon for dinner and we can talk to Mr. Butler."

So Martha wandered behind Mary, up one aisle and down another, looking at merchandise they had no way to pay for. At the back of the store, before a display of the brand new pointy-toed, high-heeled boots cowboys all seemed to love nowadays, two men crouched, blocking the narrow walkway.

"Excuse me, please," Martha said as she squeezed by them.

The men straightened up, giving her room to pass. They were tall men, trail worn and covered with dust.

"Not at all, ma'am," a smooth, soft voice replied.

Martha looked up, way, way up, into the face of the man who had spoken and was caught in eyes of deep twilight blue under dark, straight brows that dipped slightly on the outside corners. Those eyes were somehow familiar. Looking more closely at his face, she tried to decide if she knew him.

He smiled at her. She was sure he did, though his heavy beard hid any movement of his lips.

"Thank you," she croaked and hurried on by him. But she could feel those eyes following her up toward the front of the store.

Mary caught up. "I wonder what they'd look like all cleaned up?" she whispered, glancing back, none too subtly.

The cowboy's chuckle at Mary's indiscretion caused Martha to laugh in spite of herself.

"Mary Ellen, you are so bad." Martha felt her spirit rise from the chilly, gray place where it usually dwelt. There was far too little to laugh at lately. But even as she enjoyed the warmth of the feeling, she caught a different pair of eyes, those of Clarissa Butler, following her. Clarissa quickly cut her eyes back to the pile of money she was counting, pretending, of course, that she wasn't watching. Martha's mirth faded. This was not going to be a good trip to town.

Deciding she could delay it no longer, Martha walked up to the counter and waited for Clarissa's acknowledgment. Clarissa kept her eyes on the growing pile of money in front of her, pointedly ignoring her customer. Raising an eyebrow in irritation -- a bad habit her mother had tried in vain to curb -- Martha dropped her reticule on the counter, scattering the precious pile of paper money.

"Perhaps, Clarissa, if you don't want my business, I should take it elsewhere."

Martha heard Mary's skirts swishing as she hurried to stand by her elbow.

"Molly, I could hear you back by the shoes," Mary warned in a whisper.

Oh, sugar, Martha thought, chagrined that she was about to make a scene. And it had been such a promising morning.

THE TALL COWBOY heard the little woman's offer to take her business elsewhere and he stood up from his crouch to turn toward the sound of her voice.

"You do as you think best, Martha," the woman behind the counter replied.

So, her name's Martha. He liked it. It was a strong name, a pretty name. Somehow, he knew it suited her.

The proprietor rushed by to get to the front of the store, his face wrinkled in worry.

Looks like too good a show to miss. The cowboy followed. The shopkeeper slipped behind the counter as the cowboy crossed his arms and leaned against the display of pocket knives where he could watch.

The view wasn't bad. The small woman standing in front of the counter wasn't much more than five feet tall. However, unlike a lot of short women he'd seen, she was perfectly proportioned. When she'd passed him back at the boots, he'd been favored with a look at her perfectly oval face, perfectly smooth, peachy skin, perfectly straight nose that was just the right size, perfectly full, sweet lips. All that perfection was topped by golden blonde hair she had carefully hidden under her hat, except for a couple of wayward, wavy tendrils that gave away her secret.

"Your account is overdue." The woman behind the counter narrowed her eyes. "We aren't a charity institution. You must understand we have to be careful to only extend credit to those who will be able to pay."

Martha looked her accuser right in the eye.

"Our account is no more than any other rancher has here." Her voice carried not a single quiver, but it did carry all over the store. "Now, Clarissa, do you want my business, or should I take it over to

Austin?"

"Why, Miss MacLannon, of course we want your business." Butler interrupted his wife before she could say anything more. The harpy behind the counter rewarded him with a withering look. Wearing a tired smile, he turned toward Martha.

"Thank you, Mr. Butler," Martha said. "Here's my list. Could you have it loaded in my buggy?"

"Now, wait just a minute, both of you." Clarissa turned to her husband. "Conrad, I can't believe you're going to extend her credit. She'll never be able to pay."

Butler shifted from foot to foot, then raised his beaten-dog eyes to Martha.

"I'm sorry, Miss MacLannon, but your troubles are well known around town." He spread his hands in a little gesture of helplessness.

The cowboy dared a peek at Martha's face. Her lips had tightened into a thin line and her eyes were narrowed. A lot of fire and spit in this one, he thought. A lot of woman. He hoped his beard would hide the smile he could no longer suppress. It wouldn't do for her to think he found her amusing.

"Now, Miss Martha," the shopkeeper began.

"Don't you 'now, Miss Martha' me, Conrad Butler." Her voice started out low, but everyone in the small building had already gathered round. "My father did business with this store for forty years before you and your carpetbagger wife came out here. Now you have the nerve to decide MacLannon business isn't good enough for you."

"Just one minute, Martha. You can't talk to us that way," Clarissa said. "It's fair for us to ask how you propose to pay when you're not making a drive this year. Where are you going to get the money to meet your obligations?"

"Who said we're not making a drive this year?" Martha asked, her voice low.

"All your hired hands are gone and you don't have any menfolk to get the cows to market. The whole county knows you only just made your tax payment at the last minute." Clarissa looked around, making sure that her audience had heard every word. She seemed to enjoy making this news public to any who didn't know it yet. "Why you're hanging onto that ranch is beyond me, especially when you have the chance to marry and become a decent woman."

Marry? The thought of her being another man's wife bothered the cowboy. The fact it bothered him bothered him even more.

"Molly, let's go." A younger woman laid her hand on Martha's arm to calm her down. But it seemed Martha'd had enough of this overbearing, self-important, Yankee carpetbagger hag. She shook off the gentle, restraining hand.

"You Yankees have some nerve calling me indecent. You come here and buy up everything for a pittance from people who worked all their lives to build something for their children. As for my getting married, that's none of your business. My father came out here with Stephen Austin and he fought for this land. He and my brothers all laid down their lives for this land. It's all I have left of him and I'll do anything I must to keep it." She looked Clarissa Butler right in the eye. "What did you ever have to fight for, Clarissa?"

"Molly, please." Her sister's hand was back on her arm, this time with effect.

Never taking her eyes off the storekeeper's wife, Martha nodded. Gathering her dignity and her heavy wrap around her, she turned with deliberate slowness and went through the door and out onto the street.

He heard a few voices, mostly approving.

"Little Martha sure 'nuf put Miz Hoidy-Toidy in her place, didn't she?" whispered one of the wizened checker players.

His opponent jumped a king and shook his head. "Yep, but Miz Butler is just a Yankee. 'Spect she don't know how to act proper. Martha's mama and daddy brung her up better."

Mrs. Butler didn't hear this last comment. She was still fuming.

"Conrad! Are you just going to let her get away with that?"

"With what? We are Yankees, and I for one, am proud of it." He turned to his wife and continued in a tired voice. "Do you want me to run after her and call her out?"

The cowboy approached the counter.

"I'll tell you what," he said with a chuckle, "I'd think twice before I called that woman out."

"Humph!" Clarissa remarked as she resumed her counting.

Butler laughed. "You'd be smart not to, stranger. What'll it be?"

"Eight ounces of tobacco," he answered, handing Butler two leather pouches.

Conrad measured out the tobacco and divided it between the two pouches. "Anything else?"

"Well, I was looking at your boots back there, but I believe they'll have to wait." He handed Conrad what he owed and took his tobacco. "Know of any ranches hiring hereabouts?"

Conrad considered for a moment.

"Not unless Garret is hiring."

"Garret? I don't believe I've ever heard of a 'Garret Ranch'." He sniffed his tobacco before pulling the draw string shut. "Has he been in these parts long?"

"Nope, showed up late last summer. Said he was relocating from up 'round Dallas. Came in with plenty of money, too. Bought up a big ranch to the east of town."

"What about Miss, what was her name, MacLannon? Where are her menfolk?"

Butler shook his head in sympathy. "All her family, her father and every one of her five brothers, got killed in the war. From what I've heard, they fell one right after the other. Her mother withered away from grief. So, now, it's just Martha and her younger sister. You can ask her, but it's true what my wife said. Miss MacLannon is somewhat cash-poor, right now."

"What happened to all her hands?"

"She sure has had a run of the worst kind of luck. Last year's drive wasn't much for anybody, with the rains and all, and Miss MacLannon got hit worse than most. Then, in October, somebody started taking shots at her men. It was mostly a nuisance until just before Christmas, when whoever it was got her foreman. Two days later, the old German she had cooking for her men was hanged in the tree in front of her house. The few hands she had left quit after that. She and her sister had to bring old Otto into the undertaker."

The thought of her dealing with a corpse chilled him. "Sounds like the little lady has had a mighty bad time."

Clarissa huffed. "She wouldn't be having such a bad time if she'd do the sensible thing and marry Mr. Garret and hand over the running of that ranch to a man."

He stifled his reaction and only raised an eyebrow. "So, Mr. Garret is courting her? Tell the truth, I was wondering why such a handsome lady isn't already married."

A reedy thin woman, dressed in brown and looking for all the world like a sparrow, came up to the counter to put in her two-cent's-worth.

"It's her own fault Martha has no husband. She had plenty of offers and thought she was too good for any of them. If her father had done his duty by her, she'd have been married well before the start of the war." The woman tipped her sparrow-like head. "In my opinion, her parents indulged her too much. She finally accepted my brother's suit, but she put him off for so long, he had to go off to war without even the comfort of knowing he'd leave his name behind."

Clarissa looked heavenward. "Please, Esther." She turned to the cowboy. "Mr. Garret is courting Martha, though why he'd want to wed such a complete harridan is beyond me. Especially when there are so many other younger women who would make more pleasant mates to a man with Mr. Garret's responsibilities."

He didn't allow his irritation with this spiteful woman to show. "Still seems like Miss MacLannon might be able to use a couple of good hands."

"You're wasting your time. She won't be able to pay you."

"Thank you for the advice, ma'am." He turned to Esther and tipped his hat. "And thank you, too, Miss." Giving her what his mother had always called his politician's smile, he left her blushing and giggling.

He left the store and stood with his silent companion on the rough-hewn boards of the walk. Martha MacLannon was rounding the bend out of town.

"Well, what do you think, Sam?"

"I think the situation is tailor-made for our purposes, Jake."

Jake Bowman nodded. "So do I."

"PULL THE BACK rope tighter, Mary. He's still squirming too much. I can't get the iron down on him."

Mary tossed her hair back and glared, before pulling with all her strength on the rope. "Just do it, will you?"

Martha took a deep breath and rammed the iron home, turning her head and trying not to hear the pitiful cries of the calf as the intertwined A-A -- from her parents' first names -- marked the animal as Double A stock. The stench of burning hair and searing cowhide made her stomach twist in knots. Swallowing the bile in her throat, she dropped the branding iron back into the fire and rubbed her lower back before mounting Mary's big gelding.

She turned the horse toward the corral. Selecting her next victim, she circled the lasso over her head a couple of times and threw it. It dropped cleanly over the calf's head. Looping the tail of the lasso in a few efficient dallies around the saddle horn, she let the rope tighten.

"Come on, Chief, back," she cooed as she backed him away from the narrow gate, pulling the calf closer to the fire.

Mary snared the calf's back feet and pulled the rope taut around a fencepost. After securing it, she pushed the calf over onto his side and tied his front feet together using a shorter length. Chief held the calf's head with a steady backward pull.

"Stay, Chief," Martha commanded the horse. Then she dismounted and said wearily to Mary, "This is the last one for today."

Martha's shoulders ached and her back felt as though it would never completely straighten. She wiped the sweat from her brow with the back of her hand and shoved the tendrils of hair that had escaped from her old felt hat back into their confinement. With a silent hope she would have the strength to bring in water for a bath, she reached for the iron.

"Molly," Mary's voice came in a low warning. "Visitors."

Martha let the iron fall back into the fire as she looked up to see two riders coming from the main road. Mary was already at her back with their weapons, necessary protection for two women living alone. Reaching behind her, Martha accepted her Henry rifle from her sister's hand. Mary stood easily, her own double-barreled shotgun resting in her arms. Martha let the barrel of her rifle drop toward the ground, a sign of guarded welcome to their unexpected company.

The riders were mounted on two nondescript cow ponies. Trotting a little ahead of them was an enormous, grizzled, gray dog, flappy ears slapping time to his gait. The men reined in their mounts a few yards away, close enough to hear the words that were out of her mouth before she could stop them.

"That is the ugliest dog I have ever seen."

One of the men, with a bushy beard and wearing a coat of trail dust like a second suit, sat back in his saddle.

"Excuse me, Miss, but that is not the most hospitable greeting I've ever heard."

The softness of his voice surprised her, as did the fact that she recognized him.

He tipped his hat back and Martha could see his eyes. Yes, they were the same eyes. They held hers for a moment, and again, she could swear he was smiling at her, though it didn't show on his face.

These two looked rough, and most folk would have turned them away, especially with that dog. But the man returned her gaze directly, with no attempt at evasion. He sat with extreme ease on his buckskin pony, giving her time to look them over and make up her mind. Her instinct told her they meant no harm, and it had been right so many times over the years she trusted it without question.

"I'm sorry. I meant no offense to you or to your," she looked doubtfully at the animal, "ah, fine dog there. Welcome to the Double-A. I'm Martha MacLannon and this is my sister, Mary."

The man tipped his battered black hat courteously.

"Name's Bowman, ma'am, Jake Bowman. My brother, Sam."

The other man tipped his hat using the back of his left hand. The arm didn't bend right at the elbow and his motion was stiff. Sam let his arm fall quickly back to his side.

Martha looked away in embarrassment at noticing his disability and turned back to Jake. He made no show of awkwardness and only continued the introductions.

"And this," he said pointing to the dog, "is the best cow dog in Texas."

"Cow dog?" In spite of trying not to be amused, Martha felt her lips rise at the corners.

"Oh, yes, ma'am." His dark blue eyes glinted with boyish mischief. "This dog can herd cattle better than many a cowpoke I've seen. He can't brand 'em yet, but we're working on that." He looked down at the dog, who sat calmly on his haunches and returned his gaze adoringly. "Ain't that right, Dave?"

"Dave?" she repeated with a laugh.

Jake smiled outright. She liked his smile.

"Well, you see, Miss, I won him off a boy named Dave in a poker game in Fort Smith. Dave hated to part with him, too." He leaned forward in his saddle. "To tell the truth, I think he was using this poor fella to rustle cattle. Must not have been too good at it, though, 'cause Dave here was all he had to pay up with." He looked again at the dog. "Go over and say hello to the lady, Dave."

The dog turned his baggy brown eyes toward her and rose. His long legs covered the five yards between them in three bounds. He sat down in front of Martha and, with all the dignity of a Southern gentleman, raised his right paw. Martha bent slightly to take the huge appendage.

"Hello, Dave. It certainly is a pleasure to make your acquaintance," she said graciously, shaking the dog's paw.

Still smiling, she straightened up and found herself again gazing into the man's eyes. Her heart started an overtime beat and her throat got dry. Why in the world would she react like this to a saddle tramp? She focused on being sensible.

"What can we do for you, Mr. Bowman?"

Jake's eyes roamed over her yard, house, barn.

"Well, Miss, I heard tell in town you have a need for some ranch hands. My brother and I are looking for an opportunity."

Martha looked them both over again, returning her gaze to him briefly before she forced her eyes away from his.

"Does either of you know anything about working cattle?"

Sam Bowman made his first sound, a snort that was probably supposed to be a laugh. Jake exchanged a smug smile with his brother before he answered for them both.

"Miss, there ain't nothin' we don't know about cattle. We've been doing ranch work since we were just little bucks."

He was telling the truth, she was sure. She was equally certain they would expect to be paid at the end of every month with US greenbacks, the one thing she was shortest of.

Jake shifted slightly in his saddle and glanced over at his brother.

"Miss MacLannon, my brother and I didn't come out here exactly by accident. We came out here to make you a proposition. One that Sam and I believe will be mutually beneficial." He was closely watching her reaction.

"A proposition," she repeated. There had been a lot of those during the last few years, most of which she would never have repeated to a soul. She still considered herself a lady, even if most of Travis County didn't.

"Well, Mr. Bowman, I don't know if we can do business, but it's been a long time since we've had company. Why don't you and your brother stay for supper? We can talk over your... proposition." She gave the word a sarcastic edge. "Maybe we can even find enough scraps to fill this hairy elephant you brought along with you." Waving her hand toward the well beside the two-story ranch house, she said, "If you gentlemen care to clean up a bit, Mary and I will make us some supper. I hope you don't mind that it will be simple fare."

"No, ma'am, just as long as it's not canned beans."

"Mr. Bowman, I assure you, there isn't a bean in the whole house that I didn't put up myself."

"Well, hallelujah," he said with a smile.

Martha returned his smile and turned away. Her heart was getting too old to work overtime like it did when she looked into those eyes. She turned and pulled a knife out of her boot to cut the still-tethered calf free. He stood on shaky legs and, catching sight of the best cow dog in Texas, took off toward the corral, crying for his mama.

As the women continued toward the ranch house, Dave followed slowly and serenely in their footsteps. Martha gave Mary a glance and they burst out laughing.

Their laughter carried on the evening breeze to where the Bowman brothers, still mounted, watched them enter the house. Sam chuckled.

"Looks like Dave likes the ladies. Don't think he might stay when we leave, do you?"

Jake didn't answer. He stared at the porch and wondered why his luck had been so damned terrible for the last decade.

"C'mon, Jake. You know what we're here for. There won't be any time for what's on your mind."

"Sure, Sammy, sure. Well, at least we'll die in Texas." He dismounted. "Rope that calf. We might as well make ourselves useful while we're here."

MARTHA STOOD AT the window and watched as the Bowman brothers branded the last of the thirty calves milling in the corral. It would have taken her and Mary at least another whole day to get the job done.

"Too bad they didn't show up sooner," Mary said from the stove where she stirred the green beans.

Martha only smiled in answer and returned her attention to the corral. It had taken less than two minutes to rope and mark the animal. They, indeed, knew their business. She'd seen a lot of cowhands, but none as efficient as Jake Bowman.

She turned to find Mary watching her. Martha often found Mary's gaze disconcerting, never quite knowing what she was thinking. As usual, though, Mary kept her own counsel and asked no questions, except an innocent one.

"Will you make the coffee, or shall I?"

Martha laughed. "Thank you, dear. I'll make the coffee."

"Just what is wrong with my coffee?"

"Nothing, honey, nothing at all, if you're trying to make roofing tar."

"Well, maybe I just won't make coffee for you anymore!"

"Promise?" Martha asked.

They laughed together at the old joke and talked about nothing of importance while they finished cooking supper. By the time everything was ready, Martha was relaxed and completely unprepared for the sight that greeted her when she went to the door to call the men in for the meal. She stopped in her tracks when she saw them, washing up as ordered. Jake had taken off his jacket.

"Oh, my," she whispered.

He was well over six feet tall and built to every inch of it. His shirt clung to his broad shoulders where it had gotten wet and, even from the kitchen door, even in the fading sunlight, she could see the shadow of the dark hair on his chest. She could stand and look at him forever.

He turned. "Yes, ma'am, Miss MacLannon?"

Those smiling eyes never left her face. She felt the heat of a girlish blush rise up her neck. The smile in his eyes finally reached his lips.

"Oh, my," she whispered again. Then she remembered why she was standing there at the door. "Supper's ready, gentlemen." Her voice grated and she cleared her throat. "Whenever you are," she added in a more dulcet tone. At least, she hoped it was.

"Yes, ma'am. Just as soon as I change my shirt. Been riding in this one for too long to sit at a lady's table in it."

She knew that was the only warning she'd get, but she didn't avert her gaze. Even the realization that she was must appear a man-starved spinster didn't make her go back into the house where she belonged. Jake stood by the well and reached for the buttons of his shirt, his eyes never leaving hers.

What an arrogant thing, Martha thought, flaunting himself in front of a decent woman.

But, you are looking, Martha. And he warned you.

As the first buttons came open, she came to her senses. Jake's smile was still in place as she assumed the most indifferent expression she could and closed the kitchen door.

Once behind the door, she collapsed against the wall, furious with herself.

"What is your problem, Martha?" she fussed at herself. She'd never behaved like that before. What was worse, he didn't seem to mind her attentions. That's all she needed, another man chasing after her, when she'd decided she didn't need any at all. Set the table, Martha. Feed him and send him on his way.

Martha set out a proper table, just as she and Mary had stubbornly continued to do, even when it was just the two of them eating in the kitchen. Tonight, she did it more out of spite than habit, intending to regain the upper hand with the too-handsome Mr. Bowman and keep him at a distance with decorum and cool correctness. To her great dismay, the men didn't even blink at the formality.

"Gentlemen, please have a seat."

Jake came up behind her. "Oh, no. Ladies first." He pulled out a chair and stood there until she sat, then gently pushed her chair under her. Mary received the same treatment from the younger Mr. Bowman.

Only when Martha picked up her napkin did Jake take his own, shake it gingerly, and lay it on his lap.

Though their table manners were surprisingly civilized, they obviously had not been served home cooking for some time. With little talk, they efficiently took care of it all, from the home canned green beans to the smoked ham. The huge pan of fresh biscuits and the dried apple pie Martha had thrown together had also disappeared.

Dinner conversation had been sparse, only a few murmured words of praise or a request for seconds -- and thirds. Martha had been surprised at the easy familiarity, as if they were old friends. Mary, too, seemed to be comfortable with them. There had been none of the need to talk to fill the silences. That was fine with Martha. Speaking of the past only exhumed memories better left buried.

"Miss MacLannon, that was as fine a supper as I've ever had," Jake finally said as he sat back, lifted the napkin from his lap and laid it carefully at the side of his plate.

Martha felt her face warm with pleasure. It had been a long time since a man of any description had praised her cooking. It had also been a long time since she could remember having blushed so much in one day.

Fool, her spinster's mind chided. He wants something from you. Better find out what it is and stop getting all jelly-kneed every time he looks at you.

Wishing she could strangle the old lady who lived in her head, Martha joined Mary in clearing the table, sparing Jake only a small smile of thanks for the compliment.

But as aggravating as her spinster self was, Martha knew she was right. She knew nothing about this man. Start with an easy question, she thought.

"Where are you from, Mr. Bowman?" Martha asked as she poured him a fresh cup of coffee.

"Near Dallas. Our daddy had a spread between the Trinity and the Sabine," Jake said. He paused as though he would say no more. Then, he sat back, took a long sip of his coffee and continued. "There were about twenty-five thousand head of horses and cattle on the place when we left in '61. We joined the army as soon as the war broke out. In '63 I was in Virginia and got ambushed by a Yankee scouting party while my company was foraging for supplies." He took a deep gulp from his coffee cup. "Most of my men were killed. I ended up at Point Lookout."

The mention of the well-known prison camp sent a shimmy down her spine. One of her brothers had died at such a place in New York.

The look that passed over his face reminded her of her own nightmares, where she imagined what her brother had suffered.

He smiled over at Sam. "My little brother, there, tried to get me out and ended up sharing the accommodations."

Sam snorted.

"Mama and Daddy died before we got back from the war. The county took the place for taxes and a Yankee from Chicago bought it up for five hundred dollars." Jake chuckled, but it was a bitter sound. "Five hundred dollars for two hundred thousand acres of the sweetest grassland in Texas."

Silence again fell over the little group. Finally, Martha asked, "What did you do then?"

"We hired out for a while on a ranch, up in the Indian Territory, working for a Cherokee woman." Some cloud passed over Jake's eyes. He quickly raised his coffee cup and sipped.

Sam jumped into the conversation. "She was real good to work for. Knew her business, that one did," he said with quiet admiration. "She could ride as well as any man I ever saw. And when she threw a rope, it caught what it was aiming at."

"Why did you leave?"

The men exchanged a look and for the first time, Martha felt uneasy. They were hiding something.

"Well, ma'am," Jake said, favoring her with that wonderful smile, "you know how things are with ranch hands. We never stay in one place for long."

His offhand statement evoked a feeling of loss that went straight to her heart. Martha wouldn't allow herself to examine it, but only pushed it aside as she did anything that threatened to remind her of all her long-discarded dreams.

They sat in silence for a few minutes finishing their coffee. Then Jake got comfortable, leaning back in his chair and stretching his long legs out under the table. Martha crossed her arms on the table and waited. It was his proposition and she let him take his time.

"Well, Miss, it seems to me that we can help each other," Jake began, his eyes never wavering from hers. "'Bout how many head do you reckon you have ready for driving?"

"Right around two thousand at last count."

He sat up straight, put his elbows on the table and leaned toward her. She was so intent on his eyes, she almost didn't hear him when he spoke again with that soft voice of his.

"We can take your cows to Kansas for you."

"What? Just the two of you? How in the world can two men drive two thousand head of cattle? And I don't mean to be cruel, but your brother...."

Sam only smiled and tipped his head a bit toward his left arm. "Miss, I took a slug some time back. Caused a little stiffness, but it works most of the time. The only thing I can't do is draw a gun. You needn't worry about me getting the job done, though."

Jake was watching her reaction to Sam's explanation.

"He's telling you the truth, Miss. Besides, it's not just the two of us. Dave, there, is worth any three men." The dog raised his head at the sound of his name and his tail thumped against the floor. Jake leaned a bit closer and added, his voice full of conviction, "And Sam and I, beat up as we are, are worth any ten. Each."

Was he offering to stay? Martha sat back. She needed to put some distance between herself and Jake. Amused at the cowboy's cockiness, she was also convinced that he wasn't just bragging. These two men might be help enough to keep the wolf from her door for one more year, but she couldn't lead them on.

"Mr. Bowman, I can't hire you. I'm sorry."

"Miss MacLannon, you misunderstand me. What I'm proposing is a partnership. You have two thousand cows to get to Kansas. Sam and I, and Dave, can get them there. In exchange for our services, we would expect to be fifty-fifty partners."

"What?" Mary exclaimed from the sink. "You must be crazy. No cowpoke makes that kind of money."

"Sixty-forty," Martha interrupted. It was too good a deal to pass up, but she wasn't about to accept his first offer. Jake opened his mouth to argue and she raised her hand to stop him. "Mr. Bowman, we have two thousand head. At the current price, which if I'm not mistaken is eighteen dollars a head, that would be thirty-six thousand dollars. Even if we only get half of them to market, that would still be eighteen thousand. Now forty percent of that is, ah, seven thousand two hundred dollars. If you think you can beat that punching somebody else's cows for twenty-five dollars a month, go ahead."

"No wonder you don't have anybody working for you, Miss," he said with a wry smile. "The going rate for an experienced hand is thirty." He looked over to Sam, who gave a nod of approval. Extending his hand, Jake said, "You got yourself a deal, lady."

Martha stopped just short of shaking on it. "There is just one condition."

She saw the uneasiness flicker in his eyes.

"It won't be just you and your brother and Dave."
He looked at her, waiting for her to finish.
"Mary and I are coming."

Chapter Two

"I'M NOT TAKING any women along on a cattle drive." Jake sat back and crossed his arms over his chest as though the subject were closed.

"Then we have nothing more to discuss, Mr. Bowman." Martha rose. She lay her hands, palms down, on the table to signify that the subject was indeed closed.

He laughed. "So what'll you do, Miss MacLannon? Drive them yourself?"

"That's exactly what we'll do, and," she gave him her sweetest smile, "we'll keep all the money for ourselves." She saw the skeptical look on his face. A very handsome face. "We might not get the whole herd through, but we'll at least get some of them there."

"Or get killed trying." He stood and towered at least a foot over her, looking down into her eyes. "There're five hundred miles between here and the Kansas railheads. In that five hundred miles are Indians, Mexican banditos, and just about every other kind of varmint you can think of, waiting for the chance to take what they can get. And Miss Martha," he leaned down until she could almost feel his breath, warm with the faintest touch of coffee and dried apples and tobacco, brush her face, "when they get a look at you, you might just wish killing was all you were in for."

Martha gasped at the veiled crudity of his threat. She hadn't kept her virginity for this long without having at least a passing awareness of some of the ways to lose it.

"Mr. Bowman, there is no reason to be vulgar." She thought Mama would have been proud of her restraint. "Let me spell it out for you. If this drive doesn't pay, we're out of business. Now, I don't mean to question your integrity, but I can't risk everything it took my father his whole life to build on a man I've known for less than three hours. Mary and I come along, or we go alone. Take it or leave it."

"I don't doubt your grit, Miss, but we'll have all we can do keeping the cows in line without watching out for you ladies."

Martha was not amused.

"I've run this place ever since my father and brothers all went off to fight in that cussed war. I've roped, branded, herded, done everything that needed to be done, when it's needed to be done. I don't need some cocksure, know-it-all stranger to come in here and tell me that he doesn't have the time to watch out after me!"

Though she really had tried to remain calm, her voice had risen with each word until the last of her little speech had been shouted up into his face. Jake didn't attempt to cut off her tirade. He just gazed down at her, half-smiling.

Well, she'd probably ruined everything now. Might as well try to retain some of her dignity.

"Mr. Bowman, you're welcome to spend the night in the bunkhouse, but in the morning I expect to find you gone with the first light."

Jake cleared his throat and surprised her with his next words.

"Miss MacLannon, I apologize. Of course, they are your cattle and you have every right to make sure your investment is secure. If you're sure you want to do this, I'll be proud to ride with you." He once again stuck out his hand. "Still offering sixty-forty?"

"Deal," she said, quickly shaking his hand before he changed his mind.

JAKE TOSSED his saddle blanket onto the rough wooden bed and sat down to pull off his boots, placing them at the foot of the bunk. Then, he got his pipe and fresh tobacco from his saddlebag, stretched his legs out on the bed, and leaned back.

His mind turned to the woman who was now his partner. He smiled as he remembered her tirade in the kitchen, how she wasn't at all intimidated by his size or the unpleasant way he'd stated the dangers on the trail. No, sir, she'd been mad as a wet hornet and she'd let him hear her opinion of his attitude. Lightning had flashed in those blue sky eyes. She'd been hot, all right, and the rosy scent that followed her around had risen right up on that heat, filling his senses to overflowing. He concentrated on filling his pipe, all too conscious of her effect on him, and unable to put her out of his mind. Wil sure had stumbled on a prize, all this land and beautiful to boot.

"Ah," Sam sighed as he lowered himself into the next bunk, a freshly lit pipe between his teeth. "Good as a Sunday afternoon."

Twin halos of smoke soon filled the long room as they enjoyed their first night in many not spent in a bedroll on the cold ground. A real bed, even such a rough one, had become an unaccustomed luxury.

"I can understand why he would want her," Sam said.

"Um-huh." Jake puffed on his pipe, savoring the bite of the tobacco on his tongue, studiously avoiding turning toward Sam. Maybe he'd just give it up and go to sleep.

"She sure is pretty. And all this land."

"Um-huh." Damn, Jake thought. He knows exactly what I'm thinking. That was one disadvantage to riding with your brother.

"Smart, too. Talked you right into what she wanted." Jake heard the creak of Sam's bunk as he leaned over. "Jake, are you listening to me?"

He puffed at his pipe. No use, then. Sam wasn't going to let it go.

"Yes, Sam, I'm listening. I was just thinking how bad my luck is."

Sam's smile faded as he nodded in understanding. "Um-huh. I thought so."

Jake knew he was about to get a talking to, so he spoke first.

"Did you see her hands, Sam? A woman like her ought not to have to work like a field hand."

Sam threw his legs over the edge of the bunk. "You listen to me, Jake. We came here to settle up with Wil. We'll be doing her a big favor by killing the bastard before he can get his hands on her."

Jake had to agree with that, but just the same, he wished he'd gotten here, first.

"MOLLY, ARE WE doing the right thing?" Mary asked as she sat cross-legged in the middle of Martha's bed.

Martha stood brushing her hair in front of the long oval mirror her mother had brought from Louisiana as a young bride. She heard Mary talking, but she didn't answer.

"I mean, we don't know anything about these men, except what they told us. How do we know what kind of men they are?" Mary paused, then said peevishly, "Molly, you aren't listening to me."

Martha pulled the brush through her hair again. "Don't you worry about them. They are exactly what they say they are."

"How do you know?"

Martha knew Mary didn't understand her intuition about people. She tried to describe how she just knew.

"Take Wilson Garret." She shivered as she spoke the name. "You don't trust him, either."

"I don't have to listen to some intuition. I know a rotten coyote when I see one."

"Same thing," Martha said.

Mary slid off the bed and stood, stretching like a cat. "I hope you're right, Molly. We need their help. Goodnight."

Martha watched her bedroom door close. She blew out the lamp, went to the window and looked out toward the bunkhouse. Maybe the tall man sleeping out there had come along at just the right time. She only hoped he was as competent as he thought he was. Even Mary didn't know how desperate their situation had become.

With a sigh, as though her weariness could be breathed out, Martha rested her forehead against the window frame. If only there were someone to share some of the burden, even for a little while. Mary tried, but a sister wasn't the same as a husband.

Martha started at the thought.

"My goodness, wherever did that come from?" she asked out loud. "I must really be going dizzy." An attempt at dismissive laughter failed as her eyes drifted across the yard to the bunkhouse and the man who, in the course of a single day, had become her last hope.

AFTER BREAKFAST the next morning, Jake saddled their horses and waited in front of the house for his new partner to take him on a tour of her ranch. Martha appeared on the porch wearing a heavy corduroy riding skirt and a calico shirt with its long sleeves rolled up. Her golden hair was pulled back in a leather tie and left to hang down her back. In spite of her best efforts, a few tendrils had escaped and framed her face.

"Ready?" she asked as she put on her flat-topped, wide-brimmed hat and stepped down to the yard. After handing him a large burlap bag, she put her foot into the stirrup and mounted her horse with ease.

He hefted the bag. "What have you got in here? Gold?"

"Don't I wish?" She laughed as she took it back and tied it to her saddle horn. "It's just something to keep us from starving to death as we survey my vast empire."

There was something different about her this morning. He couldn't quite decide what it was, but her mood seemed lighter than yesterday. A man could find himself thinking things he shouldn't be thinking when Martha smiled at him like she was doing now.

Jake pushed the thought aside where it belonged and mounted up. "Lead on, ma'am."

Martha flashed him another smile and turned her horse toward the road. A gentle nudge of her heels set the small chestnut mare to an easy canter.

Riding slightly behind her, Jake admired the way she sat her horse. Hell, he admired her seat, in general.

Along the way, Martha kept up a nervous chatter, pointing out this or that bit of Texas flora or fauna that he probably knew better than she did. For all the world she sounded like a girl slipping off from a church social with the town's bad boy. Considering what was on his mind, he deserved the charge.

He said little, only asking a question or making a comment occasionally. The sound of her voice was so pleasing, her company so natural, he simply enjoyed the ride. When they'd reached the Colorado River, they turned upstream and followed its winding course.

"The Colorado marks the northern line." Martha pointed toward the north. "Just on the other side is the old Montoya place." She smiled. "I guess it's the Garret place, now. Hard to get used to. We have ten miles of the river front here and ten on the Blanco down in Hays county. We're just about split right in half by the county line."

Jake watched the river work its way past them toward the Gulf. "How'd your daddy manage to get frontage on two rivers?"

"He bought the section to the south in '35 when the owner decided he'd had enough of the adventure of Texas."

Jake shook his head. "I can't imagine ever leaving Texas."

Martha looked at him. "But you've left Texas...during the war."

"The war wasn't my idea. Going to the Indian Territory, well, that was just until things got back to normal down here and a man could get back to his life."

"What life were you waiting to get back to, Mr. Bowman?"

Jake pulled his reins and brought his horse to a stop. "Miss MacLannon, I have a little request to make of you, if you don't mind my being so forward."

She turned and pushed back her hat. Waves of sunny hair spilled out. She brushed them aside. He watched and wished he could do it for her.

"What is it, Mr. Bowman?"

He smiled. "Well, we're partners. Don't you think we could be a little more friendly? My name is Jake."

She answered his smile and nodded.

"I suppose it would be all right. Jake."

"Thank you, Molly."

Her smile disappeared. "Not Molly. My name is Martha."

"But, your sister...."

"That's right, Mr. Bowman, my sister has called me Molly all her life and because she is my sister, I allow her much more familiarity than I will allow an almost perfect stranger. I stopped going by that name a long time ago. Molly is a little girl's name. I am not a little girl."

"No, ma'am, you surely are not. I apologize for overstepping,

Miss MacLannon. I would still like you to call me Jake."

She turned away from him and as he leaned over to see her face, he wondered if maybe she was playing the simpering Southern belle, if maybe he'd misjudged her. If she was that kind, he'd find it much easier to keep his distance.

She looked down at her hands. "I suppose it'll still be all right."

"Forgiven then, partner?"

Martha smiled again and looked over at him. "I suppose."

"I suppose...." He waited for her to say it.

"Jake," she added.

"Thank you, Martha."

They started moving along the river again, their easy camaraderie partially restored.

"Jake," she asked, and he thought he heard some hesitancy in her voice. "Before I got so touchy...." Her white teeth tugged at her full bottom lip and he could see in her eyes the humor she now directed at her own behavior. "I asked you about what you said, about waiting to get back to something. What was it?"

He hated not telling her the truth. Bad as it was, it would be worse if she found out some other way. He didn't think she'd like being lied to, even if it was a lie of omission.

"Like I told you, I worked for my daddy," true so far, "learning how to be a crackerjack rancher." Also true, as far as it went. He looked out to the northwest, anxious to get the conversation back on business. "We're only about, what, ten, twelve miles to Austin from here?"

"'Bout that," she answered. "Have you been to Austin before?"

"Yes, ma'am. I've been there a time or two. Got some friends over there."

"Really? Daddy often had business in Austin and he took us with him sometimes. Maybe we know some of the same people."

Jake laughed out loud. "No, Martha, I don't believe you'd know the friends I'm thinking of. They aren't exactly the kind of people your daddy would have been likely to introduce to his womenfolk."

"I believe you're teasing me, Jake." A smile brightened her face.

His hands itched to touch that face, to see if her skin was as smooth and soft as it looked. She must really have been something to see when she was eighteen. She was really something to see right now.

"You'd probably be very surprised, Miss, what kind of people I've had dealings with."

"Like who?"

He was used to being the one doing the questioning.

"You brought some food in that big bag you have there, didn't you?"

She got the point, because the smile faded. When she turned her face from him, he felt like clouds had blocked the sun. Pointing to a grove of post oak and pecan trees perched on the bank of the river, she said, "There's sweet grass and water, there, for the horses."

They rode on side by side, though they might as easily have been riding on opposite banks of the Colorado.

MARTHA WONDERED about it all day. Why wouldn't he talk about his past? What did he have to hide? Maybe, this once, her intuition had been mistaken.

You're being silly, Martha. There doesn't have to be some sinister reason he won't share his past with you. But, darn it, he was the one who'd said he wanted to be more friendly and she was hurt that he'd shut her out, even while she admitted she had no right to be. She was nothing to him.

But his eyes followed her every movement as she cleared away the supper dishes and it sure looked like interest to her. Not that she minded. It was flattering to have a handsome man pay attention.

When the dishes were done, Mary hung the damp dish towel over the pump. "I think I'll go on upstairs." She hugged Martha. "Good night, Molly."

Sam stretched his long arms over his head.

"Think I'll turn in, too. 'Night, Miss MacLannon." He slapped his brother on the shoulders and went out the door.

They were alone.

Now that the safety of numbers was gone, the scrutiny of those eyes made her uncomfortable. She wanted to tell him to look at something else.

What a lie!

Martha untied her apron and busied herself folding and laying it as gently as satin across the back of a chair.

"Well, I have some sewing to do."

"I picked up a newspaper in Travis City. If you'd like, I could read to you while you sew."

Careful, Martha. He offered to read to you, nothing more.

"Thank you. I'd appreciate the company."

They retired to her father's library. It was still her father's library, even though he'd been dead for more than eight years. She supposed it would have become her husband's, if she'd ever married. That thought captioned the picture of Jake standing before the tall bookcases, looking almost reverently at the hundreds of books her father had collected over his sixty years. He looked so comfortable in this room devoted to reading and contemplation, just as he looked perfectly comfortable riding his Texas cow pony and branding calves.

Where had he really come from and how did he happen to be in the vicinity when she so desperately needed someone like him?

"He loved books, didn't he?"

Jake's question brought a flood of memories of her father, who had been the most important man in her life for so long. But the pain was gone now, replaced by the comforting memory of her father's love. She nodded.

"You know, it's been so long since I could even come in here without going to pieces, even though it's been so many years...." She let the statement hang. "Jake, if you'd like to use the library, it would be all right. It would be a shame to let all these fine books go to waste."

He smiled, genuine pleasure lighting his eyes as he turned back to the shelves. "I would. Thank you, Martha."

She watched him touch the books, gently stroking the leather bindings, and she thought she heard him sigh. He pulled one volume down. A small puff of dust flew up his nose.

"Oh, my." She snatched the book from his hands and quickly dusted it with the skirt of her dress, then returned it to him with an embarrassed smile. "I'm afraid I haven't had much time to keep house, lately."

"You don't have to apologize, Martha. This little bit of dust is nothing compared to what we'll choke down on the trail," he teased with a wry twist of him mouth.

He made her smile so easily.

She sat in her sewing chair and picked up the bodice that had been in her basket for weeks. Jake took a book from one of the top shelves, where the novels were.

"Did you find something to your liking?"

A half-smile played at his lips. She wondered what he was thinking and was sure his next words couldn't have caused that expression.

"Yep, he had a copy of The Whale up there. I haven't read it in years. Thought I'd start with that one."

"Melville was one of Daddy's favorites."

He reached up. "Here's Wuthering Heights."

"Don't tell me you read romantic novels, Jake."

"It's a romantic novel? I thought it was about mountain climbing."

She laughed out loud at his foolishness.

He opened the book and skimmed the first page. "Well, I haven't read it yet. Is it any good?" he asked.

"It's my favorite, even though it's very sad. Jane Eyre is better for a happy ending."

He looked dubious. "I guess that's a romantic novel, too? Well, I reckon I'll just have to give them both a look." He glanced around. "But don't let Sam know. I'll never hear the end of it."

She snickered and shook her head as Jake sat down in her father's chair with the week-old paper.

"Do you mind if I light my pipe?"

There it was again, the courtesy, the gentility that seemed to her to be part of his being.

"Not at all," she answered.

He smiled his thanks and filled his pipe. As he tamped down the tobacco, he was very careful that none of it fell out. His hands fascinated her. They were strong, lean, callused by years of working cattle, but somehow she knew they were also capable of gentleness. She actually shivered at the thought and quickly turned her attention to her work.

Jake lit his pipe and leaned back in the chair. His eyes were closed and a look of complete satisfaction settled on his face as he took his first puff. She had to smile at how something so simple could make him so content.

"I always wondered why men so love their tobacco."

He opened his eyes. "Oh, Miss Martha, tobacco isn't just tobacco. It's an experience." He closed his eyes again, puffing with relish.

Martha let him enjoy his pipe while she enjoyed watching him.

After several minutes, Jake lay his pipe aside and opened up the Travis City newspaper.

"Let's see here," he said as he shook it and held it up to the light of the oil lamp that sat on a table between them. "Butler's just got a shipment of patent leather shoes from Chicago. How 'bout that? And the Dove's Wing Saloon is putting in a new billiard table."

She sewed buttonholes and attached buttons and finished seams and listened as he read the rather uninteresting news of Travis City. His voice, though soft and quiet, was strong and clear. He read well, never stumbling over words, not at all like a poorly educated cow hand.

The clock struck eleven just as he was finishing up the last page.

"Goodness, I didn't realize how late it was getting." Martha put her work back in her basket and stood up, flexing her shoulders to work out the stiffness. Closing her eyes, she rubbed the back of her neck with both hands and raised her arms over her head, stretching luxuriously. "Ummm."

When she opened her eyes, she met his gaze. As she lowered her arms, she saw in his expression something she didn't dare put a name to, but it fired a response in her body and soul.

Several long moments passed and neither made a move nor a sound.

"I think I'd better be getting out to the bunkhouse," he said at last, folding the paper and rising. His face showed nothing, though she fancied she saw in his eyes reluctance to leave.

Martha, get hold of yourself.

"Good night, Martha." Jake's eyes made one quick trip down and up her body before he turned and walked to the front door.

The last man who'd looked at her that way had received a thorough tongue-lashing. What Jake's perusal made her want didn't bear pondering.

With a sigh, she blew out the lamp and went to her room, knowing it would be near dawn before she'd be able to sleep.

JAKE WALKED slowly down the front steps.

Damn it all. Why hadn't he and Sam come south instead of going north? They could have avoided all manner of trouble, and maybe he'd have found her before it was too late. He kicked a clod of dirt, knocking it all the way to the barn. The thud it made against the walls reminded him of how dull he felt most of the time. Especially lately.

"Out for a walk?" Sam's voice broke through the dark. "Or just waiting until your little embarrassment passes?"

Jake ignored the barb. "I thought you'd gone to bed."

Sam emptied his pipe. "I thought I'd fill you in on what I found out in town today while you were squiring Miss MacLannon around her domain."

"What the hell were you doing in town? We agreed it would be better to just lay low for now. If Wil finds out we're here, we can just mark time until we get shot in the back."

"I was real careful."

Jake sighed. "All right, what did you find out?"

"Wilson is for sure trying to court the worthy Miss MacLannon. He's got title to ninety-six thousand acres of land across the Colorado and aspirations of becoming a powerful land baron. With Miss Martha's spread added to his own, he would have a tidy little ranch."

"So, is the worthy Miss MacLannon leaning toward accepting Wil's proposal?" Jake knew what answer he wanted to hear.

"No, and people think she's crazy for not marrying up with him and letting him take care of her."

"Over my dead body."

"Believe me, I understand what you're feeling, but we won't be able to stay here, no matter how things turn out."

He heard the accusation. "Don't worry. I'm not going to let you down."

"I never thought you would." Sam leaned against the fence. "You know if I could, I'd do it."

"That's the one reason I'm willing to. I'd just rather do it legal-like."

Sam laughed bitterly. "C'mon, Jake. You can't kill a man legally."

Jake turned to face his brother. "You can if he draws on you first."

"Wilson may be mean and no-good, but he's not stupid. That bullet in the back is a lot more likely."

The men stood silently for a long minute. Jake measured his words carefully.

"I've been feeling real bad about what we're doing to her, Sam. She believes we're going to take her cows to Kansas." He leaned against the corral fence.

Sam grunted unsympathetically. "You knew when we rode up here there'd be no drive. Don't start feeding me any bull about feeling guilty."

"She's going to lose everything. I do feel guilty."

"So what do you want to do about it?"

Jake stood there, considering options, like he always did. "We can try to make the drive. Once she has the money to hire some hands, pay her taxes, then we can kill Wil."

"Oh, no. No, Jake."

Sam's voice was getting louder. Jake shot a glance toward the house, wondering if she could hear. Sam looked, too, and lowered his voice. "He's had long enough of the good life. It's time for him to pay."

"All right, Sam. Let's saddle up and ride on over there and shoot him like a dog in his bed."

Sam stared him right in the eye. The grim expression on his face chilled Jake's blood.

"Let's go."

Jake stood there, unable to believe what had become of his younger brother. "You'd really go breaking into a man's house and murder him?"

Sam shook his head. "A man, no. But a killer animal you hunt down and if you find him in his den, you kill him there. This isn't murder. It's justice."

"Let's call it what it is. Revenge."

"All right. Revenge. I don't have a problem with that."

"You used to," Jake said softly.

Sam snorted a mirthless laugh. "I used to have a problem with a lot of things." He was silent for a few moments. "Look, Jake, if all you're worried about is her not losing her ranch, we can take care of that real easy. I'll go over to Austin tomorrow."

Jake shook his head. "She'll never accept pity money."

Sam shrugged. "What pity money? We entered into a contract. We can explain it as a penalty for not fulfilling our part of the bargain."

Jake felt empty. "Then she can marry someone who can offer her what she deserves."

Sam laid a hand on Jake's shoulder. "Look, I know what you wanted. It's too late for me, but I wish you could go back to the way things were before the war."

Jake had no comment. That life was over, thanks to the war. A pang shot through his middle as he counted all he'd lost. Home. Family. Profession.

"Do you ever think about Mama and Daddy, Sam?" The edge of yearning in his voice startled him.

Pipe dangling from his fingers, Sam stared at the ground. "I try not to." Without another word, Sam headed toward the bunkhouse.

Studying him, Jake tried to see the freckle-faced, tow-headed boy in the hardened, bitter man Sam had become. And he missed Mama more than he ever had. She would have gathered Sam to her breast, big as he was, held him and comforted him and helped him to heal. Feeling like a lost little boy himself, Jake clenched the stem of his empty pipe between his teeth.

Mama was dead. And Daddy. And, most likely, he and Sam would soon join them. The world would forget the Bowman family had ever existed.

Once, he could have told himself at least he still had his honor. But Wil had stolen even that. Jake was honest enough with himself to admit it was the real reason he wanted Wil dead. But it would be nice to leave a bit of himself behind.

A deep sigh caught him unaware just as Martha lit the lamp in her bedroom. Jake stood by the corral and snorted a self-derisive chuckle at the ache that plagued him, watching her move around her room getting ready for bed.

"Too late for you, boy," he whispered, tearing his eyes away from the window and forcing himself to his own bunk, where he knew she would join him in his dreams.

Chapter Three

IT TOOK MORE than three nights of reading and sewing to get through all the newspapers and magazines around the house. Then he started reading to her from the storehouse of good books that lined the library shelves.

She'd stopped thinking of it as Daddy's library and felt a little guilty ceding the territory to Jake without so much as a skirmish. But the guilt didn't prevent her from enjoying the time she spent with him there. Her mind feasted on the sights and sounds of hunting whales on the stormy ocean, the English moors, the Spanish countryside. Her heart drank in the heartache of Cathy and Heathcliff, and the joyful reunion of Jane and Mr. Rochester. He read anything she asked and never made fun of the romantic ones. Well, he'd teased her a little, but still took the book down and started reading. While she listened, her hands were busy as well. During the last week, she finished that long-neglected dress and a matching bonnet for herself, and she started on a dress for Mary's birthday.

"How's it coming? Are you going to finish it in time?"

"If you read a little faster, I will." She looked up. "Maybe you should select something a little more adventurous. I sew faster when there's some excitement."

Jake laughed. "I don't know if there's anything fit for a lady that moves that fast." He leaned against the mantel, rubbing his right leg.

"Jake," she felt his discomfort in her own body, "are you all right?"

He barely masked the grimace of pain that flashed across his face. "It's nothing," he chuckled, "just my war wound. Every old soldier has one, you know. It gets worse when the weather's wet. Usually, I don't even notice it."

Her concern for him forced the question out, right past stodgy old Martha's defenses. "What happened?"

"Prison. They had us digging graves." He quickly looked over at her. With a nod, she gave him leave to continue. "They were really trenches, not proper graves at all. The dead would be brought out and dumped in. Sometimes they had a preacher say a few words. One day I fell in, or got pushed, never knew which, and hit the ground wrong.

Broke my leg right here." He touched just above his knee.

"Didn't they get a doctor to set it?"

He laughed. "It was a prison camp during a war, Martha. The people they called doctors were nothing of the sort. He did the best he could, I expect, but it never did set quite right. Still, it works. Sure am glad it was my right leg." At her puzzled look, he said, "If it had been my left, I wouldn't be able to mount a horse. I'd'a had to find myself a desk job."

"I can't see you behind a desk."

"No?" He smiled a half-smile, the one that always made her think he was playing some joke on her.

He lowered himself into his chair and stretched his leg out in front of him. She got the small footstool that she usually put her feet up on. Kneeling before him, she gently raised his leg and set the stool under it. It was done so quickly, she was back in her seat before she knew she'd even done it.

"Thank you. You didn't have to do that."

"I have to keep you healthy."

A smile spread over his face, a display of even, white teeth and, my heavens, she delighted, dimples in his cheeks. She'd not seen those before he trimmed that beard of his. How in the world could a man be so handsome?

"I'm glad my health is important to you."

"You have to get my cows to Kansas, Mr. Bowman."

He lay a hand over his heart and let his head fall against the back of the chair. "Are you saying you only want me for my ranching skills?"

This was getting dangerous. She could see he knew it, too. It was a heady thing, stronger than drink.

"What other possible reason could there be?"

"You're a hard woman, Martha MacLannon. I'd better watch out or I'm going to get my heart broken."

"I expect your heart can stand the strain."

Careful, Martha.

His eyes narrowed. "You know, ever since I first met you I've wondered something." He paused. "How come you never married, Martha?"

Stodgy old Martha had it right on the tip of her tongue to tell him it was none of his business. It wouldn't come out, though. She knew it was Molly, the part of her that was still young, still hopeful, who answered him.

"I was engaged once. I don't think I'd have gone through with it, though."

"Why not?"

She met his eyes because he willed her to. "He wasn't the right man."

Jake looked at her for a long time. She wanted to look away, but he held her tight.

"What happened to him?"

"He was killed in the war."

"I'm sorry."

It was the conventional, polite reply, but somehow, even though he might be sorry a fellow Confederate had fallen in battle, she sensed he wasn't really sorry the marriage hadn't come to pass.

They were silent for a moment.

"Well, Jake, I've got a dress to finish. What are you going to read to me?"

He picked up Don Quixote from the table next to the chair.

"To Spain, my lady?"

She nodded and picked up Mary's dress.

"DAD-BLASTED broomtail! Get yourself in that stall."

Martha entered the barn, certain she knew the cause of Jake's displeasure.

Sure enough, there he was, conducting a staredown with her saddle horse.

He turned on her. "This blasted, ill-tempered mule of yours just kicked me. Why won't she go into a stall like a nice little girl? Did you give her cantankerous lessons?"

A month ago, that would have earned him a demonstration of just how cantankerous Martha could be.

"Sunbeam sort of has the run of the barn." She bit her lip to stop her laughter. "Nobody makes her do anything. Except me, of course."

"Except you, of course? Well, then, why don't you put this fat cow of a horse in a stall? I've got other things I can be doing." He tossed her the halter and started out to the corral.

That did make her mad.

"Fat! She's not fat. What kind of a rancher can't tell a mare is in foal?"

He stopped. "In foal? She's in foal?" He looked again and lay his hands against the mare's belly. "She's not showing very much is she?"

"No," Martha said before quickly biting her lip again.

"Oh. When is she due?"

"Any time now."

"That soon?" He looked again, measuring the mare's girth. When he straightened, he avoided Martha's eyes. "I'll keep an eye on her," he promised and returned to all those other things he had to do.

His behavior was so unlike what she'd come to expect that she knew, crazy as it was, he was troubled by something. She followed him out into the corral.

"Jake," she called after him. "Is something wrong?"

He didn't meet her eyes.

"No. Course not." Then he grinned. "If I'd'a looked at her beam, I would have seen it. I thought she was just being stubborn. And," he looked away, "I apologize for calling you cantankerous."

"I am cantankerous."

He laughed. "Only when somebody deserves it."

She wasn't satisfied. "There's more. What is it?"

"Now, Martha, if there was something wrong, wouldn't I...." He looked past her. "What the...." He strode to the fence and stared out toward the northeast. "What's over this way, Martha?"

"Travis City. Austin, if you go far enough. Few thousand acres of range...."

"Are there cattle out there?"

"Probably." Before she was finished, he was in the barn.

"Where are you going?" She had to run to catch up.

"Didn't you see the smoke? Somebody's got a fire going out there." He looked up from the cinch he was tightening around his horse's belly.

Martha looked out again and sure enough, the thin wisp of smoke was clearly visible.

"Could it be a range fire?" She ran past him to get a bridle.

He shook his head as he led his horse out of the barn.

"Not dry enough, and the smoke is too concentrated. If it were a range fire, it would be spreading." He pulled his horse around. "Tell Sam to follow me, if he gets here before I come back."

"Wait for me." She had her saddle pulled down from its peg on the wall before he could turn and get back to her.

"No, ma'am. You stay here. You hear me, Martha?"

She whipped her head around to glare.

"Exactly who are you to be telling me anything? I go where I want to and don't you forget it." She punctuated her declaration with a yank on the girth.

"Martha, I don't know what's out there. Could be rustlers, bandits. It's probably nobody you'd want to meet. Let me handle it."

"Stop talking to me like I'm an imbecile. Get on out there. I'll be right behind you."

"Like hell!"

"You watch your language around me, Jacob Bowman."

"Suit yourself, Miss MacLannon." He mounted his horse and took off.

She was right behind him, hatless, riding in a skirt that was particularly indecent for this kind of excursion. It whipped up around her knees despite her efforts to pin it under her legs, causing him no end of consternation as he tried to keep his eyes ahead, facing whatever awaited them.

They approached the wispy column of smoke. There was only one fire, which meant there would be no more than a handful of men around it. He'd faced worse odds lots of times.

"Martha, stay behind me." He called to her as she moved ahead of him.

She ignored him, riding faster toward the fire.

He bit back the particularly foul blasphemy about to pass his lips.

"Do you have a will, Martha?" he yelled after her.

"What?" She didn't slow down.

He put his spurs to Buck and caught up. When he came even with her mount, he grabbed her reins and stopped her.

"If you're not going to take good advice, you're going to need a will. I can suggest a good lawyer."

"I didn't know there was such a thing as a good lawyer. No, thank you. I don't trust 'em."

His laughter exploded over the range. He caught a breath and leaned over his horse's neck. "Hear that, Buck? She doesn't trust lawyers."

"What's so funny? Does anybody trust lawyers?"

"Let me see if I have this straight. You trust me and Sam, whom you do not know, to come and go on your property at will. You give us charge of said property, to wit, your cows, horses, et cetera. You trust us to come into your house and eat at your table. You trust me enough to be out here alone with me right now...." He cast his eyes at her very, very nice legs. "...with your skirts flapping up around your knees." He chuckled at her futile attempts to jerk her skirts down to a more respectable length. "But you don't trust lawyers." He laughed again. "Come on, Miss Martha, let's see what's going on out here."

They rode on in silence. At least there was silence when Jake wasn't laughing. He almost fell off his horse during one spasm.

His hilarity died when his horse stopped about fifty yards from a small rise and refused to go any further.

"What's the matter, Buck?" He stroked the horse's short, strong neck, letting his senses take in the situation. "Martha, listen."

Martha stopped breathing and put all her concentration into listening. It was quiet at first. The lowing of cattle.

"Martha, get down and come with me." He turned to her, "Please."

She obeyed without question. Whatever was happening on the other side of that rise wasn't good and she'd been stupid enough to leave the house without getting her rifle.

"Can you handle this?" Jake asked as he held out a brand-new Winchester '66.

She looked it over. "It works like a Henry?"

He nodded. "Pretty much." She thought she saw admiration in his eyes.

"I can handle it." She took the rifle, glad for the weight in her hands.

He motioned her to follow, then crouched and moved nearly silently toward the low, mellow sound of the cattle and the smoke of the fire in front of them.

Jake dropped face down on the incline of a small rise, pulling her down beside him. She was too conscious of him, lying there so closely.

"Be as quiet as you can," he whispered directly into her ear. "Look there, by the fire."

A couple of men were moving long metal spikes around in the flames.

"Running irons," he whispered. His breath in her ear sent flames throughout her entire body. "Rustlers. They're altering the brands." He raised up to peer over the rise. She could see him looking around, making sure he saw them all.

Jake crouched back down beside her. "Martha, could you kill a man?"

Chapter Four

"COME ON, MARTHA, I need an answer."

She shook her head. "I'm not sure. Maybe in self-defense."

"Self-defense takes a lot of forms. Stealing your livelihood will kill you as effectively as a bullet. That's why rustling is a hanging offense."

She dropped her jaw in horror. "You're talking about shooting them in cold blood?"

He nodded. "They'd do the same to you. Now, look, I asked you to stay behind because I was pretty sure what was going on out here. I've seen signs that we've been hit at least twice."

He said we, her heart sang. Stodgy old Martha was about to correct him.

"Now that you're here, you're going to do like I tell you." He held her gaze with his own. "All right?"

She nodded.

"Good girl." He squeezed her hand. "If you need to kill somebody to protect yourself, do it. When the shooting starts, if you get a clear shot and can wing one or two of 'em, do it. Otherwise, stay down and out of my line of fire."

He slipped off around the small hillock that hid the band of men and their stolen beef from sight. On the other side of the camp was a makeshift rope corral where at least twenty of her cows stood, awaiting the alteration of their brands.

She counted the men around the fire and sighed a breath of relief there were only four. Would she be able to shoot one or two of them when the time came?

How good was Jake with that gun?

"Howdy, boys. Whatcha got there?" Jake stood at the top of the rise behind the men. At the sound of his voice they jumped from their crouches and reached for their guns.

Jake had his Colt Navy revolver on them before any of them could clear leather.

A low whistle escaped her lips.

He made quite a sight up there, tall, broad-shouldered, his gun leveled straight at the middle of the group of rustlers.

"Let's be nice and easy here, boys. I want to get a look at the brands on those cows you got there." He never took his eyes off them as he eased down the slope toward the fire, then sidestepped over to the rope corral.

One of the rustlers stepped forward. "Who the hell are you?"

"I work for Martha MacLannon."

"Yeah? You'd better consider a change in employment. Miss MacLannon ain't gonna have that ranch long."

"That right?" He slipped under the rope and laid his hand on the rump of the nearest cow. Still keeping his eyes on the rustlers, he slid his hand down to the brand. He made a tsk-tsk sound. "Boys, stealing from a woman. Ain't you ashamed?"

"You think you can take all of us, stranger?"

"I don't need to take you all. You don't think I'm stupid enough to come out here by myself, do you?"

Martha almost laughed out loud.

"My partner is just over the rise. There's a Winchester aimed right at your heads." He raised his voice. "Pard, give these boys a shot just to prove you're out there."

She aimed for the biggest one and neatly took off his hat.

Even Jake looked astounded. "Good shootin'. All right, friends. Who's your boss?"

"Ain't got no boss," the big, hatless one answered.

Jake looked them over. "Now, that's real convenient. Since you don't have a boss, there won't be anybody nosing around, looking for you when you don't show up." He nodded, as though making a decision, "Yep, I think I'll just save the county the cost of a trial and a hanging." He raised his gun and aimed at the middle of a man with a long weasel's nose.

"Wait, don't kill me." The weasel threw his paws up in the air.

The biggest one, the one Martha had divested of his hat, yelled, "Shut up and keep your head. He can't kill us all."

The weasel wasn't comforted. "I don't care about us all, I care about me. Look, stranger, I don't owe the boss nothing...."

A shot rang out, then another, then two more. Martha tried to jump up, but only managed to get caught in her skirts. When she finally stood on top of the rise, holding her rifle steady on the place where the men had stood, she saw only two men on the ground.

Terrified that one of those shots had found Jake, she searched for him.

"Jake, where are you?" she called as she caught sight of two horses headed for the river. Rifle on her shoulder, she took aim at the fast shrinking figures.

"Martha, let them go," Jake called to her. He still stood near the corral, his smoking revolver in his hand.

She reluctantly lowered her weapon. "We're just going to let them get away?"

"We'll let them lead us to their boss."

"I'll get the horses."

"Will you please wait?" He approached the two men on the ground. The weasel clutched his belly, his life quickly flowing from the large hole there. The other man, the spokesman for the group, was already dead. Jake kicked the gun out of the weasel's reach and knelt down beside him.

She carefully made her way down to the campsite, looking around all the while, wary that more rustlers might show up.

"Pard," Jake said to the man who lay in an expanding pool of blood, "you're dying. You know that, don't you?"

The weasel looked into Jake's eyes, pleading. "I'm gut shot?"

Jake nodded. "Yep, I'm afraid you are. It might go better for you on the other side to come clean now."

The man managed a sloppy sounding laugh. His skin already had the greenish gray pallor of a dead man. "You a priest, too?"

Jake chuckled. "Not even close. Who's your boss?"

The weasel didn't answer, but only rattled his last breath. Jake closed the man's eyes, then went to the fire and pulled the irons out. He held them up, examining them closely.

"Damn," he muttered in a nearly silent whisper.

"What are you looking for?"

He kicked dirt on the fire and stirred the ashes with one of the branding irons. "Just looking to see if there is anything to see. Let's get our horses and drive these cattle back to the house."

"What about the rustlers?"

"It's getting dark. We'll track 'em tomorrow. First, the cattle. There's almost four hundred dollars standing in that corral. Forty per cent of it's mine. You can leave your sixty here, if you want to." He moved past her up the slope to get their horses.

His words hit her like a blow right in the heart.

The sensible, responsible spinster she'd become was right there, needling. He's only in this for the money. All that flirting and joking in the library is just talk. You'd better protect yourself, or you're going to look like a complete fool.

Not to mention that your heart is going to shatter into a million pieces.

Too late to worry about that.

HE'D HURT HER feelings, he could tell by the way she rode so quietly, only speaking to urge the cattle on. He could, he should, tell her the truth -- why he didn't need to follow them.

The running irons were his own. He'd kept them in his saddlebag. Only one person could have brought them here.

Jake looked across the space between them, filled with cows, wondering what she'd say if he told her about his past. Would she understand how it all happened and forgive him?

He slowed his horse and moved behind the cattle so he could ride beside her. The sun had gone down and the air was chilly. He shrugged off his jacket and rode close enough to put it over her shoulders.

"Keep your coat. I don't need it." She yanked it off and threw it at him.

"Martha, I know I said some things back there that made you angry, or hurt your feelings."

She jerked around. "You sure do give yourself a lot of credit to think you can hurt my feelings. We're business partners, right? Well, you were right, partner. The most important thing is getting these cows back in a safe place." She kicked her horse to a canter and moved away from him.

Now he was the one feeling cold.

She had the corral open by the time he got there, but was nowhere to be seen. He got the cattle into the corral and his horse taken care of, then headed for the house.

"RUSTLERS?" MARY whispered. "How many did we lose?"

"None, this time. Jake got the drop on them." Martha quickly told her the story.

"Jake's fast, huh?"

"Yep, sure is."

"That's just my luck, to be stuck here doing wash while you're out having all the fun."

Martha laughed. "Chasing rustlers is your idea of fun?"

"Beats the heck out of wringing out your unmentionables."

The kitchen door squeaked, announcing Jake's arrival. Martha immediately clammed up, her earlier grievance still fresh enough to kill her good humor. He noticed, too. Well, good. Let him wonder if she'd ever speak to him again.

"I think I'll go finish the laundry," Mary said before making herself scarce.

Jake whistled out a breath and rested his hands on the back of the nearest chair, easing the weight on his leg. She wanted to tell him to sit, but her mouth wouldn't cooperate.

"Martha," he started, his eyes showing uncertainty, "Sam and I are going out at first light to track the two who got away."

"Fine." For the life of her, she couldn't make herself say more, even for the sake of hiding how hurt she was.

Jake turned his face away from her for a moment, then straightened, took off his jacket, and hung it on the peg behind the door. He sat down and grimaced as he stretched his right leg out in front of him.

"Look, Martha, I didn't go after them because I was worried that you might get hurt."

She turned and fixed him with her very finest glare.

"The day I need you to worry about me, Mister Bowman, I'll be sure to let you know."

"Now, don't be like that."

"Like what?" She forced herself to turn and face him.

"You're being," he paused, for once at a loss, "unreasonable."

"What?"

"We've been getting along real well, Martha, and now, just because I wanted to protect you, you're treating me like," again he paused, uncertainty heavy in his voice, "like a ranch hand. I thought there was more than that between us."

She wanted to believe what she heard. But she'd been dominated for a long time by the part of her that kept everyone except Mary at bay. It was easier now to hold him at a distance, too, now that she'd pushed him outside the little walled place of her heart.

"We're partners, right? Just partners."

She walked out before he could call her bluff.

JAKE SKIPPED supper that night. He even stayed away from the library. He wasn't sure he'd be welcome, but more, he didn't think he could go in there and read to her and watch her as she sewed for someone she loved.

It almost killed him to stay away.

He slouched against the fence, both elbows resting on the top rail, and puffed his pipe while he gazed at her bedroom window. Looked like she couldn't face the library tonight, either. She walked across the room and he knew from previous evenings she was standing before a mirror, brushing her hair.

"Man, you sure do have it bad, don't you?" Sam leaned against the fence with him. He, too, had his pipe pulled out and puffed like a train going up a hill. "You missed a grand meal tonight."

"I don't want to hear about it."

"Yessiree, that old hen was just right, though Mary said she had to cook her for, oh, six hours, I believe." Sam smacked his lips in sadistic glee. "Mighty fine cooking."

"Do you have a point?"

"Nope. Well, only that you missed a fine meal." He turned and rested his arm on the fence. "What happened out there?"

"We've been hit, at least twice that I know of. I found a cold camp to the east a ways and today we came upon a bunch of boys altering brands on the river near the property line." Jake chewed on the stem of his pipe. "They were using my irons."

"We got him, then. We have proof Wil's their boss."

"How exactly do we establish that? Waltz into the sheriff's office and identify the irons? 'Yes, Sheriff, they're mine. Oh, what was I doing with running irons?'" Jake shook his head. "If we turn him in, we go to jail, ourselves. I am not going to jail, Sam. I've been in prison once, and that was more than enough for me."

Sam was about to argue and Jake was in no mood to go through the whole thing right now.

"You go out tomorrow and track 'em. If the buzzards haven't gotten to the bodies, see if there's anything that could link them to Wil."

Sam looked greatly offended. "Jake, I'm not an amateur, you know."

"I'm sorry, Sammy," Jake said with a laugh.

"Do you want to come with me?"

Jake shook his head. "Nope, no reason to. You're a better tracker than I am. I'll ride out south tomorrow and see what's going on down there. If all our losses can be pinned to the north, we'll know who's behind it."

Sam snorted. "We already know who's behind it. Well, I'll be getting to bed. I think Martha put a plate up for you." He pushed away from the fence and sauntered off toward the bunkhouse.

Jake knocked the ash from his pipe and tried in vain to convince himself that plate of chicken wasn't calling him. He crossed the yard and went around to the kitchen door, mindful of the squeak that Martha never had fixed. The kitchen was dark, save for one lamp turned down low, and empty, save for him. A peek in the warming oven on top of the stove revealed that, sure enough, there was a plate of chicken and dumplings and a cup of coffee.

As he pulled his supper from the oven, he was suddenly aware of the ghost of roses circling around his head and he knew she was standing in the doorway.

"Hope you like it," she said.

"It's my favorite."

"Well, don't just stand there like a cigar-store Indian. Sit down and eat." She got a napkin from the linen drawer and pulled out a chair for him.

He sat and watched her move around her kitchen getting pie for them both and coffee for herself. He savored the sight of her in her nightgown and a thick flannel wrapper. Her hair was down and braided into a plait that hung just past her shoulders. This was a sight he'd like to see every morning.

They sat in silence. He ate his chicken. She flicked the crust of her pie.

"Jake," she said softly. "I was very ungrateful this afternoon. I've just had to take care of myself for so long, it's hard to give anything up to somebody else."

That cost her, he knew. "Are we friends again?" he asked, his stomach twisting a bit as he waited for her response.

She nodded. "Jake, do you mind, now that we're friends, again, if I ask you a question?"

He immediately put up his guard. "No, of course I don't mind."

"Have you ever been married?"

Not what he expected. He felt such relief, he laughed.

"Is that funny?"

"No, no. I just didn't expect that question." He took another bite. "No, I've never been married."

She smiled. "Not even close?"

"Not even close."

"Why not?"

"Never found the right woman."

She stabbed a piece of apple. "How would you know the right woman?"

Raising his eyes to meet hers, he wanted to say he would just know, then add, after an appropriate pause, and I just know it's you.

She'd proved skittish enough, though, that he was damned if he'd ruin this little truce.

"Well?" she prompted.

"Let me think, now, it's a hard thing to put into words. I guess, it would be someone who's intelligent...."

"Beautiful isn't first on your list?" she interrupted, teasing.

"Well, honey, beauty is transitory, but stupid lasts forever." He smiled, imagining the two of them forty years hence, sitting at the kitchen table, gumming pie together. "I can see myself with an, ah, unattractive woman before I could see myself with a stupid one."

"You were about to say ugly, weren't you?"

"No. Every man knows there's no such thing as an ugly woman. Every woman is beautiful." He cocked his head a bit. "It's just that not every woman is equally beautiful."

"I see," she laughed. "What else?"

"What else? Strong-willed, determined, brave, good-hearted, ah, yes, she'd better be a good cook." If he hadn't been sure before, he was now. He'd just described Martha MacLannon.

"You're going to have some trouble finding a paragon like that."

"You might be surprised."

They sat with their arms crossed on the table in front of them, their eyes locked together.

It started to look like they'd sit there all night.

"Well," Martha said at last, "I'd better get these dishes cleaned up and myself to bed." She got up and went to the sink where she ran warm water from the reservoir into the dishpan.

"I'll do that," Jake said as he came to stand beside her. When he took the cloth from her hand, their fingers touched. The feeling of her hand, so small against his larger one sent a crackle of need through him. Her eyes displayed her similar reaction. His voice was gritty when he added, "You go on to bed."

She didn't leave, but remained there, not touching him, though he could feel her presence. "You know, I didn't get anything done on Mary's dress tonight. Will you read to me tomorrow?"

"Sure thing." When the last of the small stack of plates was done, Jake exchanged the dish cloth for a towel. She took the cloth and wiped off the table.

He dried the dishes while he watched her taking her time about the table. After it was clean down to the bare wood, she went to the stove and examined the black painted iron surface, then devoted a couple of minutes cleaning it to her satisfaction.

She's going to take the black off that stove and expect me to fix it for her, he thought. And, of course, he would.

As he dried the last of the plates, he decided he ought to be getting to bed, himself. He'd see her tomorrow, and the day after, and every day until he either had to run for his life, or was dead, or sitting in jail waiting to be hanged.

Yep, he'd just go on out and see her tomorrow.

"Anything else, Martha?"

She turned around the room. "No, that looks like everything." With a teasing smile, she came to him and took the plate and towel from him. "You're rubbing the flowers off."

The clock in the library chimed ten.

"Thanks for saving me supper."

"Thanks for helping me clean up."

Nodding, he went to the door and took his jacket, which was still hanging there. With one last look at her, he smiled a goodnight and reached for the doorknob. He knew he was moving mighty slow and he knew why. Some part of him wanted her to say something, anything, as long as it would keep him there with her longer. When he could think of nothing more to say or do, he opened the door and went outside.

Martha blew out the lamp and took one last peek out the window. He stood under the tree, staring off to the north.

She'd seen him in similar poses often in the last few weeks, usually after supper and before he came to the library. He'd go out with Sam to smoke a pipe and talk over whatever it was they talked over. Then, he'd come in to her.

But sometimes, he'd stand there alone for a few minutes, just looking north.

She wondered what, or who, kept catching his attention.

Not that it was any of her business. She pulled her flannel wrapper tight around her and made herself go to bed, wishing she had some excuse to call him back.

Chapter Five

JAKE SAT BACK, enjoying the pleasant sight bustling around the kitchen.

"It's time to get out and see what we can find. Might be able to pick up some mavericks. And, we need to geld the calves." He laughed at Martha's grimace. "It isn't a pretty job, but it's got to be done."

"I know. I just didn't have the heart to take the knife to the little ones." She refilled his cup. "From what we have so far, it looks to me like we're going to come up short, too, unless you find a whole mess of cows out there."

He hadn't told her, yet, the full extent of the losses they'd suffered to the rustlers.

"We'll see what turns up." Jake sat up and rested his elbows on the table. "Are you planning on some spring grass?"

Martha nodded. "I've not been looking forward to it, though. I don't think much of following that mule."

"Sam and I'll plant the grass."

Jake ignored the glare Sam threw his way, but Martha saw it.

"We'll plant the grass, Jake," she said, casting a wary glance at the younger brother.

"No, ma'am, that's no job for women." He was amused that she raised no argument. "We can have all the planting done in a couple of days. The cattle can wait."

Even though Sam looked as unenthusiastic about the prospect of following a mule as Martha claimed to be, no one argued with Jake's decision.

The men started out for the field right after breakfast, followed by the faithful Dave. Martha wasn't sure why the dog tagged along, except that he could probably pull the plow if the mule gave out.

Martha stood at her bedroom window, watching them, when the sound of approaching hoofbeats drew her attention toward the other direction. She turned and saw the approach of a lone rider mounted on a tall palomino. It was a toss-up as to which one was in charge. The animal pranced and tossed his head, only earning himself a sharp swat with the end of the reins.

She stood, hand to her forehead. Her neighbor, Wilson Garret, had come visiting.

"Damnation!" She covered her lips with one finger, instantly contrite. "Don't let him get to you, Martha."

Garret stopped the horse in front of the house and dismounted.

"Please, get back on your horse and leave," she prayed out loud. A heavy sigh escaped her when he didn't and she headed for the door. "I'd better get out there. Mary's liable to fill his fancy hide full of buckshot." For an instant, she considered letting her sister do just that.

As Martha came out onto the porch, she noticed his eyes were directed toward the two men leading the mule away from the house. He looked confused, then anxious, then, as he became aware of her presence at the screen door, he assumed an expression of calm.

"What is going on in that rattlesnake's mind?" Mary asked as she came to the front door.

Garret warily tipped his hat to the younger MacLannon sister.

"Good morning, Miss Mary," he said.

Turning to Martha, he removed his hat and looked her up and down. She guessed she ought to be flattered by the attention.

She wasn't.

He put on what he must have thought was a most winning smile. "Miss Martha, don't you look lovely this morning?"

"What do you want, Mr. Garret?"

"Well, I heard all your hands up and quit on you. Thought I'd come and see if there was anything I could do to help you out."

"Isn't that neighborly?" Mary sneered. "But the last ones quit over three months ago. You're just a tad late, aren't you? But then, you know exactly when they left, since you're the one who ran them all off."

"Now, Mary," Martha said, "why would you say something like that? Mr. Garret has been trying to get his hands on our ranch ever since he arrived in Travis County, but that's no reason to accuse him of murder and intimidation."

His stony green eyes glittered with anger. His jaw clenched and a muscle in his cheek jerked. But as quickly as the fury appeared, he masked it. Martha admired his control.

"Ladies, I swear on my honor as a gentleman I had nothing to do with those unfortunate and cowardly attacks." His voice was calm and carried a sincerity she didn't believe for an instant. He looked in the direction the men had taken shortly before. "I see you found a couple of new hands." He motioned in the general direction of the hay field. "Anybody I might know?"

She was put on guard by his manner, the nonchalance of his innocent question. Why would he ask if he knew them?

"No," she answered. "They're not from around here."

He stared after Jake and Sam as they disappeared over a rise. Then he shook his head and turned to her, giving her another thoroughly insulting once-over.

"Martha, aren't you going to invite me up for a cool drink?"

He made a move to step up on the porch. Martha moved into his way.

"Actually, no, I wasn't. And I don't recall giving you leave to call me by my first name." There, she'd set him straight, for all the good it was going to do her. "We have quite a lot of work to do." She crossed her arms across her bosom, shielding herself from his roving eyes. "What can I do for you, Mr. Garret?"

He stepped back into the dust of the yard. "In addition to offering my help, as any good neighbor would, I thought I would reiterate my offer to buy your property."

Martha gave him a pained look. "What, no proposal of marriage? Why, Mr. Garret, I'm crushed."

"I'm sorry, my dear," he replied. "A man's pride can take rejection only so many times. Perhaps, when I've had a rest from the sharp edge of your clever tongue, I'll consider courting you again." His eyes moved over her, making her feel stark naked. "If the scenery stays this pleasant around here, I'll definitely be back."

"Don't hurry on my account. I'm not for sale and neither is my land."

His eyes narrowed and he started up the steps again, only to be met at nose level by the business end of Mary's shotgun. He stopped and glared along the barrel to the woman holding it. After failing to intimidate the younger sister, he returned his attention to Martha.

"One day, Miss MacLannon, you'll come begging me to take this miserable piece of ground off your hands. You'd just better hope I still want it."

He jerked the reins free of the hitching post and, mounting quickly, yanked the golden horse around toward the north in the direction of his ranch. Without even a tip of his hat, he set his heels to his mount. The dust settled before Martha relaxed, leaving her with a nagging certainty she'd see him again, much too soon.

AT NOON, MARTHA took a basket of food out to Jake and Sam. She enjoyed cooking, especially for an appreciative audience, which they certainly were. The basket yielded more than even two big, hungry men could polish off, though they did their best.

Sam sat back on the ground and pulled out a tobacco pouch.

"Miss Martha," he said, "you are about the best cook I've ever had the pleasure to be fed by."

"Why, thank you, sir."

Jake stretched out on his side and looked her over. It was an appreciative appraisal. Now it was clear to her why Garret had left her feeling dirty. Jake's gaze, openly admiring, was also filled with respect. He didn't look at her like a thing to be possessed.

"The cook sure does look pretty, too," he said.

Warmth flood her cheeks as she looked down at her dusty rose-colored dress. She didn't trust her voice to even say thank you, but only risked a little smile.

The three sat in silence, Sam puffing on his pipe, Jake looking at Martha, and Martha trying to look like she didn't notice him looking at her. Sam finally rose and knocked his pipe on a tree.

"I believe I'll take a little walk," he said. Tipping his hat to Martha, he headed off toward a small stand of trees.

When Sam was out of earshot, Jake asked, "Who rode up after we left?"

"Wilson Garret." She smoothed her skirt, wiping off some imaginary dirt.

"Still wanting to court you?" At her questioning glance, he explained, "Folks in town don't have much else to talk about, so we heard plenty. I can certainly understand his interest."

She looked at him, hoping she understood him, wanting to hear him say it. He obliged her.

"You're a very beautiful woman, Martha."

The words thrilled her to her toes, but she tried to remain cool, at least on the outside.

"Oh, don't be ridiculous. He doesn't want me. Even if he did, and I shudder to ponder the possibility, I wouldn't have him."

Jake smiled. "Why doesn't he go after Mary then?"

"Mary would shoot him." She enjoyed making him laugh. He was so handsome when he laughed. "Actually, it wouldn't do him any good. Daddy's will left the ranch to the oldest surviving child. I never thought it would be me."

"Only the oldest? What about the rest of you?"

"Each of the boys was to get money and stock to get started ranching. Mary and I were to get a...dowry...I suppose you'd call it. He didn't want everything dissected into pieces." She sighed. "Now I have a ranch, and Mary had a real nice bank account. But we've just about used it up. I have to start paying her back from this drive."

"You shouldn't be telling me all this. I could be a thief," he teased. "Or a rustler. I could be rounding up your cows just to steal them from you."

"Tell you what? That we're cash poor and one season away from destitution?" She smiled at him. "As you say, that's no more than you could have found out in town. Clarissa Butler would have been happy to fill you in on my financial situation. Anyway, you're no thief."

A cloud passed over his face, closing him off from her. He got up and said, somewhat gruffly, "Sam and I had better get back to work. Thanks for dinner, Miss."

He quickly covered the distance to the mule resting under the shade of a tall cottonwood nuzzling the last of the grain from the bag tied around his head.

As she packed up the remains of the dinner, she watched him, a little confused by the sudden change in his manner, and especially by that *Miss*. She cast one last look toward the man trailing the mule and wondered if she'd ever understand him.

WILSON GARRET was still in a rage when he returned from the MacLannon ranch. Barely able to eat, he kept thinking about her. Never had he had such a time with a woman. How was it that she, unlike all other women he'd ever met, resisted him?

He turned slightly in his chair at the head of the massive Spanish dining table. In the large mirror on the wall, he saw a thick mane of blond hair now neatly pomaded and framing his high brow. His mother had always said a high brow was a sign of high intelligence. His clean-shaven jaw was firm and strong. The widely spaced eyes of green were brilliant, and many a young girl had lost her virtue after looking into their depths.

He sat up straight and patted his stomach. His body was still trim and fit, even after nearly forty years of hard living. All in all, there was no reason a woman should find him unattractive.

But Martha did.

That dried-up, sharp-tongued old maid had just about exhausted his patience. His mood improved slightly as he recalled her standing on the porch in that pink dress. She still filled it real good, he thought, imagining what she looked like under it.

Damn her to hell! "She probably has to be tied up in a corset. Bet she looks like a sack of flour when she gets unwrapped."

Even as he spoke the words to no one, he acknowledged they weren't true. He had once held her in his arms. There had been no disguising the firmness and arousing strength of her body. She had fought him, of course, which only excited him more. He would have that woman, and her ranch, if it was the last thing he ever did. Nothing and nobody would stand in his way.

Suddenly, he thought of the two men who had been walking up the path to the hay field. There was something about them that unsettled him. The taller one had a beard, and there was that almost unnoticeable limp, just like.... He broke into a chuckle.

"That's crazy. They're both dead. I killed them myself. Any man can grow a beard. And lots of men came back from the war with a limp."

But the icy finger of doubt moved along his spine, raising the hair on the back of his neck.

"Damn! I should have put a bullet in his brain and buried the bastards. Then I would be sure!"

He rose from the table so rapidly the chair flew out and fell on its side. Garret strode to the veranda door which faced the bunkhouse. Spying his foreman enjoying a smoke in the shade of a pecan tree, he grew even more agitated. Everything falling apart and there was Monroe sittin' on his rump.

"Monroe! Get your lazy ass in here!" he shouted. "It doesn't matter who they are, anyway," he continued to himself. "They'll be out of the way soon enough."

He went into his office, muttering, cursing women in general, the beautiful and well-placed Miss MacLannon in particular. He kicked the wastebasket by the desk, sending paper all over the room. He was pacing the floor of his study like a big cat in a cage when Monroe entered.

"That woman's found herself some hands. Go kill the sons-of-bitches. Now!"

Monroe nodded. "I've seen 'em. They were riding out pretty regular, but they've been staying right around the house, ever since the big one and Miss MacLannon caught the boys out there with them cows. We'll have to wait until they get out on the range again."

"All right, just get the job done. Soon."

Monroe started to leave the room.

Turning away from the foreman, Garret fumed around his desk. A thought occurred to him and he called to the man.

"Monroe, do it yourself. I'm sick and tired of your hired men and their screwing up."

He calmed down a bit.

"And don't leave any witnesses."

Monroe's face said he'd never be so stupid.

Garret resumed his pacing. His sense of unease increased. It was times like these when he thought maybe, much as he hated to admit it, Jake had been right...again. They should have gone on to Mexico in '70 and bought a ranch there. At least he wouldn't be so worried, now. In spite of himself, he remembered something Jake had said to him one fine spring day just last year.

The only unforgivable sin, Wil, is turning on your friends.

Chapter Six

THE LIGHT FROM the sooty oil lamp wasn't nearly enough. A midnight blackness had settled over the stall in the back corner of the barn, but Martha could have had a thousand lamps and the situation wouldn't have been better.

Her saddle horse, Sunbeam, had been laboring for hours with no sign that the foal was moving out of the womb. Something had to be wrong. A swelling sense of dread threatened to keep Martha paralyzed there on the floor, but she forced herself to get up. She washed her hands in the bucket and let the water run down her elbows. With a few softly spoken words, Martha crouched down by Sunbeam's tail and gently slid her hand inside the birth canal.

"Oh, no." Panic started pushing out the dread. It was as she'd suspected -- the foal was breech. She removed her hand.

The mare sensed her fear and flailed her legs. Martha spoke quietly while she stroked the smooth chestnut flank, calming her.

"You won't die," she vowed. "You're going to live and so will your baby."

Before she could think any more about it, she again gently slipped her arm into the birth canal, feeling for the thin legs. When she had them, she slid her hands along them to the tiny pasterns. She wrapped her fingers around the little legs and pushed inward and upward as far as she could reach, trying to twist the little body toward his mother's backbone, making him turn in the womb. The mare protested, weakly kicking to stop the torment.

"Please, Sunbeam, be still, honey," Martha whispered, pushing desperately on the spindly legs. After several minutes with no progress at all, Martha tried to pull the foal from his mother's body.

When this also failed, a scream of frustration tore at her throat. Taking a deep breath to swallow the fear, she withdrew her arm from her horse's body and flopped on her bottom in a huff. After almost a year of waiting for this baby, he was going to die because he was turned around backwards. And Sunbeam would die along with him.

She looked out the barn door toward the bunkhouse. Not even thinking, she jumped to her feet and ran across the yard. As she yanked the door open, silvery moonlight flooded inside, illuminating the bearded face on the bunk. She ran in and knelt by him.

"Jake. Wake up, Jake." When he didn't answer, she set her hands on his shoulders and shook him.

Then she removed her hands and sat back on her heels, as she looked down the octagonal barrel of a Navy Colt.

"Martha?" he said, quickly coming to full consciousness, and lowering the weapon. "Dammit, woman, don't you know better than to wake a man up like that?"

"Please, come to the barn and help me. It's Sunbeam. She's in trouble."

She was up and out the door before he could acknowledge her.

A few minutes later, they were kneeling by the mare and Martha had explained the situation.

"Poor little girl," Jake said, as he stroked her neck and down her legs. "She's so tired." His voice, gentle and concerned, almost made Martha give in to her own fatigue, fear, and desperation.

"Jake, please, I can't do it. I'm not strong enough to turn him or pull him out."

He only paused for a second. "Is there some clean water in here?" he asked.

She dashed to refill the bucket and get a clean towel. By the time she had them on the bench at the end of the stall, Jake had his sleeves rolled up over his elbows. After he'd washed his hands and forearms thoroughly, he knelt down by Sunbeam's side and felt the mare's belly.

"There are the legs, and," he moved his hand upwards, "there's the head." He sat back and sighed. "I'd hoped...." He shook his head. "But as usual, you were right. This baby is sure as hell coming into the world bass-ackwards." He grimaced. "Might as well get to it, then."

He spoke softly to the mare, keeping her attention on his voice, while he reached in and felt for the tiny hooves. Sunbeam was too exhausted to even kick and just lay still as he invaded her body. Martha's heart froze.

Jake breathed a sound of relief. "It's small, Martha. I've got the back pasterns."

He reached his other hand around to feel the mare's belly. With each contraction, he gave a slow, steady pull on the little legs.

She sat beside Sunbeam's head. His voice calmed her, as it calmed the mare. They both were completely obedient to his direction.

"Come on, you sweet thing."

She stroked Sunbeam's long, beautiful face while she sat waiting. Her attention was divided between the laboring mother and the voice of the man dragging the baby into the world. The minutes crept on and on.

When at last the little head appeared, Martha sat back on the sweet clean hay and allowed herself the luxury of a few tears of relief and gratitude. Jake rubbed the foal down with a clean towel, clearing away the membrane from the nose and gently warming the baby until its exhausted mother could get her second wind and take over.

"Good thing these things fold," he said with a grin.

Sunbeam finally got to her feet and nuzzled her foal. Then, she put her muzzle to Jake's cheek as though to thank him for his help. He reached up and stroked the velvety nose, the barest hint of a smile given away by the lines at the corners of his eyes.

Martha moved out of the mother's way, nearer to Jake.

They sat side by side, sharing the pleasure of watching the baby, already standing on its own and nosing around his mother's belly for some food.

"I didn't even think to ask," Martha said. "What is it?"

"It's a horse."

Though his face bore the serious expression of a schoolmaster, his eyes glinted with mischief. She slapped at his shoulder playfully and laughed, sure she had never heard anything so funny.

"No, stupid! Is it a colt or a filly?"

"A filly," he smiled as he looked at mother and daughter, "a real pretty one, too. What are you going to name her?"

"I haven't even thought about that. I'm just so glad they are both all right." She wiped away a stray tear. "You must think I'm very silly, just a typical female, crying over every little thing."

"Martha, 'typical' is a word I would never use to describe you." He went to the bench and started to wash the bloody remnants of the birth from his arms.

Not knowing why, she went to stand beside him. He reached around her for the towel. She didn't, couldn't, move away from him, even as his arm brushed her back. He wiped his arms dry.

She wondered how those arms would feel around her.

"Thank you, Jake."

He dropped the towel and pulled his sleeves down.

"I'm always glad to help you. You know that."

They stood just inches apart. Martha tilted her head way back to look into his eyes, feeling them draw her in. She knew she should go. He'd as much as said he'd be leaving after he got his share of the profits from the drive. She was too sensible to knowingly make trouble for herself.

Did he want to kiss her? It might be nice, just once, so she could remember it later. Should she let him, just once?

Wouldn't that only make it hurt more when he did leave?

She recognized the look of desire in the depths of his eyes. She'd seen the same look before in other eyes, but she'd never welcomed it as she did now.

Maybe just once. Just one kiss.

He looked deep into her eyes, seeking permission.

She didn't even realize she had given it. He moved even closer, collapsing the distance between them to only a breath, and lay his hands on her shoulders, stroking her arms down to her hands and then back up. His touch caused her heart to flutter like a bird in a cage, while every muscle relaxed as his hands passed over them. He moved up along the sides of her neck and, hesitating for the barest second, he touched her face, a tentative movement as though testing the feel of her skin.

He moved slowly. She knew he was giving her time to stop him. He'd not force anything from her. He was her protector, after all, the man who'd arrived when it looked like all was lost. She was safe.

Only when she'd closed that final tiny distance between them did his arms surround her, those same strong arms that had saved Sunbeam and her baby moments before.

He lowered his lips to hers. He demanded she open herself to him and she obeyed, welcoming the entirely new sensation of the warm probing touch of his tongue. Somewhere deep inside, she heard a nagging voice of warning, but she didn't try to break out of his embrace. Her arms, like snakes under the spell of the charmer's flute, stroked the strong muscles of his shoulders before encircling his neck.

Jake tightened his arms around her and lifted her until her face was on a level with his own. He held her firmly, yet so gently, like a priceless treasure. She allowed him to touch, taste, explore her mouth as no other man had ever done. And even though she had never experienced it, she recognized the yearning that began deep within her, then grew and spread as an ache throughout her whole body. His desire was obvious and she wanted to yield to him. She held onto him, begging him with her arms, her hands, her lips, not to leave her.

Jake set her feet back on the ground. He lifted his mouth from hers and kissed her face, her eyes, then returned to her lips, devouring her. Still holding her in his arms, he murmured her name as he caressed her.

His words reached her consciousness.

"Molly, darlin' Molly."

Both her hands flew to his chest and pushed him away.

"Molly," he began.

"I told you before," she said, her voice brittle and hard, good sense restored. "Don't ever call me that."

She turned and without another word walked almost at a run to the house, leaving Jake in the barn door looking after her.

MARY WAS ASLEEP in Jake's chair, but she lifted her head when Martha came in.

"How is she?" Mary asked sleepily.

Martha didn't answer, but went straight into her bedroom, where she closed the door and threw herself on the bed. The tears were ready enough, but she refused to cry.

She still felt his lips on hers and his strong arms holding her tight, his large, gentle hands caressing and possessing her. The aching want still filled her, crushing her from inside.

The door opened and Mary came in and sat down on the bed, stroking Martha's hair.

"I'm sorry, Molly. I wish you'd called me. Maybe we could have done something together."

"What?" Then she shook her head as she understood Mary's meaning. "Everything went fine. The baby was breech, but Jake was able to get her out."

"It was a filly! Oh, Molly, how wonderful!" Mary leaned over and embraced her, then suddenly sat up. "Jake was out there? Molly, what happened?" she asked, a slight smile indicating she already knew.

Martha didn't answer and wished that Mary would disappear, just for a little while. Guilt clutched at her heart at such a thought, at least until Mary opened her mouth again.

"What did he do?"

"Who?" She hoped Mary would just let it go. No such luck.

"He kissed you, didn't he?" Mary giggled with glee.

Martha rose on one elbow. She was somewhat chagrined that Mary seemed more excited about the prospect of Martha getting kissed than Martha, herself, was.

"Well?" Mary demanded.

"Yes, Mary."

"Ooooohh!" Mary fell onto the bed beside her and asked in a whisper, "Was it good?"

Even in her present misery, she had to smile, especially since it had been. Very good.

"Yes, in fact, it was."

"So, what's the problem? The horses are fine. You got kissed by a good-looking man, and I might add," she continued archly, "it's about time."

Martha rose from the bed and went to stand by the front window. His shadow moved across the big double doorway of the barn.

"I hate this place."

"What? How can you say that?"

"Why are we holding on to this piece of dirt? Neither of us is likely to marry. We don't have any relatives who'll want a ranch in Texas. Who is there to leave it all to?" She sat heavily in the big chair by the window, where she had often found comfort as a child on her mother's lap. "You know what they say about me in town, don't you?"

"I'd have to be deaf not to." Mary puffed her bosom out and, one hand on her hip, one at her throat, she mimicked the local hens discussing the local scandal.

"'That Martha MacLannon is a disgrace. Wearing pants and herding cattle like a man!'"

Martha huffed with indignation, which only made Mary's eyes glint with wicked mischief as she continued.

"'And she is such a bad influence on her sweet little sister, too.'"

Martha snorted at that. "I wonder if they'd be happier if we wore party dresses and rode sidesaddle?"

"You know why they hate you, Molly. They're plain jealous. Every one of those old hens wants Wilson Garret as a son-in-law. He hasn't paid the least attention to the other young ladies."

"None of the rest of them have clear title to one hundred twenty-eight-thousand acres of prime ranch land."

"That may be, but I think he's just as much after you as he is the land. I don't think many women have rejected him like you did."

Martha suddenly heard her mother's voice warning her she would be an old maid if she didn't make up her mind which one of the dozens of marriage proposals she was going to accept. How different her life would have been if she'd just listened. A husband, home, children. She'd always refused to fret over what had never been, but the thought that now she really was running out of time kept nagging at her.

"Maybe I should just give in and marry him, if he would still have me."

"No!" Mary actually shivered. "The thought of you with him makes my skin crawl."

"Lots of women marry men they can't stand."

"Molly, nothing is worth that. However, you shouldn't give up on finding a man who would make you happy and," she had to stop to take in a breath, "you are not too old to have those children to leave all this to."

Martha laughed out loud. "Just who is going to marry me? All the men in Travis County are either already taken, or I wouldn't have them, or they're scared of me."

With a look of contrived innocence on her face, Mary said, "Maybe there is somebody, though. Somebody right around here who has shown a considerable interest in you? Maybe someone who has kissed you recently? Like maybe in the last hour?"

"Forget it, little matchmaker. He's not for me."

"Come on, Molly. I've seen you two sitting in the library talking, and him reading, and you pretending to sew while you're mooning over him." She looked out the window toward the barn. "He's still out there. Why don't you take him a cup of coffee? He could probably use it."

Martha threw up her hands in total exasperation.

"What do you want, Mary? Do you want me to go out there and give him what I've kept from every other man in Travis County for thirty-five years? A man I've known for barely a month?"

"Yes."

Martha laughed grimly at her sister's boldness. "Well, Miss, let me tell you something. That man is going to get on that horse of his and he and his brother and that big, ugly dog are going to be gone before winter comes. I've lost everyone I ever loved except you, and I certainly won't knowingly put myself in the position of falling in love with a man who won't stay. I'm not so stupid that I'm going to be left here with a child to raise by myself."

"Does he strike you as the kind of man who would leave his child?"

Martha gaped at Mary. "You're serious! You'd actually be happy if he got me with child."

"I'm dead serious. I've watched him look at you, the way his eyes follow you around the room. If he leaves, it'll be because you haven't given him a reason to stay."

"You heard him that first night, Mary. He's a cowhand, a drifter. He'll get his stake and move on."

Mary was about to argue, but Martha cut her off. "Mary, please, just drop it." Martha was suddenly very tired. She stared out the window.

Mary's footsteps stopped at the door and Martha heard the grating of the doorknob, but she didn't turn around. Her eyes followed his shadow as he moved around in the barn and her fingers stroked her lips as her thoughts followed her tall, Texas cowboy.

Chapter Seven

JAKE HAD TO REMIND himself to keep his mind on the cattle he was trying to round up and not on the woman who owned them. He was grateful for his pony, and that chasing cows didn't take too much brain power on a man's part, because all morning he'd not been thinking about much else but her.

She'd not even given him a glance at breakfast. He knew because he'd not taken his eyes off her. She was one beautiful woman! Her hair shone like gold and felt like silk. Her skin was so smooth and warm. He could still smell her scent and feel the firm softness of her body. She'd reached up to hold him and he knew she'd wanted him as badly as he did her.

Then he had to go and ruin everything.

But, damn it all, all he'd done was call her Molly. It had come out so naturally, so easily. His Molly. His saddle became uncomfortable and he shifted miserably.

"C'mon, Jake, let it go," he said to himself. It didn't matter what he called her. He couldn't give her what she deserved.

Before they got here, before he'd seen her, before he'd held her, he'd accepted the inevitable result of the path he and Sam had chosen. If they succeeded and were caught, as was most likely, they would hang.

He literally owed his brother his life, but as much as he loved Sam, he wasn't so sure anymore he was ready to die. At least, not this way.

Dismissing the risk, Jake decided to ride out a little further. His best thinking was done alone, riding the open range on a good horse. With a kick to his mount's sides, he got the pony moving. The wavy grass and bright bluebonnets blurred with their increasing speed. As he hugged the buckskin's neck, he thought about Beau. Buck was a sure-footed, game little fellow, but Beau was the finest piece of horseflesh Jake had ever seen and he missed him. Another item to add to Wilson Garret's bill.

He rode until he reached the Colorado River and Martha's northern boundary line. Just on the other side was Wil's ranch. So close, he thought. It would be so easy to ride on over there, catch Wil alone, kill him. He walked his winded pony along the river, all the while plagued by the temptation to end it once and for all.

Then what? He knew the only reward for him would be the end of a noose or permanent residence in Mexico. After last night, neither prospect was pleasing.

Jake turned toward the west. The sun just touched the horizon -- about six. Time to be getting back home.

Home, he thought, wishing it really was. This would be a fine ranch with a man who cared running it. Martha did her best and her best was a sight better than most men were capable of, but he knew her heart, at least, wasn't in it. He thought he knew what she wanted out of life. He wished he could give it to her.

"Damn," he thought, shaking off the self-pity that had settled over his shoulders like an old lady's shawl. "Just think about her cooking." He smiled and turned his horse, about to start back, when something, a feeling, a premonition, made him pull his mount to a stop at the top of a rise. Feeling exposed and alone, he knew he was being watched. His gut told him it wasn't idle curiosity.

He pushed his hat back from his brow and nonchalantly reached for his canteen. Just as he leaned forward, he heard the shot and was knocked from the saddle by the impact of the bullet.

His only thought as he hit the ground was, Not again.

SUPPER SAT ON the stove but there was no one around, yet, to eat it. The warm April breeze carried the smells of the kitchen out to the porch as Martha headed to the barn to check on her mare and the foal. The air was filled with the feeling of life reborn. She breathed it in deeply, fortifying her own soul.

Martha lay her arms on the top rail of the fence and watched as the filly, less than a day old and a bit wobbly, to be sure, trotted after her mother around the paddock. A miracle that wouldn't have been, if not for Jake. He'd saved them both.

Like every other free moment she'd had today, she thought of him, remembering the feel of his arms, the touch of his mouth upon hers. She also remembered the way she'd hardly looked at him this morning at breakfast. The fact was, she was embarrassed by her behavior last night. All he'd done was call her Molly, after all.

How could she ever explain that stodgy old Martha, fearful and overcautious and overly comfortable with being an old maid, had taken over? It really was like she was two people, sometimes.

The filly approached the fence, trusting and unafraid. Martha reached through to pet her. Stroking the foal's oversized ears, she said, "Maybe Jake ought to name you. He saved your life after all." She wondered what would have happened if he'd not been there....

A chill began working its way up her spine, a clawing, ripping chill of terror the warm spring air couldn't thaw.

"Jake," she whispered, turning away from the fence and looking out at the rolling acres to the north.

She gathered her skirts and ran to the house, tearing her dress off on her way to her room. Dread knotted into a ball in her stomach as she pulled on the boy's pants and worn calico shirt she worked in and yanked on her boots. Out in the front hall, she picked up her Henry rifle, making sure it was loaded. On her way out the front door, she grabbed her battered hat and slammed it on her head.

Nearly running across the yard to the barn, she looked for any sign of Sam or Mary. She was consumed with certainty that Jake was hurt and she knew she couldn't move him by herself.

Martha fought her rising fear. She had to be rational and think. Both their lives might depend on it. She rushed into the barn and grabbed a bridle from the rack. Mary's big bay gelding nickered at her touch.

"Come on, Chief. Help me find him."

Whispering encouraging words, more for her own sake than for the horse's, she threw her saddle onto Chief's back and pulled the cinch tight. She slipped her rifle into the leather scabbard on the saddle and led the horse out of the barn.

Should she tell Mary where she was going, though she didn't know herself? Should she take the time to get her medical bag? Should she wait for Sam?

The chill slid up her backbone again, like a call, a summons. She mounted and started off in the direction her intuition indicated. Chief shied as a huge shadow came from the direction of the bunkhouse. Dave caught up, keeping stride with the horse. She was glad to see him. She'd need whatever help she could get.

Riding hard, she reached the northern boundary of her land. Martha strained in the twilight for some sign. So far, the tracks of Jake's pony had been clear and easy to follow through the scrubby grass, but with the fading light and the rougher terrain, she was afraid she had lost him.

She saw Dave looking off in the distance.

"Go find him, Dave."

As though he had just been waiting for the word, Dave bounded off. Trying to keep the dog in sight, she continued north. The fact that Garret's ranch lay in this direction only made her more apprehensive.

The hair on the back of her neck rose at the gunshot in the distance.

"Jake." She put her heels to Chief and took off at a dead run toward the sound.

She almost ran up on top of them, but managed to get Chief stopped about twenty yards away. Jake lay on his back on the ground. Her heart stopped when she saw him lying so still. A man stood over him, gun drawn, pointed at Jake's head.

"Look there, Al," a second man, still on horseback, called.

Al looked up from his job. "That's Miss MacLannon. We'll have to take care of her after we do this one. Get her." He returned his attention to Jake.

Martha pulled her rifle from the scabbard and raised it, bracing her feet in the stirrups.

The second man started toward her. "Looky, she's got herself a little gun."

She ignored the second man and concentrated on the one standing over Jake. One shot was all she'd get. She took a deep breath. As she released the air in her lungs, she squeezed the trigger. Her ears were so full of the pounding of her own blood, she didn't hear the sound of the shot. Al dropped to the ground.

"Be damned!" the second man yelled. He had his gun out and started toward her.

"Stop where you are, or I'll kill you, too." To emphasize her intent, Martha raised the rifle, drawing a bead on the man's chest.

An unearthly sound came to her ears. Dave closed the distance before she could fire. The man's horse reared at the appearance of the huge hound. He flipped backwards out of the saddle, but his right foot was trapped in the stirrup.

"Help me," he shouted as his horse shied and ran off, dragging him along the rough ground.

"Serves you right," she whispered, dismounting and running to Jake.

Only a brief moment of guilt passed through her mind when she stepped over Al's dead body. She'd never killed before. But, there was no time. Pushing aside all concerns other than Jake, she knelt beside him.

His breathing was ragged and shallow and he showed no signs of consciousness, but occasionally grimaced as though in pain. Martha was glad for that. As long as he was in pain, he was alive.

She began a businesslike examination of his wounds. The blood crusted around his face came from a cut on his head -- not attractive, but not serious. She passed her hands over him, shoulder to wrist, along each leg. Struggling with his weight, she slipped her hand behind his neck and felt for the stickiness of spilled blood.

It didn't take her long to find it. A brown-red stain marked the place on the back of his right shoulder where the bullet had entered.

Cold rage came upon her as she suddenly understood what had happened. He had been shot from behind. She sighed as she realized that besides testifying to the cowardice of his attacker, the lack of an exit wound in the front meant the bullet was still inside.

But he was alive! The words rolled through her mind like far-off thunder. It gave her a sense of peace and purpose. With a task ahead of her, even one as gruesome as this, she regained some feeling of control.

She needed clean cloth for bandages. He was still bleeding and it had to be stopped.

"Why didn't you get your bag, Martha?" Glancing around, making sure she was alone, except for Jake, she pulled her shirt out of her waistband. She took her knife from her boot and slit the bodice of her chemise at the waist, then cut the shoulder straps and pulled the material out from under her shirt. Trying to ignore how naked she felt, she tore the material into strips and folded them.

"Jake, why do you have to be so big?" She struggled with him to get his jacket pulled down far enough to pack the wound with the strips of her unmentionables. "I suppose I'll blush like a fool as soon as I have time to think about this." But instead of thinking of her intimate clothing touching his skin, she suddenly thought of all the people she had loved, and how she had lost most of them.

How she'd almost lost this one, too.

Martha pushed the thoughts from her mind. There was more than enough to worry about right here and now. She took stock of her resources as she considered how to get him back to the house.

"All right, Martha. How are you going to move a man who outweighs you by at least a hundred pounds?" She looked around. One horse, one big ugly dog, one rifle. One saddle, with a blanket roll and a rope. The answer came. "A travois. Poles. What can I use for poles?"

About thirty yards away, a small stand of post oak beckoned. A tree lay on its side at the edge of the stand. She eyeballed the limbs, finally settling on two about fifteen feet long. She and Chief managed to break them off with enough length to do the job and dragged them over to where Jake lay like a two-hundred-pound sack of sugar. She constructed the stretcher next to him, laying the poles on the blanket, then folding the blanket over them.

"Okay, Jake," she grunted, turning him on his face and laying her travois-stretcher over him. She got on the other side and pushed him the other way. His weight would keep the blanket and the poles secure. She tied the two poles to the saddle horn, one on each side of the horse.

"Hold on, Jake. I'll get you home."

BEFORE CHIEF was completely at a standstill, she jumped down and ran to Jake. She drew her knife from her boot top and cut the ropes holding Jake on her travois.

"Where have you been? I've been worried out of my mind." Mary demanded as she ran out of the house. Then she saw Jake on the improvised travois. "What happened?"

Sam stood on the top step. "Martha, is he...?"

"He's alive. Come help me. We'll take him into my room." Between the three of them, they got Jake into Martha's bedroom and into her bed.

"Mary, get me some water and a couple of long knives." Martha set about getting clean cloths and her medical bag.

Within minutes she had everything she needed and she set to work. She carefully soaked the dried blood that glued her chemise to the wound. Then, with both Sam and Mary helping her, she removed his jacket and shirt and pulled the top of his long underwear from his upper body. They turned him onto his stomach and stepped back to give Martha room.

She studied the man lying in her bed. The entry wound looked worse up close. As she started probing for the bullet, the weak moans from her patient both reassured her and made her nervous.

Mary washed the wound once more while Martha went to the basin and poured fresh water, then washed her hands and the two long, thin knives.

Satisfied that everything was as clean as possible, she went to the bed and stood beside the wounded man, steeling herself for the task ahead. Jake's breathing had steadied and was now fairly deep and even, though every now and then a breath would come a bit ragged.

Taking the sharper of the two knives, she inserted it into the bullet hole and, with a quick motion of her wrist, extended the opening. The only sound from her patient was a weak moan. The knife slid easily into the wound and she immediately located the slug.

"Sam, hold him still."

Sam moved quickly to do her bidding and took a position on the opposite side of the bed. Luckily, the bullet was lodged against his shoulder blade and wouldn't move around much. Martha slipped the second knife in and used the two blades as forceps to pull the bullet from his body. Though it seemed to take much longer, it was only a minute before the misshapen mass of lead lay on the night stand.

Martha then turned her attention to the wound, pouring in warm water and watching the mixed fluid of blood and water run out. When it appeared clean, she poured carbolic acid into the wound to kill any infection before it started. He had lost a lot of blood and an infection might succeed where the bullet had failed. Taking a small jar from the medical bag her mother had given her on her sixteenth birthday, she opened it and withdrew a small, threaded needle.

"This is the part I hate!" Mary said as she and Sam turned their heads from the sight. Martha smiled at them.

"Cowards!"

She stitched the muscle and fat layers and it struck her that Jake would carry her stitches inside his body for the rest of his life. When those few stitches were done, she again washed the wound with carbolic and proceeded to the outer skin. Pressing his skin together gently like her mother had shown her, she closed the wound with several small stitches. She washed the wound and covered it all with a clean bandage. Only as she stood up did she notice the ache that had settled between her shoulders and radiated down her back.

Martha touched his forehead. He wasn't feverish, yet, and she gave thanks for that favor. She pulled a light spread over him and went to collapse into her chair by the window.

Mary brought her some supper and she ate, though she really wasn't hungry. Sam sat with her by his brother's bedside, but asked no questions until she'd finished.

"What happened, Martha? Did you see who did it?"

"Yes, though I didn't recognize them. They knew me, though."

"How many were there?" he asked.

"There were a couple of men looking him over when I rode up. I killed one, just as he was about to put a bullet in Jake's brain." She shivered. He would have killed Jake, she told herself, but the guilt of taking a life nagged at her conscience. "The other one got dragged off when Dave frightened his horse. I think he thought he was being chased by a hell-hound."

Sam was silent. "Well, I'll just mosey on out there and collect the body. There might just be a reward on the old boy." He rose and started for the door.

Martha took his hand as he passed her. "Sam, please be careful. If they went after Jake, they'll be after you, too."

"Why do you think they were after Jake?" He seemed suspicious of her question.

"Because you work on my ranch. It's got to be Garret's doing. I'd bet my last cow on it."

Sam nodded and started out the door. He stopped.

"Martha, thank you for finding him and saving his life."

His face was turned away, so he didn't see Martha's guilty flush at his statement. If it wasn't for her, she thought, Jake wouldn't have been hurt in the first place.

"You know, ladies, it's been a long time since we've been with folks like you. Jake and I both feel, well, real comfortable here and we don't want to cause you any grief." He stopped, apparently suddenly embarrassed. "Good night, Misses. See you in the morning."

They watched him close the door behind him.

"Molly, they deserve to know what's been going on here."

Martha leaned wearily against the back of her chair.

"I know. I'll tell them as soon as Jake wakes up."

Chapter Eight

JAKE WOKE WITH a killer of a headache. He didn't remember being in a saloon, but the last time he'd felt like this was after a bender in the Silver Slipper in Fort Worth and the ensuing evening's pleasures in the arms of a soiled dove named Sue.

I must be dreaming, he thought as he drew in a deep breath. He smelled Martha.

Coming to complete consciousness, he realized he was lying on his stomach. He tried to turn over, but a sharp pain in his right shoulder warned him to stop. The accompanying groan escaped his lips before he could catch it, waking the small figure curled in the chair by the window.

Then, he realized where he was. He had spent many evenings in the doorway of the bunkhouse, watching her as she sat by that window on the side of the house, combing her hair, reading, or sewing by the light of the oil lamp. The remainder of those evenings had been spent trying to get to sleep. After an hour or two of his tossing and turning, and cussing and groaning, Sam would move to the other end of the long building to get some peace.

He was in her bed.

He would have laughed at the irony if his head hadn't felt like it would explode if he did.

She stirred and stretched. Seeing him awake, she smiled. As he tried again to turn over, she rose and came to the bed.

"Don't try to move, yet. I don't want those stitches to break. There won't be much of a scar if you're careful." With gentle, but firm hands, she pressed him back down to the bed. "You ought to try to stay on your stomach."

"I hate laying on my stomach," he said.

She looked amused. "Are you going to be a difficult patient, Jake?"

"I'm not going to be patient at all, Miss MacLannon."

Laughing, Martha reached across him and helped him turn over and sit up. "Well, come on, then, if you insist. Here, let me get the pillows behind you."

Her face was close to his and he looked up into the perfect oval framed by a halo of wavy blond hair, free for now of the usual combs and pins that restrained it. From the outside corners of her blue sky eyes lines radiated, reflecting the wide, beautiful smile on her lips. He forced himself to look away, quickly. She noticed the grimace that passed over his features.

"What's the matter? Did I hurt you?"

"No." At least not in a way he'd tell her about. "What happened?"

She brought him a glass of water and sat by the bed as he drank it as ordered.

"Two days ago, you went out to round up some of the stock. I...." she stopped. "Well, I got a feeling there was something wrong and went out after you."

"What? Are you crazy, woman?" The pain in his head stopped him. "Why did you do something that stupid?"

"Stupid? If I hadn't gone out there, you would be dead now."

"You shouldn't take chances like that. I don't want you hurt because of me."

She cast her eyes toward the floor. He expected her to yell or something. The half-guilty look she wore confused him.

"So, where was I?" He held out the water glass.

"Out near the northern line." She took the empty glass and put it on the night stand. "I heard a shot. When I got to you, there were two men about to finish the job. I shot one and Dave chased the other one off."

"Two days, huh?" Jake cast a sidelong glance at her.

She nodded. "Sam went out yesterday to collect the body...."

"You killed him?"

"Yes. Sam said it, the body, was gone when he got out there."

Her fingers nervously picked at the yellow-checked material of her dress as she avoided his gaze. She wasn't very good at hiding her feelings.

"Is there more?" Jake asked.

She didn't answer right away. He sat back and relaxed his aching shoulder, waiting. Martha took a deep breath and faced him.

"It's time to be completely honest with you, Jake. Things out here are a lot worse than I led you to believe." She paused.

He supposed she was waiting for a question or something from him. When he just lay there looking at her, she looked away and continued.

"I know you think I was going under just because I'm a woman and didn't know how to run a ranch."

"I never thought that, Martha."

She shook her head. "Please, don't patronize me. I don't need it. I know what I can do and what I can't. The truth is, though, a year ago, we had ten year-round hands, a foreman, a blacksmith, and a cook. We weren't making a fortune, but we were just about to get back on our feet. If it hadn't been for the awful luck during last spring's drive, with the rains and all, we wouldn't be in this fix, now. We lost three fourths of the herd and the proceeds barely covered the expenses."

Jake held his peace.

"My foreman wanted to try a run to Kansas during the early fall to recoup some of what we'd lost in the spring. That was when somebody started attacking my hands. But only if they were out alone, or separated from the others."

She had risen and was pacing the floor at the foot of the bed. Her voice grew angrier as she continued.

"The first killing happened last September. That fool of a good-for-nothing, shiftless, no-account weasel sheriff wouldn't even come out here to look at what was happening. We had to take the bodies into town. He even told me...." She whirled around and leaned on the footboard of the bed. "Do you know what he said to me?" She returned to her pacing. "He said, 'Miss MacLannon, maybe you ought to sell that ranch to a man who can handle it.'"

What a picture she was when she was riled! Her breasts rose and fell faster, her cheeks pinkened, and her lips pouted, luscious as a ripe peach. Her little hands formed into fists that pumped as she strode across the room, back and forth, in her agitation.

"Well," she said, "nobody is running me off my land! No, sir!" Again, she turned to Jake. "Especially not a coward who shoots from ambush."

As she got to the next part of her story, she paced more slowly. Her hands resumed their worrying of each other, just in front of her waist.

"The men stayed longer than I expected them to. Four of them were killed. The coyote even killed Otto, the best damned trail cook in Texas!" She suddenly realized her choice of words and a deeper blush covered her cheeks. "I'm sorry. I didn't mean to be profane."

Jake almost laughed, but he could see her genuine embarrassment, so he just nodded and continued to listen in silence.

"Finally, in December, they got my foreman. The rest of the hands left, then." She sighed deeply. "I couldn't blame them. There was no reason for them to stay and risk their lives."

"So, whoever it was, is still out there and tried to kill me?"

She nodded. "That would make sense."

"Do you have any ideas who might be behind it?"

"I'm sure it's Garret, though I can't prove it. It started right after I turned down his first marriage proposal."

Jake agreed. It could be no one else.

"So, if you and Sam want to leave, I'll understand. And I'd like to try to pay you for all the work you've done around here."

What he wanted was to pull her into his arms and hold her, right here in her bed, to make everything right for her. But the best he could do right now was reassure her.

"Martha," he said, "we knew all about this before we came out here. You didn't think a story like this wouldn't be spread to every stranger who came into town, did you?" He half-expected her to be angry for hiding his knowledge of just how bad things were, so he continued a bit sheepishly. "Considering your circumstances, we figured you would be especially open to our offer, and we have been careful." He grinned as he inclined his head toward his shoulder. "Well, most of the time."

Far from being angry, she sat down heavily in the chair by the bed.

"You mean you've known all along? You're still going to stay?" She continued hurriedly, more out of pride and obligation, he thought, than any real desire to let him off the hook. "I'm serious about this, Jake. I won't hold you to our agreement, if you don't want to take any more chances. I especially don't want your blood on my conscience."

Jake didn't miss that *especially*.

"Honey, you didn't murder anybody."

She paled. "Actually I did. I killed that man."

"I know you feel guilty for killing even such a worthless no-account as that, but I appreciate it. You saved my life. It wasn't murder." He waited until she looked at him. "Sam and I are staying to see this through."

"Are you sure?" she asked, her voice quiet.

Jake thought he heard some other question just behind the one she actually asked.

"Yes, Martha. I'm sure."

Her lips turned up in a quick smile that as quickly faded. She got up and turned away from him, bustling around the room, picking up clothes, moving things on her dresser. Avoiding his eyes.

"Well, as long as you're sure. I just don't want you staying out of some misplaced sense of obligation."

Enough wanting, he thought. He made up his mind at that moment. He was going to have this woman. All he needed to do was convince her it was what she wanted, too. Judging by the blush on her cheeks, the still-fresh memory of her in his arms, and the fact she didn't snap his head off for calling her honey, it wouldn't be too hard. He was also going to have to find a way to kill Wil Garret and get away with it.

He watched with amusement as she puttered around the room, making all kinds of small talk.

"Martha," Sam said as he entered the room, "it looks like your neighbor is coming to pay his respects."

Martha rolled her eyes in exasperation. Muttering under her breath, she looked out the front window. Jake heard the sound of hoofbeats coming closer. He heard the crunch of the dirt at the front porch steps and the sound of leather across horsehide.

"It's criminal the way he treats that animal. Someday that horse is going to kill him, and I just hope I'm there to see it," she said with disgust.

"What kind of horse is it?" Jake asked innocently.

"A palomino. A handsome one, real tall, very big in the chest."

"What does he call him?"

"Some French name. Beau, I think." She looked back to Jake. "I'd better go see what he wants this time, as though I don't already know."

As she passed the bed, she scratched Dave between his flappy ears. His sad, brown eyes only glanced at her before returning to look at Jake adoringly.

"Dave is a pretty good nurse. He's been sitting with you night and day."

Her laughter flowed in from the hallway, and it seemed to fill the room with her presence long after she left, lingering and mixing with the delicate scent of her rose water.

Sam went to the front window, careful to stay hidden behind the frilly curtains.

The sound of voices drifted through the open window.

"Mr. Garret, what a surprise. What brings you out here so early this morning?"

"I came to look upon your beautiful face, Martha, my dear."

The blood in Jake's veins ran cold. He hadn't heard that voice in almost a year, but it was unmistakably Wil. It was all he could do to keep from taking the revolver from Sam's gunbelt and going to the window and getting it all over with, right now.

Rustler's Bride

"Help me up, Sam," he said.

Sam must have read Jake's thoughts on his face.

"Glad to, brother." He gave Jake his shoulder to lean on and pulled out his revolver and offered that as well.

Pointedly ignoring the weapon, Jake motioned for Sam to move the big chair to the window facing the front of the house, then eased himself down in it. Careful to stay out of sight, he looked once again upon the face of Wilson Garret.

He was still the dandy, all duded up and nowhere to go. Except to hell.

"Molly," the silky voice came again, "why don't you marry me? I'm rich, good-looking, smart, and I can do a lot more for you than you can do for yourself. With your land added to mine, we'll have the biggest spread in central Texas."

"Mr. Garret," came her sweet voice, "if you ever call me Molly again, I might just take Mary's shotgun and fix you so no woman would have you."

Jake chuckled in silent amusement.

"As far as marrying for property, if you want the biggest spread in Texas, why don't you mosey on over to old man Henderson's ranch and marry him?" She paused. "But I suppose you'd rather have a woman, wouldn't you? Well, let's see, oh, yes, I do believe he has a daughter. Mary, what is the child's name?"

"Hester."

"Oh, yes, dear, little Hester. Lovely girl, only eighteen. Word is she wouldn't be at all uncomfortable in the marriage bed."

Jake could see the veins standing out on Wil's neck.

"But, Martha," he pleaded prettily, "I want you. But I'm a patient man. I'm willing to wait for you to come around and see the sense in our union." He fixed her with a gaze Jake had seen reduce women to stuttering, blushing jelly. "And Martha, I always get what I want."

Martha wasn't stuttering, nor was she blushing. Her back ramrod straight, she had hardly been reduced to jelly.

"Well, Mr. Garret, I never do anything I don't want to do." She stepped down to the top step. He had been left standing by the hitching post. His boots were already white from the small dust storm Beau stamped up in his impatience. She looked Garret directly in the eyes, and her words were loaded with conviction.

"I will never marry you. And before I see you get your hands on anything belonging to me, I'll personally slit the throat of every cow, wring the neck of each and every chicken, shoot every single pig right between the eyes. I'll torch every field and every building. And before I'd marry you, I would kill myself."

Jake was very pleased by this little speech, except the last part.

"Martha, you're going to think this over and you'll come to the conclusion that the only thing you can do is marry me. Nobody else will have you, with your sharp tongue and unwomanly ways. I promise you, sometime, one way or another, you'll come to me. Then you'll know how a real man handles a woman like you."

Martha calmly stepped to the front door and reached inside for her sister's loaded shotgun. Jake almost guffawed out loud.

"Don't make any promises you can't keep, Mister Garret. Now, if you don't get off my land," she said, "you're going to find out how a woman with a shotgun handles a man like you."

She raised the double barrels of the weapon to his crotch.

Garret looked uncertainly at the two barrels directed at his privates. He turned and jerked the reins free of the hitching post.

"I'll be back, Martha. You'd better think over my offer," he said as he mounted.

"You mean your threat, don't you?"

"I don't want it that way." His voice was startling in its tenderness. "I think we could be good together, you and me. You're a lot of woman and you need a man who can handle you."

"I suppose you think that's you?" she asked sarcastically, too angry to be embarrassed by the intimate nature of the conversation. "Would you handle me like you handle your horse?" She shook her head. "No, one of us would be dead inside a week, and if I were you, I wouldn't bet it would be me. I could easily decide to cut your throat in your sleep." She considered the idea as though it had real merit. "I might just do it, anyway, if you don't leave me alone."

He laughed and looked at her from his high perch atop Beau. Just before he took off, he threw back at her, "Martha, you're going to be the best I ever had. A little stringy, maybe, being as how you're so old, but you will be good."

Martha stood fuming that he'd had the last word.

Jake sat back, watching Beau race toward the road. "I'm going to kill that bastard."

"Why didn't you?" Sam asked.

He didn't answer right away. "I've been thinking."

"Jake, why do you have to think all the time? Can't you just take it like it is?"

"Why should we swing when all we're doing is bringing a

criminal to justice? He tried to kill us. Now, if we kill him, and get caught, we'll hang." His eyes dared Sam to deny his next words. "We've already accepted the fact that we will be caught, haven't we?"

"Yes, we have. Or at least, I thought we had. You of all people don't need to be told the law. But why change the plan?" Sam fixed him with a piercing gaze. "I'll tell you why. It's clear as glass whenever that woman is around. What are you going to do? You gonna marry her, yourself? Settle down here and be a gentleman rancher? Go to all the cattlemen's conventions and rub elbows with the very folks we used to steal from? You ain't forgotten why we're here, have you?"

"I'm not liable to while I have you to remind me, am I?" Jake regretted the accusation as soon as it left his lips. "I've just started thinking," and as if to stop Sam's remark before it even came out of his mouth, he hurried on, "that maybe this plan of mine goes against everything I've ever believed in. Maybe I'm not so anxious to die as I was before. Especially now when I've found a place I feel like I belong, where I'm needed." And maybe even wanted. "I want to leave something behind when I go. Maybe what a woman like that wants is what I want, too."

"Caught up in a woman's skirts, Jake? Hell, I thought you'd gotten over stuff like that."

Sam barely got the words out before Jake stretched up his strong left arm and grabbed him by the collar, dragging him to his knees beside the chair. "How stupid are you anyway?" He practically spat the question into Sam's face. "Didn't you see? Didn't you hear what he said, how he spoke to her?"

Releasing the younger man, Jake rose with some difficulty and walked over to the door. He glanced down the hallway. It wouldn't do for her to hear and misunderstand. Once he was sure they were alone, he spoke softly to his brother.

"He wants her, not just the ranch. All the respectable people in Travis City know he's chasing after her. They know she's been resisting him. If I beat his time, and especially if she comes to me willingly...." The thought of Martha standing with that shotgun directed between Wil's legs made him smile again. "What will that do to Wil's pride?" He paused to let it sink in. "He might just get mad enough to call me out in town to save face. I'll be able to kill him. Legally."

Sam thought about all this for a moment. He then shook his head.

"He'd be more likely to just shoot you in the back again, while you're riding your range, rounding up your steers, then take what he wants after you're dead. Besides, what makes you think she'll marry you, anyway?"

Jake's lips curved in a soft smile as he remembered the one kiss they had shared. He could still feel how she fit in his arms, taste the sweetness of her lips, the warmth of her mouth, how she clung to him. She had been his for only a minute, for only one kiss. One really good kiss. But she had to be handled the right way. Maybe he could use Wil's lack of finesse for his own ends.

He'd never been more certain of anything in his whole life as he was of his next words.

"She'll marry me."

Chapter Nine

"DON'T YOU THINK maybe it's a little too soon to be working cattle, again?" Sam asked.

Jake continued pulling on his pants and ignored him.

"He's right, Jake. It's only been a week. You're not strong enough to get out of bed, yet," Martha said from out in the hall. "Are you decent?" She peeked around the door frame. Satisfied he at least had his pants on, she came into the room, arms full of clean laundry.

"Why are you so anxious to keep me in your bed, Martha?"

She gasped at the provocative remark, almost dropping her load of clothes.

"That's ridiculous. I just don't want you to rush your recovery." Crimson crept up her face as she looked at his naked chest. She tossed him a clean shirt. "Put this on." Sam's choked chuckle earned him one of her withering glares. "Don't you have anything to do?"

Jake caught the shirt with his left hand and gingerly slipped his right into the sleeve. His clothes lay on her dresser, all washed, ironed, and folded neatly by soft, gentle hands. Courting Martha would be the most pleasant thing he'd ever done.

"Umm," he groaned, loud enough for Martha to hear.

She whipped around at the sound, a concerned frown on her face. He didn't even try to hide the fact he'd been looking at her.

"You see? You are trying to take it too fast," she fussed.

"No, really, I'm fine." He started to pull the shirt over his right shoulder and made a terrible face of pain. He even faked a little groan.

She rushed over to help him.

"Sam," she chided, "how can you just stand there?"

"I didn't think my help was needed, Martha." He winked at Jake. "Looks like you have things well in hand."

"It really does hurt, Miss Martha," Jake said. *Not only my shoulder, either.*

She tried to look disgusted, but he saw a touch of a smile in her eyes.

"Put on your shirt, you faker." Her voice softened. "Don't try to do too much too soon, Jake. I'd hate for you to hurt yourself, again."

He couldn't resist. "Do you really care, Martha?"

"Of course, I care. What kind of person would I be, if I didn't?"

"And I have to get your cows to Kansas."

She smiled. "Yep, that too."

"You can depend on me, ma'am, soon as you release me from this prison hospital you've got going here."

Martha nodded. "I'm sure I can depend on you. I'll be in the kitchen if you need anything." As she passed by him, her scent filled his head.

He watched her walk down the hallway.

And he smiled.

TWO WEEKS LATER, after ten hours on the range, Jake rode wearily toward the house. His right shoulder ached like the very devil and it was all he could do to pull the notepad and pencil from his jacket pocket and add in the twenty-three head he was driving. Even Dave, usually tireless, was dragging as he nipped halfheartedly at the heels of the laggards.

"Looks like you had better luck than me, little brother," he said to Sam as he rode up to the corral and opened the gate. Around fifty head milled around inside, mostly cows with new calves.

"I didn't get all of them. Martha went out early this morning, right after you did. She came in about an hour ago with," he checked the slip of paper in his shirt pocket, "ten cows and five calves." He handed the slip to Jake.

"Dadblast it all, Sam, I don't want her going out alone." Jake put the slip inside his jacket pocket and dismounted, careful of his shoulder.

"I was already gone. How was I supposed to stop her? Anyway," Sam smirked, "you ain't her husband, so I guess it don't matter much what you want." He took the reins from Jake. "How's that shoulder?"

"It's all right."

Jake walked away from the corral, toward the last of the cattle that Dave brought up toward the open gate. When they were safely penned, he asked, "Where is she?"

"In the kitchen."

He blew out a sigh. "I'm too tired to eat even Martha's cooking." He took the reins and led his exhausted pony into the barn.

MARTHA ALMOST sent him back to her bed when he came into the kitchen. She could see his exhaustion in his eyes, the slump of his shoulders, the way his feet barely cleared the floor as he walked to his place. She poured him a cup of coffee and set it in front of him, then got his supper right on the table.

"Jake, maybe we need to take a couple of days and rest. We've all been running like slaves every day for weeks."

He shook his head. "We're going to need every head we can get. They're there for the taking, but we have to get them."

"It's not worth you working yourself to death."

He looked at her, a sly half-smile on his face. She knew she was about to get a teasing. At least he felt well enough for that.

"I'm glad you're so worried about me, Martha. But I assure you, if you can round up cows, so can I."

Casting an accusing look at Sam, she whispered, "Squealer." She turned back to Jake. "All I did was ride out a little ways and there they were."

Jake just lifted one eyebrow, unbelieving.

"All right, I went out to the Bastrop county line."

He still sat there, not speaking, just looking at her.

"Well, aren't you going to yell at me?" She immediately realized that sounded like she was acknowledging his authority to yell at her. "Not that you have the right to, mind you. It's my ranch and I can go anywhere I please."

Nothing.

"I guess that means you have nothing to say on the subject?"

He shrugged his good shoulder. "What can I say, Martha? If you want to put yourself in danger, what can I do about it?" He got a wicked gleam in his eyes. "Maybe I should tie you to your bed in the morning so I can work without worrying Garret's got his hands on you."

"What! You wouldn't dare."

He ignored her outrage. "Maybe what might be better is to make sure you don't think you need to be out doing a ranch hand's work."

"I am perfectly capable of doing any work that needs to be done."

"Now, Martha, don't get yourself all ruffled. I didn't say you couldn't. I said you shouldn't need to." He sat back and rubbed the back of his neck.

Without even thinking, she got up and went to stand behind him. She moved his hands away and started rubbing his neck and shoulders, herself. Except for changing the dressing, it was the first time she'd touched him since he'd left her prison hospital.

"Thank you. That feels good," Jake said.

He closed his eyes and let his head tip back just a bit, until the thick waves at the nape of his neck brushed her massaging fingers. She let herself enjoy the innocent intimacy and kept kneading the tightened muscles in his broad shoulders, careful of his mending wound. After all, she was his nurse.

She thought he'd drifted off to sleep, sitting right there at the supper table, his meal untouched, when he sat up a bit straighter.

"You know," he said, "I think we need more help."

She returned to her chair and got him another hunk of rare roasted beef.

"Eat," she ordered. "We can't afford more help."

"We can't afford not to have more help. There's no way we're going to be able to do this with just the four of us and Dave."

"What? I remember someone sitting right here at this table claiming that two men and a big, ugly dog could do it just fine. 'My brother and I are worth any ten men, ma'am.'" She delivered this last in a deep voice, imitating him.

He laughed. "That was before I got hurt. I'm still not a hundred percent and to make a trip like this pay, we've got to find every head that's ready and able. We need more hands and that's just the plain truth. Tomorrow, Sam and I will head down to San Antonio to see if we can find some." He turned back to his supper, his sign that the discussion was over. She hated it when he did that.

"The plain truth is, I don't have the money to pay any more hands."

He shrugged. "Then we'll just make them partners."

"You're getting mighty free with my money."

He refused to talk any more about it and he was so tired that she took pity on him and dropped it for the time being. Tomorrow, after he'd rested, he'd be more reasonable and she could talk some sense into him.

"YOU ARE AS pigheaded as any man has ever been." Martha stood behind Jake as he saddled his horse. "I don't understand why you have to go all the way to San Antonio. Why can't you just go to Travis City or even to Austin? In fact, I ought to be the one doing the hiring, since it is my ranch."

Jake tightened the cinch and dropped the stirrup, then leaned against Buck's side, crossing his arms.

"Well, Martha, we could go to Travis City, I suppose. But that is where we heard about the trouble you were having, all your men getting shot and all. Everybody there advised us to keep moving and not take work out here. Do you really think we'll find anybody there?"

She looked offended. "I'm not a simpleton. All right, you're correct about Travis City, but I still think I ought to go along."

"Oh, no, ma'am. We'll be hanging around the saloons to find idle men, surely no place for a pretty woman like you. If it got around that you owned all this ranch land, well, look at all the trouble you've already gotten yourself into." She opened her mouth to tell him what she thought about that, but he didn't even let her get started. "Martha, I'm not in the mood to argue with you. You will stay right here."

Her anger left her sputtering and him unmoved. Well, not unmoved, since her eyes flashed and her skin took on a glow that made his own skin grow warm. But it didn't change his mind.

"Of all the high-handed, arrogant...."

"C'mon, Sammy, daylight's burning." He mounted and looked down at the still furious Martha. "You keep that Henry rifle of yours loaded by the front door and don't let yourself get caught alone. We'll be back in a couple of days, at most."

He wasn't about to tell Martha the real reason he wouldn't go to Travis City. There was no telling when that upstanding citizen, Mr. Garret, might show one of his two faces. Jake wasn't ready for that meeting, not yet. Garret still thought him dead and being already dead afforded a certain protection, especially when one's enemy showed a fondness for shooting men in the back.

IN TWO DAYS, all they'd managed to find was the seediest saloon this side of Encinada, and possibly the only place in Texas where the whiskey wasn't watered down. No cowpokes had hired on, yet, not even for the outrageous forty dollars a month Jake was offering. It seemed the news of the ghost-rider who killed vaqueros on the Rancho MacLannon had reached south as well as north.

They sat, backs to the wall, and waited for their liquor. The blowsy blonde serving girl deposited a bottle and two passably clean glasses.

Her style was mighty smooth, Jake thought as she displayed her wares, cleverly dropping her shoulders while she poured them a round so the bodice of her worn satin dress gaped open, for his eyes alone. She was a nice-looking woman, for all the obvious use. At another time he might have taken her up on her not-too-subtle invitation. But he shook his head. He had another blonde on his mind.

She frowned, then winked one of her laughing brown eyes at him and turned to his brother. Jake let Sam have his fun flirting with her.

Jake concentrated on his drink. The woman stood the bottle on the table and left them alone.

"Had enough?" Sam held the bottle over Jake's empty glass.

Jake chuckled. "Nope, you're still drinking. Reckon that means I'm still drinking. Fill 'er up."

"I was talking about San Antonio. We're not going to find any hands here," Sam said as he poured.

"Yeah, 'fraid you're right. Looks like we're outta luck for this year. Don't know how I'll tell Martha."

Sam took a drink, savoring the taste of the whiskey. "This ain't too bad, you know." He turned to Jake. "Have you figured out how you're going to get her to marry you?"

Jake smiled. "You were a bit skeptical. You think I can, now?"

"Hell, I never saw a woman you couldn't have if you really wanted her." He sipped at his drink. "I reckon you want this one as bad as any before."

Jake nodded. "I want this one mighty bad." He took a long drink of the whiskey. "Bad enough to try to get over the past and make something out of the rest of my life. Don't you ever think about settling down, Sam? Raising a few children? Getting old and dying in your bed?"

Sam didn't answer right away.

"I can't think of anything but making him pay. Everything else has to wait." He tipped his chair against the wall and sipped his drink.

Jake considered Sam's words. "Is it worth your life?"

"You know it is. He deserves to die for what he did."

"By our hands?"

"I know you'd rather not be the one to do it." Sam studied his glass. "You know, Jake, I've killed a lot of men. Men who'd done nothing to me, were nothing to me. They were only wearing the wrong color. I could surely kill Wil. Maybe if it hadn't happened the way it did, I could let it go. But...."

Jake chuckled grimly. "It never was a matter of degrees with you, Sam, not about anything. You have to have it black or white, right or wrong, guilty or innocent. Life isn't like that."

"The law is like that."

Jake looked him in the eye. "Okay, Mr. Prosecutor, we've been accomplices to cattle rustling. Do we deserve to hang?"

Sam returned his gaze just as steadily. "Yep. The penalty for cattle rustling in Texas and just about everywhere else is hanging. You bet we deserve it. The law don't care why we did it, Jake."

He looked away. "Maybe it should."

"Let me ask you one. Does Wil deserve mercy?"

Jake didn't have to think that one over.

"No. He needs to die 'bout as bad as anyone I've ever seen."

Sam nodded grimly. "If I were still in a position to see it done, hanging would be my first choice. Nice speedy trial. A chance to make his case. Quick verdict. Swift justice. But only after he's spent the night in jail watching the gallows go up, knowing all that work is just for him." He nodded. "That would be good."

"Personally, I'd prefer a quick bullet between the eyes."

"I would, too, personally. But Wil deserves special treatment."

Jake poured himself another drink. "One way or another, I'll take care of it for you, Sam." He owed him that much.

MARTHA SPENT the time Jake was gone to San Antonio catching up on the housework and working in the vegetable garden, mostly to keep her mind off him. He'd said he would return in a couple of days, but now, with a couple turning into three, doubts nipped at the back of her mind.

Why should he come back? What was there to keep him here?

The roundup had been very disappointing, so the money wouldn't be nearly what they'd hoped.

His very life was in danger as long as he was here.

She had pushed him away that night in the barn. More and more she regretted that.

Would things be different if I'd stayed with him that night? Would he be in love with me now?

She straightened up and leaned on the hoe, arching her back to stretch out her stiff muscles. She rubbed the back of her neck and could almost feel another's fingers there, stroking, caressing.

"Stop it, Martha! Are you getting demented? What would he want with an old maid like you?"

She was startled that she had spoken aloud, but even more so by the pain she felt. She'd thought she had faced up to it, accepted it. More quietly, she said, "I won't start feeling sorry for myself."

She concentrated on punishing the weeds in her garden for all the disappointments and troubles of her life. The sweet smell of fresh earth filled her nostrils and she found it strangely soothing to her spirit. She enjoyed the comfort of useful work and allowed her mind to wander.

Martha had never been much for daydreaming, but lately she'd allowed herself to imagine what it would be like to wash and cook and sew for her own husband and children. Naturally, the husband's role in her daydreams was filled by none other than Jake Bowman.

Her meandering thoughts drifted to memories of her nighttime dreams, which were even more interesting. She could feel strong arms surround her, lifting her to meet firm, gentle, sweet lips that demanded, persuaded, tempted her to give in and do what she wanted to do, regardless of the consequences.

The sound of hoofbeats startled her from her fancy. A dust cloud moving up the road from Travis City had reached her front yard. She waved her hand in front of her face, trying to keep the dust from filling her nose and mouth, then she saw the familiar horse approaching.

"Oh, no."

Garret broke off from the group of men following him and rode slowly toward her, followed by his foreman. He looked her over admiringly. She would've found that look on another man's face exciting, but such attention from this one frightened her. It also made her angry and caused her to speak more sharply than she'd intended.

"What do you want? I thought we said all we needed to say the last time you were out here."

He pushed back his fancy Texas hat. The flaxen hair, pomaded as always, shone like polished gold. He put on an engaging smile.

"Well, my dear, we didn't part on very good terms, and since we're neighbors, I rode over here to make up so we can be friends, again. You can't get along out here without your neighbors, you know."

Martha's fingers tightened around the handle of the hoe. "All right, you've apologized. Now, if you don't mind, I have a lot of work to do." She looked toward the mounted band standing around her front porch. "And would you get your men off my flower beds?" She turned back to her garden, hoping he'd get the message and leave.

"I actually came over here for a couple of things." His manner turned serious, and he continued. "One of my men was killed two, three weeks ago. I heard in town one of your hired men got himself shot at about the same time." He smiled unpleasantly. "That does happen a lot out here, doesn't it? Do you know anything about what happened?"

A sudden prickly feeling moved up her spine. He knew about Jake. There was no way he heard about it in town. Since the body of the gunman had been gone by the time Sam went out to get it, they hadn't even bothered to go into town to tell the sheriff.

She answered cautiously.

"Two or three weeks?" she asked, hoping surprise was evident in her voice. "Well, Mr. Garret, why on earth would you wait so long? By now, whoever did it is long gone."

"The way we parted company, I wasn't sure you'd even speak to me."

"Of course, I'll talk to you about something like this. Just as long as you don't start up again with your ludicrous marriage proposal."

The grin faded instantly, replaced by a look of black rage that caused her blood to freeze in her veins. He got down from his horse and, tossing the reins to Monroe, approached her.

"Mr. Monroe, a bit of privacy, if you please."

Chapter Ten

MONROE SMILED an ugly, oily smile and turned, leading the palomino toward the men sitting atop their mounts in front of the house.

She was glad Garret wasn't able to read her mind, for he would have been greatly gratified at the sudden panic that filled it. Gripping the handle of her hoe tighter, she studied his face as one might a rattlesnake, poised to strike, in terrified fascination.

Even while she waited for a sign of his next move, she tried to think of a way to get Mary's attention. But Mary was working in the house and probably wouldn't hear anything until it was too late.

His plan for her was as clear as crystal, if not so pure.

There would be no witnesses, except for his band of men who would, she had no doubt, stand right there while he raped her, cheer him on, and then possibly join him in the sport. She would never know how, but she kept her face impassive and stared him straight in the eye. Her calm seemed to unnerve him, but he paused for only a moment.

Glancing over his shoulder at his men and finding he was well backed up, he turned his full attention to her as she tried her best to appear unconcerned before him. He reached out to touch her face. She jerked away and raised her hand to slap him, but he anticipated her reaction and grabbed her jaw in one hand, while his other arm pinned both of hers to her body.

"When are you going to give in and give me my way?"

He tightened his grip around her body and pulled her roughly against him. She struggled to free herself. In spite of her determination to keep her head, she became almost hysterical when he rubbed the bulge in his trousers against her thigh.

"Would you like some of this, Martha?" he growled.

She heard the howls and cheers, the shouts turning to catcalls as he caught her hair in his hand and forced her face up toward his. He ground his mouth down on hers, his kiss rough and hurtful, hardly deserving of the name. He cut her lips with his teeth and forced his tongue into her mouth.

She bit him. Hard.

"Damn you, you bitch!" he shouted, blood, both hers and his own, streaking his lips.

Still holding a handful of her hair, Garret struck her across her face with the back of his other hand. In his rage, he dragged her by the hair out of the garden and threw her down in the dust under the cottonwood tree. He fell on her, pinning her to the ground, squeezing the breath from her body. The calmness of his voice was more menacing than anything she had ever heard before.

"I'm gonna take you right here, Martha MacLannon. I won't be put off by a piece of baggage like you."

He grabbed her hair again and twisted her head around. He kissed her again, daring her to repeat her attack. She couldn't breathe. Lack of air made her dizzy and she started to panic.

"Get off me, you rotten bastard!" she screamed as soon as she could get a breath.

His weight crushed her, preventing all but the most ineffectual struggle on her part.

"Martha, you might as well lay back and enjoy it."

He rubbed his mouth along her neck. She felt her stomach churn and she thought she would retch. The feeling only made her struggle harder.

Lord God, she prayed, as hot tears washed trails through the dust that covered her face, please let me die. I can't live with this.

She remembered Mary, who would then be alone, at this monster's mercy. The tears ceased and she stopped struggling. Garret took this as acquiescence. He moved slightly to get a better position and started to open his pants.

A deep-throated growl rumbled from the direction of the barn.

"Dave," she whispered, twisting her head back toward the sound.

The huge dog was running full-out toward them, his teeth bared. Garret didn't even blink. He pulled out his revolver. The report of the gun hammered in her ears. The biting smoke filled her throat.

Martha saw the big dog fall to the ground, almost before she heard his cry. His sad brown eyes, full of apology, fluttered closed. Blood ran freely from the top of his head. She squeezed her eyes shut against the heartbreaking sight.

Garret returned his gun to its holster, then pulled her dress up around her waist, giving his men a good look at her legs. She heard more whistles and humiliating comments from several. Her anger, amplified by anguish at his heartlessness, cleared her mind. He wouldn't have an easy time of it, she vowed. She just had to wait for the right moment.

He held her down with his left arm across her chest and the weight of his leg pinning both of hers to the ground. His right hand went back to his fly. He raised himself up on his left elbow just enough to give him room to operate and Martha realized she had her chance.

Just as his pants came open and his swollen genitals were exposed, she suddenly had no greater desire than to put her knee right up into them.

So she did.

Garret bellowed in pain and rolled off her, his hands cradling his aching, now greatly diminished, manhood. Martha rose quickly and, before the men in front of her house could react, she ran to the back door. She locked the door behind her and dragged the table in front of it, then she headed for the front of the house, where her Henry waited by the door.

Mary knelt by the front door, checking Martha's rifle. Her lips parted in shock as she took in the cuts on Martha's lips, her tousled hair and torn clothing.

"Molly, are you all right?" she asked, tossing the rifle to her sister.

Martha caught the rifle in one hand and wiped the last traces of tears from her face with the other.

"Yes, honey, I'm fine. Let's go and clean up our yard."

Mary nodded and followed Martha out toward the front of the house. Garret's men were still mounted and making comments about the boss's ability to ride home. The snickering and guffaws subsided, however, when the two women came out onto the porch.

"Gentlemen," Martha said, "though I seriously doubt you are qualified to be called gentlemen, I don't want to be ungracious, but if you all don't get off my property, I'll use this rifle." Seeing the smiles on some of their faces, she levered the first cartridge into place and raised the rifle to armpit level. "I don't really care which ones of you drop."

These rough men were acquainted with the efficient Henry repeater rifle. It could kill in the hands of a small woman, especially an angry one, just as well as in the hands of a man.

Garret came limping around the side of the house about that time, hitching up his pants. Martha cast him a disdainful glance.

"You'll be sorry for this, Martha," he warned her.

"Not nearly as sorry as you'll be if you ever come around here again."

His eyes flashing fire, he reached for his gun. His hand froze just over the butt of his revolver as her shot raised a little cloud of dust at his feet.

Martha jerked the lever of the rifle, prepared to fire again. "You want me to aim a little higher, Mr. Garret?"

Silently Garret mounted the big horse. He yanked on the reins and set his spurs into the steed's side. Barely keeping his seat, he took off at a run toward his own ranch. The men, not knowing what else to do, turned and followed their boss back home. Martha heard the chuckling they dared now that the boss-man was gone.

Only when the last of Garret's men were out of sight did the women lower their weapons. Martha sank, sighing, onto the top step. Mary knelt down beside her to examine the bruises and cuts. Martha waved her off.

"Mary, please, I'm all right," she said.

"What did he do?"

Martha laughed a little, though it hurt some when she did.

"These are the marks of Mr. Garret's affection." She raised a hand to her lips, thinking of the difference between her most recent kiss and the one in the barn. It was like night and day.

"Molly," Mary asked meekly, "did he...?" She left the unspeakable question hanging in the air between them.

Martha squeezed her younger sister's hand reassuringly.

"No. My backside is sore from where he threw me on the ground and," she grimaced as she sat up a little, "my ribs might be bruised, but I'm all right. I got in a good kick and ran for the house."

"Is that why he was limping so?"

"Yes, ma'am. I'm afraid I injured Mr. Garret's pride." She looked out after the disappearing dust cloud. "I suppose all I did was make sure he'll be back."

She hoped Jake would get home soon.

MARTHA GOT HER wish near dusk that same day when Jake and Sam returned from San Antonio. Dave saw them first from his blanket on the front porch. Garret's bullet had only grazed the top of his head and knocked him out. The only permanent damage would be a scar, but he still acted like he had a headache and just wanted to sleep. Martha heard his pitiful bark and ran to the window. The dog tried to get up, but flopped back down. The effort was just too much.

"Poor Dave," she said. Holding back the gingham curtains at the kitchen window, she saw the two men riding toward the house. Without a word, she ran to her room, leaving Mary alone to finish supper.

She poured water into the porcelain wash basin and, pulling the shades over her windows, quickly stripped off the grimy, torn dress and tossed it into the corner. She washed off the dust of the day's work and other activity with rose-scented soap and brushed her hair to a sheen. After cleaning up as well as she could, she put on the pink dress Jake had complimented so often.

She stood in front of the mirror and assessed her appearance. Something was wrong, but she didn't know what it was.

"Oh, my shoes!"

Even with all the rush, she felt refreshed and tranquil when she came out onto the porch to welcome her partner back from his trip. She hoped the bruises and cuts on her face weren't too obvious.

While still far off, he saw her standing on the porch. She was tantalizing in the pink dress that made her look like a rosebud. He hoped she'd worn it for him. He kicked his tired pony to a faster trot, leaving his brother behind.

As he approached the porch, he got a good look at her face. The bluish bruise on her cheek, the swollen bottom lip, stirred up a pot of fear in his belly and boiled over into his voice.

"What the hell happened to you?"

Martha's eyes widened. "That's quite a greeting."

"He was here, wasn't he?"

"Who?"

"Don't play with me, Martha. Was Garret here?"

She didn't answer right away, only stared at him.

"Well?"

"Why are you yelling at me?"

"I asked you what the hell happened? Tell me, Martha."

She frowned. "Now, just a minute, don't you bellow at me. You're acting like it's my fault he tried to rape me." She slapped her hand to her mouth, shocked at her own language.

Jake was truly enraged as his worst fears were acknowledged. He got down from his pony and walked up to the front steps. She backed up against the porch post. He saw her wariness, but couldn't control his anger.

"He did what?"

Martha shrugged. "Well," she stammered. "Actually, I kind of prodded him to do what he did."

Jake slammed his gloved fist into the porch post right beside her head. Martha flinched.

"You're making excuses for him?"

"No," was all she could say before he yelled again.

"I'm gonna kill that yellow bastard, son-of-a-bitch right now!" He jumped off the porch and started to mount his horse, but Martha was right behind him and she grabbed his arm.

"Jake, please, don't," she said. "Your shooting arm hasn't healed completely. He didn't get what he came for. I already took care of him."

He leaned against his horse and crossed his arms over his chest.

"What did you do?"

"I...well...I kicked him," she answered, her cheeks pinkening.

"You kicked him?"

"You know..." she said, with an innocence that had the corners of his mouth twisting with the threat of a smile. Then, almost as an afterthought, she added, "And I shot at him."

"At him? You didn't hit him?"

"No." She shook her head. "I just made him dance a little bit."

"Oh," Jake replied, the smile spreading over his face. "You made him dance?" he asked with a chuckle.

She only nodded, venturing a smile. "It wasn't funny then...."

Jake gave in to the relieved laughter, throwing his head back and enjoying the mental picture of Wil hobbling toward his horse, skipping out of the way of Martha's bullets. Even as he pondered the image, though, he knew their troubles would only be multiplied. Wil had been humiliated, and what was worse, by a woman.

Yes, sir, Wil would be in a state. Ripe to make a mistake. Jake's smile broadened. Maybe it was time for the resurrection of the Bowman brothers.

"Jake," he heard Martha ask, "What is it?"

"Nothing, honey," he said, absently adding the endearment. "When's supper? I'm starving."

She looked a bit confused, but whether by his evasiveness or by the *honey*, he didn't know.

"Supper will be in about fifteen minutes, if you'd like to freshen up some." She turned and went up the porch and into the house, casting another puzzled look at him.

"She sure does clean up nice," Sam said. He laughed when Jake turned a jealous glare on him. "Don't worry, Jakey, I won't try to beat your time."

"Like you could."

Knowing Wil, they didn't have a lot of time to spare, so he'd have to move faster than he'd planned. Sometimes, she was hard to read, so he'd have to feel his way with her.

That was damn sure a pleasing prospect.

"Well, Sam, you heard the lady. Let's go freshen up."

AFTER SUPPER, Mary volunteered to do the dishes.

"Go on, Molly. I know you have some sewing to do tonight. My dress isn't finished and my birthday is just around the corner."

"That was supposed to be a surprise." She peered at Jake. "Did you tell her?"

"No, ma'am, not a word."

Martha laughed. "I'll have you know, Miss, I finished that dress last night." She took off her apron and lay it on the back of her chair. "I do have some mending to do, though."

Jake followed her into the parlor. She sat down on the horsehair settee and took up her basket. The first article she picked out was one of his shirts.

"You don't have to do that," he said softly.

Martha's smile warmed her eyes. "I don't mind. Besides, you can't go around in torn shirts."

With the lady's permission, Jake filled his pipe and sat back in the big chair opposite her. His eyes moved from her clever fingers making tiny, orderly stitches to the oval face he saw nightly in his dreams. Did she even realize what she did to him?

Would it matter to her, if she did?

They sat there in the quiet, neither feeling the need to talk, her needle working in and out of his worn work shirt, his pipe sending up a fragrant wreath around their heads. If he searched for a thousand years, he would never find the peace he'd found here. He watched her work and, for the first time, really admitted to himself that what he was about to do, he would do only because he wanted to. It was the best reason, the only reason he needed. Getting Wil's goat was just a bonus.

He was anxious to get on with it.

"Would you like to go out on the porch for some air, Martha?"

She blushed prettily at the invitation.

"It is a bit warm in here all of a sudden, isn't it?"

Out on the porch, they stood side by side at the rail, carefully avoiding any touch, and looked out at the land, the stars, the barn, anything and everything but each other.

"How is the grass doing?" he finally asked.

"Oh, fine. We haven't had much rain, but I expect it'll be all right."

He hesitated before going on with what he had to say. When he'd seen her face this evening, the smooth skin marked, the lips bruised, he'd been filled with rage. Wil had hurt her, and that wasn't made any better by the fact that she had done him worse. He had meant to rape her, to compromise her and force her to marry him out of fear and shame. If Wil had gotten what he wanted, he would surely be dead now.

My brave girl saved his worthless life, for at least one more day.

"Have you ever thought that if you were married, Garret might leave you alone?"

Martha laughed. "Where am I supposed to find a man who'd marry me?"

He answered softly, praying she would respond as he wanted.

"Right here."

She looked up at him, her eyes questioning. Jake wasn't exactly sure what to say. He sensed her unease and he was anxious that he might scare her off, so he tried to lighten the mood.

"After all, I have to protect my investment."

Her eyes went flat as glass. Whatever question had been there, he'd given the wrong answer. She turned away again looking at nothing.

The desolation on her face wrenched his heart. He cursed himself for hurting her and, again, for not knowing how to fix it.

"So, you're proposing a marriage just for appearances' sake, so it looks like there's a man looking out for my interests," she said in a monotone. She was quiet for a long time before she finally said, "I guess it does make sense. It will be just in name only. You wouldn't expect...anything more?"

He didn't like the sound of that at all. Was that really what she wanted? Jake decided to take the easiest way out.

"Whatever you say, Martha."

He saw a look he hoped was disappointment on her face. Well, it was her idea. Let her live with it for a while. Jake didn't think she would want to be a wife in name only, at least, not for long.

But, she'd run from him once already, so, until he put a ring on her finger and the papers were signed, he wouldn't do anything to make her any more nervous. He was a patient man, and when something was worth waiting for, he could wait for as long as it took.

She extended her hand.

"Deal," she said. "When are we going to do it?"

Damn! She sounded like they were closing a cattle deal. He could think of lots of better ways to seal a bargain such as this one.

"Tomorrow. The sooner the better, don't you think? "

Martha nodded.

He wasn't sure if he should, but she didn't pull away when he leaned down and kissed her gently on the cheek. She offered no resistance, nor any encouragement to proceed further.

Patience, boy. You'll have the rest of your life, if you can find some luck.

"Goodnight, Martha." He left her and started down the steps, thinking about all the things he wanted to say to her. Her whisper barely reached his ears as he stepped down onto the ground.

"Goodnight, Jake."

He went straight to the barn and dragged the canvas off the ancient buggy he'd found hidden away in a corner. It was still in real good shape and, as a bonus, he found a frilled yellow canopy wrapped in another canvas in the backseat.

"A most fitting way to bring my bride to the preacher." He pulled the lightweight vehicle out where he had room to work and got the axle grease and a pair of heavy gloves from the shelf in the tack room.

"Whatcha doing out here?" Sam ambled in carrying a large bottle.

"Getting my marriage transportation ready."

"You asked her? She said yes?" Sam was astounded. "Man, that was quick work."

"She thinks I'm marrying her just to protect my investment."

"She doesn't know you very well, does she? So, have you figured out how to get Wil dead?"

Jake looked up from the axle. "Not tonight, Sam."

Sam nodded. "All right. I guess we ought not sully the occasion by talking about him." He held out the bottle. "Brand new. Don't know about this stuff, though. Supposed to be from Kentucky." He pulled the cork and offered Jake the first drink. "Congratulations, Jake."

"Thank you, brother." Jake took the bottle and downed a big swallow. It burned all the way down. "Good," he croaked, offering it back to Sam.

Sam accepted the bottle with a grin. He scowled bitterly as the whiskey streamed down his gullet. "What you need, my brother, is one last night of debauchery before you're tied down forever, even if the other end of the rope is attached to the worthy Miss MacLannon." He took another swig. "Too bad we don't have any dancing girls out here."

Jake laughed. "That's all right, Sammy. Just don't get so drunk you start to think you can do the job."

Sam howled.

Jake listened to his brother really laugh for the first time in a long time. "Here, hyena." He tossed him a cloth. "Wipe down the upholstery. Then you can tell me that story again, the one about the one-legged saloon singer in Kansas City."

Sam hooted as he contemplated the tale. "Man, she was something."

As they worked, they took turns telling various ribald stories, some true, most fictional.

Jake finished the round. "There was this one girl in Virginia. She was a camp follower, you know." He moved along the springs of the old-fashioned buggy, scraping off rust and applying a liberal coat of axle grease. "She could lay on her stomach and bend her legs over her head and suck on her own toes."

"Go on. I don't believe that."

"I never saw her do it myself, but I did see her do things that lead me to believe the story."

"Where do you suppose she is now?"

Jake guffawed as he jumped up into the buggy and bounced. The springs were quiet and firm. "Good as new. Hand me up the canopy, Sam." They rehung the canopy, restoring the old buggy to a useful life, while Jake pondered the restoration of an old rustler.

"We'll make quite a sight," he said.

"That you will." Sam lay his good right arm across Jake's shoulders. "Come on. Let's go spend, we hope, your last night in the bunkhouse where we can get really good and drunk. I'll make up some more stories for you."

Sam was true to his word. Their voices, growing louder through the night, degenerating into hoots and catcalls, reached the house, making Martha wonder what was going on out there. It irritated her just a bit that Jake was out there enjoying himself while she was so miserable.

She lay alone in her bed and contemplated how ridiculous the whole thing was. In the morning, she was going to marry a man she'd only known for two months. If he had spoken but one word of love for her, she would be the happiest woman in the world, but no such declaration had come. He had agreed readily -- too readily, she thought -- to her proposal for a marriage in name only.

And tomorrow night, she would be sleeping alone, again. Her hand touched her pillow, and she was surprised to find it wet with tears.

"How pathetic! Crying and didn't even know it."

Well, it had been a hard day. A woman was entitled to a few tears after being threatened with rape and then agreeing to a loveless marriage, all in less than twenty-four hours. She wanted to talk, to be reassured she was doing the right thing. But Mary was asleep and, anyway, the person she really wanted to talk to was getting drunk in the bunkhouse.

Chapter Eleven

"DID YOU HEAR all the noise from the bunkhouse last night?" Mary hurried into the kitchen, where Martha was already getting breakfast on the table. "I never did hear such caterwauling."

Martha didn't respond. She wasn't ready to face Mary's questions, and what other reactions she might have, Martha didn't even want to think about.

Jake, of course, chose exactly that moment to walk in, looking like every giddy schoolgirl's dream, apparently wearing his best suit. Cut to show off his broad shoulders, the jacket of black broadcloth hung open, revealing a wine-red brocade vest. And the pants....

Oh, my. Her eyes moved down his long frame to the Navy revolver slung low and strapped to his right thigh.

He had trimmed his beard and Sam had cut his hair. It would have served him right if Sam had cut off his ear, too, the way they'd been drinking. Even as irritated as she was, she still appreciated the sight of him, strong and masculine and dangerous.

Mary whistled. Martha could have killed her. Jake smiled his gracious thanks for the notice.

"Where are you going so fine-looking? A man usually only gets all dressed up for a funeral or a wedding."

Jake grinned and took his place at the table. Martha tried hard to ignore his good humor as she practically dropped his plate on the table in front of him.

"Well, Mary, I suppose it depends on your sister," he said, digging into a plate of steak and eggs.

His intended only gave him a raised eyebrow when she plopped the coffee cup next to the plate. Mary dropped onto the chair next to Jake and eagerly waited for him to swallow. She stopped his hand on its way to his mouth with the next bite.

"Now wait just one minute. What's going on?"

"Martha has agreed to become my wife."

Mary's face lit up. "You're getting married? I don't believe it!" She jumped from her chair and almost jumped over the table to get to Martha, who was standing by the sink. Mary wrapped her arms around her sister, laughing with joy.

Martha would have none of it.

"Mary, will you please just shut up?" she pleaded as she loosened Mary's deathlock around her neck. "For heaven's sake! Jake suggested that if I were married, then maybe Garret would give up and stay away from me. So don't go getting all sloppy. We're too old for such foolishness."

Jake looked truly offended. "Speak for yourself, sweetheart."

She turned a glare on him. "I'm not your sweetheart. This is a marriage for show and nothing more."

He only smiled.

Mary looked from one to the other.

"So you're getting married just to spite Garret?"

"No," answered Jake, "but it does give me an excuse to take care of him the next time he comes snooping around here." He pushed his chair back and stretched out, calmly sipping his coffee.

Martha sighed as she turned back to the sink. She felt Mary watching her. Her younger sister, for once, let it go.

Finally, Mary said, "Well, I guess I'd better get changed, if I'm going to be in a wedding."

"Don't bother with anything fancy," warned Martha.

"Mary, get as fancy as you want. We've got to give the old biddies in Travis City a fine show, since it might be a spell before we get back to town. They'll need plenty of grist for the gossip mill." Jake rose and started toward the door. He turned around with a grin. "Martha, don't hold breakfast for Sam. He doesn't feel much like eating this morning. A bit of stomach trouble, he said." As he stepped out the door he said softly, "Wear something pink, will you?"

She watched him go. Her heart, still pounding as it had since he'd walked into the kitchen, showed no signs of slowing. It was sure to give out on her soon. Then, she could just die and be done with it. How could he come in here, looking like that, when he knew, he had to know, how he affected her? If a woman pulled a stunt like that, she'd be called a tease and most folks would say she deserved whatever happened to her.

Standing in front of the preacher with a man like him was all she'd dreamed of when she was a young girl.

"Well, Martha, you're not a young girl, anymore." She threw the wet rag into the dishpan. "Guess I'd better get my wedding dress on."

SHE STOOD AT the screen door, staring. Jake went up the steps, stopping on the porch, giving her time.

Rustler's Bride

"Your carriage, ma'am."

"It's beautiful," she whispered and pushed open the screen door, walking out slowly, her eyes never leaving the buggy. "It's been such a long time since I've even seen it." She went down the steps and walked around it, touching the warm, shiny clean leather. "How did you...."

Her pleasure filled him with happiness. And hope.

"All it took was a little bit of care, Martha." He offered his elbow. "May I help you, my lady?"

He knew what she was thinking when she spoke. "There aren't any gossips to impress here, Jake."

"I'm not trying to impress anybody but you."

She took his arm, but refused to meet his eyes.

When they pulled away from the house, they did indeed make quite a sight.

Sam rode slowly behind, his head hanging a bit. Martha supposed he was still suffering from the stomach trouble which had kept him from breakfast. But halfway to Travis City, he perked up and spoke to Mary who rode in the back seat.

"They sure are quiet, aren't they, Mary?"

"Um-humm. What do you suppose is wrong with them?" she asked.

A squinted stare preceded his answer. "I think they're bashful."

Jake snorted a chuckle, but didn't say anything.

"No, that's not it. They're not in the mood. What we need here," Sam went on, "is some entertainment. Can't have a wedding with no music. Let's see...." He tipped his head and winked at Mary. A rascal's grin split his face and he drew in a big breath. A strained tenor, shaded by a slight lisp, erupted from his mouth. "As they marched through the town with their banners so gay, I ran to the window just to hear the band play...."

Mary flopped over in the back seat, choking with laughter. Jake chuckled out loud. Martha struggled to maintain the straight face she felt this occasion warranted. Sam doggedly continued.

"I peeked through the blinds very cautiously then, lest the neighbors should say that I was looking at the men."

Martha lost her struggle, her giggle popping out, transforming into full laughter when Sam grinned and leaned over toward her, conspiratorially.

"I heard the drums beat and the music so sweet, but my eyes at the time caught a much greater treat."

"Here comes the good part," Jake whispered to her.

"The troops were the finest I ever did see, and the Captain with his whiskers took a sly glance at me."

Jake obliged, peering -- or was he leering -- at her from the corner of his eye and stroking his moustache.

Sam somehow raised his voice another octave in his female impersonation and went on with the second verse.

"When we met at the ball, I, of course, thought 'twas right to pretend we had never met before that night.

But he knew me at once, I could see it by his glance, and I hung down my head when he asked me to dance.

Oh, he sat by my side at the end of the set and the sweet words he spoke I shall never forget."

Martha knew the song well and heard the final lines reverberate in her heart.

"For my heart was enlisted and could not get free as the Captain with his whiskers took a sly glance at me."

"Bravo!" Mary shouted over her applause.

"What do you have to say, Captain Bowman?" Sam asked Jake. "Did you like my little song?"

"Sounded to me like your saddle was getting uncomfortable, Sam." Jake grinned. "Do you know Goober Peas?"

"Yes, sir," Sam replied with a snappy salute. "Join me, Miss Mary?"

Sam's actual singing voice was a strong baritone. Joined to Mary's clear alto, they proceeded to serenade Martha and Jake all the way to town.

The bride and groom were content to let the others keep the noise going. Martha allowed herself to sneak a peek at him several times during the trip and saw his eyes scanning the horizon. She, too, was uneasy about meeting up with anybody on this particular day. It was going to be hard enough without any distractions or troubles. She just wanted this thing to be over with.

As they entered Travis City, Jake finally spoke to her.

"I have a couple of things to do before we go see the preacher. Is there anywhere you need to go?"

She suddenly realized Jake probably wouldn't have thought of a ring. Her mother's wedding ring was in the deposit box at the bank.

"Yes, there is," she said.

Not asking where she was going or what she was going to do, he pulled the team up at the porch in front of the hotel and jumped down. He came around to her side.

"All right, go take care of your business. I'll meet you at the parsonage in half an hour. And Martha...." He paused and waited for her to look at him. With a smile, he added, "Don't get into any trouble."

Already acting like a husband. The self-recriminations to stop acting like a lovesick fool came immediately.

He put his hands on her waist and lifted her gently out of the buggy, setting her like a piece of porcelain on the ground.

"Remember, now, half an hour. Don't keep me waiting any longer, sweetheart." He lifted her hand and gently kissed the back of it, then smiled as he got back in the buggy and drove off down the street toward the livery stable.

Martha could only stand watching until he disappeared around the curve of the street. When he was out of sight, she turned and saw the crowd that had gathered. What a fool she was! Of course, he'd only been putting on a show for these gawkers, just like he said. Well, then, might as well take the show to the biggest theater in town.

"Let's go over to the general store, Mary," she said.

Several of the most reliable purveyors of news in Travis City must have sprouted wings. Not only had they beaten her to the store, but Clarissa had already gotten the report on the arrival of the little party from the MacLannon ranch. Consequently, there was quite a crowd milling around the counter.

Martha strolled down the aisle, stopping in front of the material. She began examining the fine, white cotton.

"Well, Martha," Clarissa said as she came up behind her in the narrow aisle. "It's been a long time since we've seen you. Wherever have you been?"

The milling crowd resembled a flock of buzzards circling over a not-quite-dead animal. The chief buzzard waited for a reply. Well, let them circle. Today, she would retain her dignity. No screeching at these busybodies. She would do nothing to shame Jake.

"Hello to you, too, Clarissa." She nodded to the other women.

"You look so pretty today. What's the occasion?"

"It isn't every day a woman gets married. I thought I ought to dress up for the occasion."

She thought she could hear the moths chewing the woolen underwear on the top shelves.

"So you finally accepted Mr. Garret's proposal?" Clarissa finally asked, her disappointment barely concealed. "Congratulations," she added flatly.

Martha's peal of laughter caught them all by surprise.

"Oh, no. I've been turning him down for the better part of a year. Why would I change my mind all of a sudden? No, you don't know my fiancé."

Women being women, they all at once began to interrogate Martha on the identity of her intended.

"Is he that tall, good-looking man who was driving the buggy?" one of the younger women asked.

"As a matter of fact, yes."

The questions started from all directions.

"Where did you meet him?"

"Where is he from?"

"Does he have a brother?"

She decided to go whole hog. Jake said the old biddies should have grist for a long time.

"Jacob is an old friend of the family," she replied. "Oh, yes, the Bowmans have been friends of ours, well, it seems like forever." Martha was starting to enjoy being the center of attention. "It just seemed natural for us to get married. But, he was years getting back from the war. He was wounded, you know, and then he had to settle his father's estate near Dallas. He's only recently been free to get on with his life."

Mary gave her a look of warning not to overdo it. She took the hint and stopped running on so, letting her sigh and just-so-slightly-dreamy expression give whatever impression it would. She lovingly stroked the cotton material, obviously meant for a man's shirt.

Suddenly, the crowd of women fluttered around her, wishing her good luck and congratulations. Felicitations and wishes of eternal happiness were not forthcoming from all, however.

"He must be very," Clarissa paused briefly, as though searching for the right word, "understanding. After all, my dear, the way you usually dress and your language. You must admit, Martha, you don't have the most even temper, do you? Most men..." -- the emphasis was interesting, Martha thought -- "wouldn't stand for such conduct from the woman they planned to marry."

"Yes, Clarissa, he is very understanding. As for the rest," Martha cast her eyes down, as though truly embarrassed. "I can't tell you the relief of not having to be so, well, so unwomanly. It's really not my nature at all, you know."

She paused for the sympathetic clucks from the swarm of biddies.

"You should all thank the good Lord you have menfolk around.

When there's no one else to do the work...." She spread her hands. "Now," she smiled happily, letting herself be swept away by her own story, "I'll turn the running of the ranch over to Jacob and leave those smelly old cows to him."

Mary almost choked. Martha put on her best look of alarm.

"What time is it? Oh, my goodness, Jacob will be waiting!" She turned to Conrad, waiting behind the counter, and smiled her very sweetest smile, the one that melted butter. "Mr. Butler, would you be a dear and cut me three yards of this white cotton, and," she looked around, "six each of the pink and blue ginghams?" She turned to Clarissa. "He likes me in pink." She waited for the swoons to stop. "We'll be back to pick it up."

Conrad was completely charmed, of course. He returned her smile, while his wife glared at him.

"Certainly, Miss MacLannon."

Turning to her sister, Martha continued her performance, enjoying it no end.

"Mary, come on now. You know how Jacob hates to be kept waiting!"

Bidding her audience good-bye, she even managed a charming little blush, though they'd never know her coloring was from the laughter she was holding in. Martha heard the sighs of the younger women as she made her way to the door.

"It's so beautiful. Their love has lasted so many years and she has waited for him so patiently."

"I'd certainly wait for a man like that. Did you see how tall he is?"

"Oh, and those shoulders!"

"Didn't she just glow?"

"If you silly geese don't stop this sickening talk, I'm going to toss the lot of you out on the street," Clarissa said before she stomped down the aisle to the back of the store.

All in all, a very satisfying shopping trip.

She and Mary walked nonchalantly down the street toward the bank, managing to keep straight faces. For a few seconds, anyway. Mary held her peace until she looked at Martha, then the two of them began giggling like children.

"He's been a friend of the family forever," Mary mocked. "Oh, Molly, you'll burn for lying like that!"

Martha giggled even harder at her sister's rendition.

"I thought I'd give them what they want, for once. A genteel, well-mannered, obedient floor mat."

"Molly, who's Jacob?"

They laughed as they walked on along the main street of Travis City. As they stepped up on the walk in front of the saloon, Mary suddenly turned serious.

"You do want to marry him, don't you? You wouldn't do it for me or the ranch?" Mary forced Martha to stop and look at her. "Molly, you love him, don't you?"

She never got a chance to answer. The swinging doors opened and Martha bumped into a man. She'd barely righted herself, when a strong hand seized her arm.

"Well, what do we have here?" Garret gripped her arm so tight she thought the blood had been cut off. "Perhaps we might finish that little talk we were having, Miss MacLannon?"

Chapter Twelve

GARRET PULLED her close. The stench of whiskey hit her in the face.

"You and I have nothing to talk about, Mr. Garret!" she cried, trying to maintain some semblance of gentility, even as a crowd gathered. She wished she could come to this town just one time and not attract an audience. His arms wrapped completely around her, trapping her against him. He wasn't about to be caught off-guard, again.

"Let her go, you polecat!" Mary yelled, squirming in the embrace of Garret's foreman.

"Shut her up, Monroe."

Monroe grinned. "Sure, boss." He tried to get himself a kiss, but only grunted in pain when Mary's heavy dress shoe caught him in the shin. "I like 'em wild, girl," Monroe told Mary.

"No, let her go!" Martha struggled against him.

"Not so fast, Molly, my girl!" Garret said as he held her like a common trollop.

"Don't you dare call me that."

He laughed at her impotent demand. His right arm tightened around her waist, pulling her up against his chest. His left hand worked its way down her side toward her bottom.

"I've told you that you and I would one day get along very well, Molly." It was a taunt. "Now's as good a time as any to get started, I think."

The whiskey had cost him his sense of caution, and perhaps because there was a crowd and he wanted to humiliate her as she'd humiliated him, he slid his free hand over her, squeezing here and there before settling on her posterior. He pressed her body tightly against his, squeezing and smiling disagreeably into her startled face. In his firm grip, she was unable to do more than squirm, which only seemed to make him smile more. She was suddenly aware of what else it did to him.

Mary must have had the same realization. She started screaming her head off. Monroe covered her mouth with a dirty hand.

Garret's hand left her bottom and moved toward her bosom. She fought and kicked like a wildcat, while the crowd surrounding them hooted and laughed.

"Let go of me!" Martha yelled at him, all thought of appearances gone. "Do you think you can attack a respectable woman right on the street?"

"Now, whether you're respectable or not is a matter of opinion, Molly. You never have acted much like a lady that I've ever seen. There is also some question as to what has been going on out there with those hired men of yours."

That brought a round of chuckles from the assembled crowd.

"What would you know about how a lady acts? Whatever I did was to keep the likes of you away from me!"

"Take your hands off her."

At the sound of Jake's voice, Garret abruptly released Martha.

"You!" The word escaped Garret's lips in a hoarse whisper.

Without Garret's arm holding her, Martha fell toward the dusty street. Jake was there to catch her.

"Are you all right, sweetheart?" He held her up and looked her over.

He paid no heed to the man staring at him in disbelief. She could only nod. She hadn't actually been hurt, and the only harm done was the embarrassment at being handled like a soiled dove in public. That was secondary, right now, to Garret's extremely interesting reaction to Jake.

Once satisfied that she was only shaken, Jake turned back to the other man. When he spoke, his voice carried a note of menace that made her breath catch in her throat. A perverse thrill streaked through her. She'd never heard him use that tone before. He sounded possessive, protective of what was his.

Protecting her.

"Didn't your mother teach you any manners?" Jake's eyes burned steadily into Garret's. "Since you didn't know the lady was spoken for, there'll be no trouble this time, though I would be justified in calling you out. I can't fault you for your interest, but she's mine and I won't be overlooking anything like this in the future." He started to turn away, but, seemingly as an afterthought, he looked back at the still-speechless man and added, "By the way, the name is Bowman. Jake Bowman." He looked steadily at Garret, his warning even clearer, more menacing, for being left unspoken. It was as much a promise as she'd ever heard.

He turned to her. "Are you ready, honey? The preacher is waiting."

She was just about to answer when she noticed the gaggle of women standing in front of the general store just a couple dozen yards down the street. They'd never come this close to the saloon, but hung back watching the altercation. They oozed envy as Jake gave her his undivided attention. She decided if he wanted to give them a show, she'd go along with the charade. It would be fun, if only for a short time, to make them think such a man was so in love with her that he'd stand up to a man with thirty hired guns behind him. When she answered, her voice was soft and full of sweetness that was no act.

"Well, actually, dear," it came out so easily, "I was on my way to the bank when I was," she glared at Garret, still standing speechless in front of the saloon, "interrupted."

"What do you need at the bank?" Jake asked. He had completely dismissed Garret and, it seemed, everybody else from his mind.

"What?" she stammered, trapped in her little fantasy. How could she admit her knight in shining armor hadn't thought of a wedding ring? So much for the little romance she'd spun in the store.

"Martha?" He had that I'm waiting look on his face.

She lowered her voice, hoping no one else would hear. "My mother's wedding ring is in a safe deposit box in the bank and I wanted to get it."

"Why?"

She was astounded by his denseness. "We're getting married, aren't we?"

"Sure, but why do you need your mother's ring? I already have one."

The words caught her completely by surprise.

"You bought me a ring?"

Jake frowned. "Of course. Wasn't I supposed to?"

She could have hugged him, kissed him, let him do anything he wanted to, right there on the street, with the entire population of Travis City looking on, and her reputation be damned. She didn't know if she'd ever love anyone like this, again.

"I didn't think you'd have time."

Jake laughed, still looking only at her. He stroked her cheek tenderly.

"For you, my love, I have all the time in the world."

The young ladies swooned at that.

She looked into his eyes and almost convinced herself she saw love there.

Jake offered his hand. "Let's go, sweetheart. As I said, the preacher's waiting."

She placed her hand in his and stepped down from the walk with him.

"Sam, escort my future sister-in-law, would you?"

Sam spared Garret only a mocking grin. Holding his arm for Mary in a stance of studied gallantry, he bowed slightly to the crowd and he and Mary followed them down the street toward the little frame house beside the church.

They arrived at the parsonage and were escorted to the parlor by the parson's wife. All the necessary forms were already prepared. Jake signed his name and stood aside watching Martha sign her maiden name for the last time.

At this moment, he was almost grateful Wil had betrayed him and Sam. Considering where he was a year ago, he couldn't conjure the circumstances that would have put him standing next to this woman right now, binding his life to hers. Even the fact that Wil wanted her so bad couldn't make getting her any better.

She smelled of roses, even after the tussle on the street. And she was wearing pink, just as he'd asked. He didn't know if she loved him yet, but he was an optimistic sort, patient and willing to earn her trust and her love.

He straightened to his full height and took her hand, then turned toward the preacher, who was now ready to make them man and wife.

IN THE HOTEL dining room, they had dinner alone. Jake watched as she kept touching and twisting the simple gold band on her left hand. She couldn't leave it alone, turning it as though trying to find just exactly the right place for it to catch the light. He couldn't take his eyes off her. She was so very beautiful, but she was also strong, brave, and had the backbone of any ten men. All in the world a man needed was a woman like this one beside him.

"Jake, I want to thank you for what you did."

The sudden break in the silence surprised him. "What'd I do?"

"The way you faced Garret down."

"I only did what any man would have done. I should've beat the stuffing out of him."

"I haven't had anybody stand up for me like that in a long time." She looked again at the golden band that encircled her finger and laughed. "It was like being the belle of the ball, again. I do believe every woman in Travis City will be jealous of me tonight." Her eyes shot up to meet his. "What I mean is...." she stammered. They shared a smile at her discomfiture. "For the first time, I almost wish I could hear the gossip this'll cause."

"It was my pleasure, Molly." He looked up warily. "May I call you Molly, now?"

The look in her eyes gave him hope. "I suppose you have the right to call me anything you want to. You're my husband."

"Yes, I am." He said it as an affirmation, just between the two of them, something she couldn't put down to trying to impress any gossips.

She nodded and he saw there was more she wanted to say. If he could keep her talking, she might say something close to what he needed to hear. He settled for something safe.

"You haven't eaten a thing."

"I guess I'm not very hungry."

"Well, I must be the only one who gets an appetite from getting married." He resumed his attack on the thick steak hanging over the edges of his plate. He looked up at her. When she'd met his gaze, he added, "I'm going to need my strength." To demonstrate his point, he took a big bite of the meat.

She understood his suggestion right away and was truly shocked. Then, he saw another look come on her face.

"Maybe you'd better order another, then."

His jaw stopped working. What in the world was she trying to do to him? He finished chewing, but suddenly felt an appetite of a different kind coming on.

He needed to get her home as quickly as possible.

Home. After twelve years, he did feel like he was home. Home with Martha. Molly, he corrected himself. Molly Bowman. He savored the sound of it in his head.

Heaven, itself, couldn't be better than what was waiting for him back in that ranch house.

"Are you ready to go home, sweetheart?"

A quiet smile lit her face and his heart.

"Yes, I'm ready to go home."

Chapter Thirteen

THE RIDE HOME was no more somber than the ride to town had been. The entertainment in this direction was the gossip Mary had collected from her friends.

"Naturally, you two figure prominently in all the stories." She leaned up to whisper to Martha, "Molly, they're green with jealousy."

"Hear that, my love?"

Martha rolled her eyes. "Don't let it go to your head."

Sam wasn't about to be left out. "They're taking bets at the saloon. The odds are you won't last six months."

Jake laughed at the news. Martha huffed in total irritation. His humor mellowed to a smile as his considered his wife's expression. Why would the opinion of a bunch of gossips bother her? Of course, she still thought this was only a marriage of convenience.

Time to start disabusing her of that notion. He took her hand and, giving it a little squeeze, placed it on his knee, holding it there when she would have moved it. She didn't return his caress, but at least she didn't fight him.

He pulled up in front of the house and stopped the buggy at the steps. She waited for him to jump down and come around to help her out. He tried to catch her eyes, so he could flirt her out of her mood.

"Thank you," she said and turned away, going into the house without ever looking at his face.

"Oh, my, my," Sam whispered, pretending to shiver as the door slammed behind her. "It's got mighty cold all of a sudden."

Jake said nothing, staring at that closed door, wondering. He wasn't about to force her to do anything she didn't want to do, but.... He got back up on the front seat and drove the buggy into the barn.

Sam followed, restraining the impulse to offer condolences. "Need a hand with that, brother?"

"Nope."

Sam nodded and went about bedding down his own horse. After Jake was left alone, he took his time getting the horses rubbed down and fed. He wiped down the buggy and removed the frilly canopy, which he carefully folded and laid in the back seat. When he'd made sure the buggy was clean, he threw the canvas over it. He fed all the stock and finally checked every animal. Twice. He checked Sunbeam and her little filly three times. Everything in his barn was in order.

Now it was time to see about putting his house in the same shape.

Once satisfied that she'd had enough time to think he wasn't in any special hurry to come in, he strolled on over. The voices fell silent when he entered the kitchen. Martha stood by the sink, watching him from the corner of her eye, like a mouse eyeing the movements of a cat.

HE POURED himself a cup of coffee and lean up against the side table, looking for all the world like a man standing in his own kitchen.

Which he is, she thought miserably, for as long as it lasts.

Not a word passed between them, but she felt his eyes follow her as she moved around the room. She glanced at him, but refused to meet his gaze.

"Martha, is there any more coffee?" Sam asked.

"You've had enough coffee, Sam," Mary piped in. "I'd like to take a walk out to see the filly. Come with me." She grabbed him by the arm and forced him to get up. "Please excuse us."

"Not exactly subtle, is she?" Martha asked as her sister dragged Sam out toward the barn.

She cleared the table and turned with the stack of dishes toward the sink. Jake blocked her way and showed no inclination to move over. She either had to go around the other side, making it obvious she wanted space between them, or pass him there by the side table and risk touching him. All too conscious of him watching her every move, she only considered a moment. He moved just enough to let her squeeze by, forcing her to brush against him slightly. Her skin tingled with the awareness of him, but she refused to look up.

"Excuse me." She pushed on through to her goal and put her dishes in the soapy water. Going about her business, she risked glimpses at him. He never took his eyes off her, sipping his coffee, leaning his long body against the side table, one hand in his pocket, like he had all the time in the world.

What does he want? In a panic, it occurred to her he might expect....

She gathered her courage and turned. When her eyes met his, he made no effort to hide what he felt. She turned away quickly.

He wanted her.

Well, she knew that. He'd never hidden it.

But he was in this for the money and he'd not hidden that, either.

Would it really be so bad? They were married. She peeked at him again.

Looking at him only made her heart ache more. Part of her knew if she let this go the way he wanted, the way she wanted, she'd be destroyed when he left her.

Mary's question popped into her mind. Does he strike you as a man who'd leave his child?

Shaking her head, she dismissed the thought. She'd never trap a man that way, and if she were wrong about his parental devotion, she'd be left to raise a child alone.

They would stick to their bargain. She would even offer, in time, to let him divorce her, if he wanted to. By that time, maybe she could get over him.

But did she have the courage to tell him so?

He'd still said not a word since entering the kitchen. She turned back to the sink, wiping it dry and wringing the last drops of water from the rag.

Maybe it was safer to act like this was normal.

"I think I'll turn in. Make sure you put out the lamp." She waited for some word from him. It started to look like she'd be waiting all night. "Sleep well, Jake."

He looked at her over his cup.

"Oh, I will," he said, smiling ever so slightly.

Martha studied his face. Was he going to let her go? She chided herself for deep down hoping he would at least try to change her mind.

"Good night," she said, leaving the kitchen and going to her empty room and her empty bed.

JAKE STOOD there in the quiet, listening to Martha's footsteps move almost silently down the hall to her room. The door closed with a gentle, but very final sounding click. He lifted his head slightly, listening for the turn of a key in the lock. There was none.

He sat down at the table to finish his coffee and try to figure out the best way to proceed. How long should he give her? Maybe he should just act like this was normal and let her come to him when she was ready. Even as he considered it, he knew it was the wrong tack.

Everything she'd said today, everything she'd done, pointed to a lack of trust. She had some cockeyed idea that he was a transient husband. Her reaction to Sam's offhand comment on the way home was more than irritation with a bunch of gossips. Was she really afraid he'd not be around in six months? She ought to know him better than that.

But how could she? She'd known him less than two months, not to mention she'd maintained a certain formality even while she flirted with him nightly. But, she'd risked her life to save his on no more than a feeling.

"So, I've got a wife who has somehow got the idea I don't want to be a husband. What do I do about that?"

What would she do if he went to her? How bad did she want to keep him at a distance?

A few minutes later, he heard the front door open and Mary go up to her room. Sam would be in the bunkhouse by now, probably figuring the odds that Jake would end up joining him later.

"Well, hell," he said to the air, "this is stupid. She's my wife and I love her. I just have to prove it to her." He drained the last of his coffee, blew out the kitchen lamp, then started down the hallway to the bedroom he fully intended to share with his wife.

MARTHA WAS already in bed when Mary's footsteps echoed from the stairs. Minutes passed as she lay there, her ears straining for the sound of the squeaky kitchen door that would signal Jake had gone out to the bunkhouse.

Maybe he'd gone out the front. She jumped out of bed and ran barefoot to the front window.

High and full, the moon bathed the yard in a silver glow. To the left she could just see the cottonwood where Jake often stood, puffing his pipe and looking off to the north. He wasn't there. Her gaze passed across the yard, first examining the barn for any sign of his presence. She moved to the side window, which had a much better view of the bunkhouse, where a lamp had just come on. Probably Sam, she thought. She looked back along the path to the house, but if Jake was out there she couldn't see him.

She wanted to see him one more time tonight, just a look would be nice. Somewhat put out, she got back into bed.

What was wrong with the man's timing, anyway? Why couldn't he have ridden up here ten or fifteen years ago, when she was still young and looking for a husband?

Mama had always worried that Martha didn't know what she wanted. The problem was she knew only too well. The first time she'd laid eyes on him, she'd recognized Jake as the one man she could belong to.

A dull pain reached into every part of her body. It was a hunger, a need, one she had long feared would never be satisfied.

It was more than simple lust. She wondered, of course, what it would be like to lie with a man, especially a man like him. But, more than that, she simply wasn't meant to be alone. Some women could handle it. Some women were able to live full lives by themselves. But Martha recognized her nature was best suited to the role of a wife, to love, to help, to share, to give a man a peaceful, comfortable home, well brought-up children, warm companionship. All she wanted in return was to be loved and cherished.

She'd refused every man who'd proposed because she couldn't imagine herself as his wife. But when Jake suggested this crazy idea, she knew how right it would be with him. She had wanted to refuse his offer, since she knew it had been prompted by pity or, perhaps, even greed. He'd said he was only protecting his investment. But part of her had hoped for more. She knew Jake could help her discover everything there was to know about the love between a man and a woman, a husband and a wife. It wasn't that she didn't know how. She was a rancher, after all. But they weren't animals.

He'd shown her, that night in the barn, how different it was between people who cared for each other. He'd held her, kissed her, made her feel free and safe and cared for. That was what she wanted.

In that instant, she could feel him holding her tight against him, again. Night after night, alone in this room, she'd relived the wonder of that embrace, wanting him more than her next breath, knowing she wasn't bold enough to give or take what she wanted.

It was the man's place to pursue the woman. But Jake had kept his distance, never trying to touch her, never trying to get too close, as though he, too, were wary of becoming too involved. As though he wanted it to be easy to leave. He no more wanted to be tied here than she wanted to tie him.

She was so occupied feeling sorry for poor Molly, she never heard him coming down the hall. The door opened and, almost as a disinterested observer, she watched him come into her room.

No, I want him here so badly, I'm imagining this. Then, he lit the lamp and turned the light down low.

With a start, she realized it was no dream and jerked the covers up to her chin. He looked at her and smiled that smile of his. Her heart jumped, but her brain, ably assisted by her overgrown pride, blast them both, took over her mouth.

"What are you doing? Get out of here," she demanded in a harsh whisper.

He started at his shirt buttons.

Be calm, Martha. "Jake Bowman, just what do you think you are doing?"

He looked at her calmly, his fingers steadily moving down the front of his shirt.

"I'm getting ready to go to bed."

Chapter Fourteen

YES, THAT WAS exactly what he was doing. She watched in silent fascination as his fingers separated the last button from its hole, then pulled the shirttail from the waistband of his pants. Plopping his backside down on her bed, he yanked one boot off, then tugged at the other, but it wouldn't budge.

"Honey, will you help me?"

She gasped, clutching the bedclothes more closely to her chin. "No, I will not help you! Pick yourself up off my bed and get out of my room!" She turned away from him. The rest of his words hit and she whipped her head around again. "And don't call me 'honey'!"

"You said I could call you anything I wanted to. I am your husband."

She didn't need the reminder. She also didn't intend to let him renege on their bargain.

He made no move to get off her bed or vacate her bedroom. In fact, he continued with the business of getting his boots off. She placed her foot against his backside and tried to push him off. He didn't budge.

"There we go," he said triumphantly as the boot came off, quickly followed by his socks. She noticed he placed them neatly by the side of the bed. He rose and began unbuttoning his pants.

"Stop!" she cried, jumping from the bed.

He turned and looked at her, his eyes moving slowly and appreciatively from the top of her head to her feet. With the wisp of a smile touching his lips, he repeated the caress in the opposite direction, even more slowly, back up along her body.

Martha wasn't up to being undressed like that. Much more of that look on his face and she wouldn't be able to control the situation. She walked to the door and, with all the dignity she could muster, considering she was standing barefoot in her nightgown, she opened it.

"Jake," she said, as to a child, "I sincerely appreciate the protection of your name, but, you remember, we had an agreement. This," she waved her hand toward the bed, hoping he'd get the idea, "was not part of the bargain. Now, I insist you leave my room at once."

He looked at her rather like she had once seen him look at a recalcitrant calf, a stubborn creature fighting him in futility. Then he nodded slightly and she sighed in relief as he started toward the door.

She never saw it coming.

He slammed the door shut, then brought his arms up on both sides of her, trapping her against it. She tried to duck under, but he was too fast, grabbing her arm and bringing her up hard against him with his other hand.

"You conceited goat! Let go of me!" She kicked at him, though he easily prevented her reaching her target. "Damn it all to hell! Are you going to force yourself on me? You think you can get away with it just because I signed a piece of paper? Is that all your word is worth, Jake?"

He loosed his hold a little, but she was still held fast.

"I'm just trying to protect myself, Molly. As to my word, you can either trust me or not. Please, honey, tell me what you're afraid of."

She tried to get her hands free for a fresh assault. "I am not afraid of anything!"

"Molly," he asked again, "what are you afraid of?"

So angry she could barely think, she answered, "I will not be used for a man's pleasure, only to be cast off when he gets ready to move on. I'll bet you haven't even thought about the fact that you might leave me with a child to raise alone."

"Ah, so that is it. Don't you know me better than that? Don't you trust me?"

She stopped struggling, but held herself as stiff as a fencepost. "As a business partner, yes."

He still held her against the door. She wasn't afraid, though. She could never fear him. He looked into her eyes, exerting his power over her, forcing her to return his gaze.

"Why do you think I'm going anywhere?" he asked quietly.

"I'm only taking you at your word. When you got here, you as much as said you were looking for a stake and you would move on when the drive was over."

"When did I say that?" he asked, infuriating her to speechlessness.

Her fist escaped and he caught it again, this time in his ribs. He gasped for breath. With a grimace of pain he grabbed her hand.

"Damnation, Molly! You throw a pretty good punch for such a little woman." He paused to catch his breath. "Now, you listen to me, my girl, and you can believe this," he said as he held her trapped against the door, "I'm not going anywhere. You're stuck with me til death do us part."

She stopped fighting, desperate to believe she'd heard him right.

"What did you say?"

He rubbed his thumb gently over the knuckles that had just bruised his side, then he kissed each finger, slipping the tip of her index finger between his lips, sucking on it, caressing the pad of her fingertip with his tongue. A small gasp escaped her and she shuddered with the deliciousness of the feeling.

A smile appeared around her finger. "Ummm, sweeter than penny candy." He sucked each fingertip before answering her question. "I don't know when I said anything you could've misunderstood like that. I never intended to leave here. I wanted you the first time I ever saw you."

She looked at him, eyes wide with disbelief. Only one word escaped her parted lips. "What?"

He smiled as he released her hand and stroked her face, his fingers moving along the line of her jaw, up the smooth plane of her cheek. She leaned into his caress and saw the look of desire flash in his eyes.

"Yep. In that store when you set down that Butler woman. Then, when I saw you with your foot up on the rump of that calf, all dressed in boy's clothes, with a red-hot branding iron in your hand, well...." He smiled. "I thought to myself, 'there is the woman who's going to have my children'."

Her eyes widened even more at this revelation.

All the while he talked, his voice soft and slow, his hands explored her body in the same way, softly and slowly. He stroked her shoulders and down her back. The thin cotton of her nightgown slid beneath his hands. She felt herself relax, protected and safe for the first time in many years.

"That night in the barn, when you pushed me away, I didn't know why you were scared, or of what. It didn't seem you were afraid of men, since you aren't afraid of much of anything, but there was something keeping you from me. So, I let you think I accepted that hair-brained scheme of yours of being married in name only," he pulled her tighter against him, "as though I could ever keep my hands off you."

His eyes swore to the truth of his words.

"Molly, I swear by all I hold holy, nobody'll get to you without going through me, first." He placed kisses in her hair and breathed deeply, sighing with pleasure. "You smell so good." Holding her gaze tight, he raised her hand, kissing each finger as he continued. "Now, wife," he said, "do you want me to sleep out in the bunkhouse tonight?"

"No." Her response was quick, earnest.

"Where do you want me to sleep, then?" he asked, slipping her finger between his teeth. His eyes smoldered with want.

She could only look at him, into his eyes, at the lips pulling on her finger. Only one answer came to her mind.

"With me."

The words barely got out of her mouth. He swallowed them as he lifted her in his arms. They kissed, light, fleeting, swiftly flying motions, each tasting and sampling the other after so long a fast. She clung to him, holding on for her life. His hands moved along the lines of her body, down past her waist, where he touched and kneaded her flesh. At first he ministered to her tenderly, patiently, but as the fire of his need for her burned hotter, his touch became more insistent, more intimate.

He reached down behind her knees and pulled her legs up to encircle his waist. They leaned against the door, his weight adding another caress, this one covering her entire body. When he pressed the evidence of his need against her belly, she felt no panic, no fear. Her own body ached just as much for him. He wove his fingers through her hair and turned her head to fit his mouth more perfectly upon hers. His tongue moved, slow and gentle, around her mouth. It slipped along hers, rubbing, sparring, twisting. Their mouths parted only for an instant as he slipped her nightgown between them and over her head.

"Molly," he whispered into her mouth.

His hands on her bare skin warmed her all the way through. It was pure delight.

Wanting to give him that joy in return, she grabbed the shoulders of his shirt. His lips never left hers as he pressed her against the door with the weight of his body and dropped his arms, so she could pull the shirt off. When she began to pull clumsily at the rest of his clothes, he laughed into her mouth and wrapped his arms around her to carry her, still twined around him, over to the bed. After laying her down, he quickly removed the last material barriers between them, then stood looking down at her. For the moment, not touching her, except with his eyes.

"Jake." She held out her arms for him.

He knelt over her, his kisses feather-light on her lips before he lay down, covering her body with his own. His weight pressed her into the mattress, but it was no burden, their nakedness no source of shame. The freedom she gave him and took for herself was the creation of God. She wanted to tell him how she loved him and she did, but the words were silent ones, expressed as soul-scorching, heart-bursting kisses. Even if she'd had free use of her mouth for a few seconds and the breath to form words, knowing how he wanted her took away any rational speech. She could only whisper his name, and touch him.

He whispered to her as well, words of love and lust and desire. Words that came into her ears through his kisses and the nibbling roaming of his mouth over her skin. Words that caused new flames of desire to lick at her mind driving her to a state of near madness. When he covered the peak of her breast with his mouth, she couldn't believe the wave upon wave of pleasure drowning her, pulling her farther under.

"Touch me, Molly," his whisper rough in her ear.

She did, unhesitating. Her fingers closed around him and she reveled in his smooth hardness. The feeling of power as she watched his face was like nothing she'd ever felt before. She instinctively knew how to give him pleasure. He threw his head back, a sound, much like a growl, coming from deep in his chest.

"Molly, I love you," he whispered between her parted lips before he claimed them with a kiss hotter than any branding iron. He marked her with that kiss. He tasted and stroked her soft inner mouth and pulled her tongue into his own, sucking and nibbling. She mimicked his motions and sampled the taste of him.

He left a trail of hot, searing wetness down her throat to her breasts. His lips closed over one taut nipple, then the other, then back to the first. She arched, pushing her breast even deeper into his mouth.

"It's too much, Jake. I can't stand it." Her voice was strained and, to her own ears, unrecognizable. Her eyes, long closed, opened to look into his, those beautiful eyes she'd never tire of.

"This is nothing. You'll stand a lot more before I'm done, sweetheart," he promised.

She'd never have believed the explosion just those words could cause. Threading her fingers into his hair, she dragged his mouth to hers, her lips claiming him, branding him, burning him, as his had done her. He was hers.

He eased her knees apart and moved between them. His sleek aroused flesh moved easily into the wet, warm haven of her body. Stopping just before the final stroke that would make her completely his, he brushed her lips with his and whispered, "I'm sorry for the hurt, sweetheart."

She stroked his face and held for another branding kiss. He buried himself inside her. She welcomed him. Even the pain was a cause for greater celebration. It was over so fast and was replaced by a greater pleasure than any he'd yet shown her. The joy of being one with him was nearly too much for her to bear. She could only call out to him, then he collapsed on her, spent, whispering her name.

She didn't know how long they lay there, Jake's long frame draped over hers, his head pillowed on her breasts. Their breathing was labored for some minutes, their limbs drained. They might have slept, but she wasn't sure.

She gazed down at the head resting upon her so intimately. Her fingers played with the gray-streaked dark brown waves at the nape of his neck. He made a sound of contentment, like the purring of a big tom cat, well-fed and content. She kissed the top of his head. She purred, too.

AFTER LONG MINUTES, he raised up on one elbow. His free hand smoothed the wavy tendrils of golden hair while she smiled at him through a hazy happiness he'd never seen in her eyes. He was glad he'd been the man to put that look on her face.

"Molly," he asked when he finally had the strength to speak, "I need to ask you something."

"Ummm?" She turned her cheek into his caress.

"That night in the barn, why did you run out?"

She laughed softly. "You called me Molly."

Her actions that night, the initial eagerness, then the anger, had made him wary of pushing her too fast. Now that she was somewhat compliant, he thought to get an explanation, but her offering left him really confused.

"I just called you Molly, now, too. Are you mad at me?"

"Of course not. That's my name."

"Please explain that to me."

"All my life, I was Molly. Nobody, other than my mother, ever called me Martha and she only called me that when I'd really irritated her, usually after I'd refused another marriage proposal. I was quite the belle in my day." She gave him a smug smile.

"I'm not surprised. I'd be willing to bet there were a thousand others who wanted you but didn't think they had a chance."

She combed her fingers through his beard. "They didn't. I was waiting for you to show up." She pulled him down for a kiss, then sighed with pleasure as she sucked on his bottom lip. "Ummm, sweeter than penny candy," she murmured.

He chuckled and sucked back.

Martha fingered the hair on his chest. "Everybody loved me, doted on me." She laughed again, more heartily this time. "I think that's why my temper took everyone by surprise. Nobody ever saw it before, because nobody ever crossed me."

He had to laugh. "So you got your way all the time?"

She nodded. "Yep." Then, her face became somber. "Until the first telegram arrived. The government of the Confederate States of America regrets...." Her voice trailed off. "We couldn't recover from the grief of the first before the next one arrived, then the next. I decided Molly was a ridiculous name for a woman with my responsibilities." She shook her head. "No, it was more than that, really. Molly hid. Martha came out and protected us. Sounds crazy, doesn't it? It was like there were two people in here." She frowned and touched her temple. "Martha did what had to be done. When you called me Molly, it just reminded me that I couldn't be irresponsible."

Jake rolled over and pulled her into his arms. "I'm glad Martha is there. We might need her from time to time."

She smiled broadly. "I don't think I want her here right now, though. She's too much a prude."

He gave her a stern look. "I'm your husband, woman. Whatever we do, I'm sure Martha would approve. Now, come here."

His Molly obeyed, rolling into his arms and they proceeded to test stodgy old Martha's forbearance.

Chapter Fifteen

MARTHA WAS awakened the next morning by the first rays of sunlight filtering around the shades at her window. In the twilight between sleep and wakefulness she was seized by a sudden fear that the whole incredible experience had only been a dream. Her attempt to sit up caused the man in her bed to stir and tighten his arms around her. She immediately relaxed and snuggled into his embrace.

As she lay there in his arms, she lightly rubbed her hands across his chest, playing with the dark hair, tickling the ribs covered with hard muscle.

She wondered if his body was as sensitive as hers. As a test only, she placed a kiss on a convenient nipple, then slipped her tongue out to lick it. When she opened her mouth to nip at it, a big hand covered the tender spot.

"You'd better be ready to finish what you're starting."

His threat was considerably softened by the smile in his dark blue eyes.

"How long have you been awake?" she asked. Her hand continued its lazy exploration of his broad chest.

"Long enough." As though she weighed no more than a feather, he pulled her to lie atop him.

"So, you're a mind reader, too," she whispered as his mouth caught her words in their first kiss of the morning.

"No, I'm just hungry." He turned her onto her back and dipped his mouth to hers. His lips traveled in a gentle caress down the length of her neck, to that tender place where her shoulder began.

"Jake?" Her breath in his ear caused him to shiver. She smiled.

"Ummm?" he answered. His voice was already getting rough.

She ran her fingers through his hair. "Am I too old to have children?"

"Honey, you'd know more about that than I would." His lips never left her skin.

"No, I don't mean can I. I still can. But, do you think I'm too old to?"

"No, my darlin', you are definitely not too old." He kissed her gently. "Now, stop interrupting me when I'm busy."

He returned his attention her body. She knew he was more interested in making love than in any possible consequences.

"Wait, Jake," she said, stilling his roaming hands with her own, "you said you wanted children. I don't want you to miss out on that because you married an old woman."

He smiled. "Sweetheart, why don't we just let nature take its course?"

His lips nuzzled the place where her pulse throbbed faster and faster in her throat. From there his tongue traced a line up to her earlobe. She shivered in reaction and even more so when he nibbled at the tender morsel. The discussion was over for now. His voice was husky and hungry in her ear as he covered her body with his own.

"Until nature decides, why don't we stay in practice?"

THE SMELL OF coffee startled her from a sound sleep. Her jerk to wakefulness brought Jake along with her. It was late, probably almost eight o'clock. She started to rise, but strong arms pulled her back.

"Nope, not yet."

She found herself lying on him again, his mouth lazily tasting hers.

"You sure are sweet," he whispered. "I just can't seem to get enough."

She responded, returning his kisses, barely taking time to breathe. Finally she had to push herself up.

"You, sir, are no gentleman!"

"But, you, madam, are most assuredly a lady. Leastwise," he added as he made a test of his assumption, "you sure do feel like a lady."

She bubbled with laughter as she pushed away and rolled to lie beside him.

"Jake, stop. You don't seem to understand how serious our situation is." She paused for effect. "Mary is cooking!"

"Oh, heavens, no!"

Trying to maintain her mock seriousness, she said, "Don't joke. Mary's cooking could kill us all." Her lips briefly sought his and she continued. "Besides, I need some rest. Something less strenuous, like mopping floors, maybe."

"You'd rather mop floors than spend the day in bed with me?"

She raised an eyebrow cynically. "I doubt I'd survive the whole day with you in your present mood."

A suggestive smile came to his face. "What a way to die."

Martha rose from the bed and crossed the room to her dresser. It seemed the most natural thing in the world to be naked before him. And she could feel him following her every move. He watched her as she bent over the open drawer and pulled out fresh underclothes, as she poured water in the china washbasin, as she took a fresh cloth and washed. She never knew it was possible to feel heat like this just from a man's gaze.

After the torture had gone on long enough, Jake grunted.

"You'd better hurry up with that, woman, or you'll find yourself back over here."

"Yes, sir."

As she finished dressing, Martha watched him rise and stretch his arms over his head. Several scars ran across his back including the one left by the wound she had tended in this very room. It had healed well and, she thought with a smile, he certainly seemed to have full use of the arm.

She sat on the edge of the bed and studied him. It was the first time she had seen a man naked...in the daylight. Last night, there hadn't really been much time to look at him. Now she looked her fill.

He moved like a big cat, confident and graceful. His body was hardened by work, but still there were subtle signs that it was not the body of a very young man.

"Jake, how old are you?"

"Forty-three last August," he answered without hesitation. He glanced at her. "Too old?"

"No sirree. Not that I could tell, anyway."

He laughed. "Thank you, Mrs. Bowman, for that testimonial."

She continued to watch him as he dressed. No, it was certainly not too old, at least not for him. He was hers and he was perfect.

"MARY, COULD I have some more of your coffee, please?" Jake asked. He finished off his eggs and wiped his mouth on his napkin. "I don't know why, but Molly seemed to think you couldn't cook." He threw a sly look at Martha.

"Well, I wonder why she would say a thing like that," Mary answered, pouring him more coffee. "Sam?" she offered a refill, which he took with thanks.

Martha was a bit chagrined, in fact. Mary had learned to cook, somewhere, sometime. She suddenly had the suspicion that she had been duped for these many years by her younger sister.

Maybe Mary would find herself cooking more often, now.

She didn't know if it was just her own good mood that made everybody else's seem lighter this morning, but even Sam, who hardly had more than ten words to say at any one time, was gabbing like an old lady at a sewing circle.

"Well, brother, I see you survived your first night of married life." Jake sat there, smiling and taking the ribbing in extreme good humor as Sam looked him over. "Where's the blood, man? From what I heard, I figured this woman would have turned you into scraps for the dog by now!"

"Sam Bowman!" Martha said. "How can you say things like that?"

He was unabashed. "My dear sister-in-law, I only said I heard that, not that I believed it!"

"You'd better believe it. I worked very hard to earn my reputation."

Her husband's laugh betrayed no apprehension. "Well, let them say what they want to, but they'd better not say it to me." Jake got up and went over to the door where he took his gunbelt from the peg and strapped it on.

Martha held his jacket. So many nights she'd dreamed of doing such wifely favors for him. The reality was even sweeter.

"Thank you, honey." He shrugged into his jacket and stood obediently as she straightened his collar.

"Daylight's burning, Jake," Sam said. "Kiss her, already, and let's get out to work."

Jake grinned in answer and gathered her into his arms. His kiss was no goodbye peck, either. Her arms circled his neck and she pulled herself up tightly to him. Her lips answered his, tug for tug. When they parted, he held her.

"Don't get yourself all tired out mopping those floors, Molly," Jake said, giving her a wink. He looked unnaturally pleased with himself at her shiver of anticipation. His hands squeezed her bottom before he released her and walked out the kitchen door behind his brother.

Watching him all the way to the barn, she whispered, "Oh, my." She'd never get tired of looking at that man. He disappeared into the barn and Martha knew she had to get to work. Turning to clear the table, her jaw dropped to her knees. Mary already had the dishes in a dishpan of hot water.

"What?" Martha said in mock confusion. "Why, I think I am going to faint."

"Don't be so sassy, Molly. You said it was time I learned to cook and do housework."

"What's brought on this sudden desire for domesticity?" Martha took a damp cloth and wiped the table clean.

Mary only shrugged. "I guess you and Jake getting married just got me thinking. You're going to have a family to care for and I have to start doing my part around here."

Martha looked up from her wiping.

"Mary, you've always done your part."

Mary shook her head. "Most of what I did before is being done by the men, now. They can do it faster and better than I can. Anyway, when you and Jake start having children, you're going to need help around the house." She sighed. "It looks like I'm the one who's going to be the spinster aunt around here."

Molly tried not to laugh. "Don't be silly. You don't have to be a spinster aunt." She put both hands on her sister's face and turned her. "You're very beautiful, Mary, and you have a more beautiful spirit than anyone I've ever known. Someone will see that and someday you'll have your own children to take care of."

Mary turned toward the window as Sam rode by on his way out to the range. She smiled sadly. "Sure, Molly. But when?"

THE PILE OF wanted posters lay on the dusty, scuffed desk, among the refuse of hundreds of greasy meals crusting the surface of the darkly lacquered wood. Coffee stained many of them and some had been gnawed by the rats infesting the jail. But the sheer number of them gave Monroe hope he could find something to improve Garret's disposition. He'd been like the very devil, himself, ever since the day a month ago when Martha MacLannon had married that Bowman fella.

The sheriff flattened out a poster and held it up, beady eyes squinting, struggling to make out the words.

WANTED FOR RUSTLING CATTLE AND HORSES
MURDER, RAPE, VANDALISM

"Hey, Monroe," he asked, a quizzical look on his jowly face, "what is," he stumbled over the word, "van-dawl-izm?"

Monroe wasn't in the mood to play teacher.

"Just find the damned poster!" he yelled at the other man. "Jackass," he muttered under his breath.

"Well, I might just have found it," the sheriff crowed. He waved the yellowed paper under Monroe's nose. "I do happen to know what rustling, murder, and rape mean." He screwed up his piggish face in confusion. "What's Garret planning on doing with it, anyway?"

Monroe snatched the poster from the sheriff's grimy hand. He'd been wondering that very thing, himself.

"What do you know," Monroe said softly. He read the same words the sheriff had already read. But the poster continued:

SUSPECTS IN A MURDER IN THE INDIAN TERRITORY SOLD STOLEN CATTLE IN KANSAS: FIVE WHITE MEN, BETWEEN THE AGES OF TWENTY AND FORTY-FIVE. ONE RIDES TALL PALOMINO. REWARD OFFERED, $2,000.00. CONTACT OWEN TUCKER, CARE OF THE FEDERAL COURT, FORT SMITH, ARKANSAS.

Monroe added it up. Garret told him the Bowmans were rustlers, then told him to go find some paper he could pin on them. Monroe had wondered just how he knew that. He didn't know much about his boss's past, except that just before settling in Travis County the previous summer, Garret had been up north. Monroe looked again at the poster and checked the date: July, 1871.

Everybody had seen that tall palomino.

A low whistle erupted from the foreman's lips. This little piece of paper was sure to set him up for life. Garret had plenty of money to buy the second largest spread in the area, with enough left over to hire the guns to enjoy as much serenity as a man could have in this life. There weren't many places where a Reb could get that kind of money legally these days.

Now, he had a pretty good idea where this particular Reb had come by his wealth. It was time he shared some of his good fortune, Monroe decided, pawing through the papers scattered across the desk.

He found a second poster, practically identical to the first, with more detailed descriptions of the men, missing only the reference to the horse. He picked this one up and noted the descriptions could fit the Bowman boys. He laughed. These descriptions could fit a lot of people. But, if he knew cowfolk, as most of the people in this town were, all you had to do was give them a start and they would find the evidence, themselves. The necktie party the boss wanted to throw for Bowman was practically a done deal.

Turning to the sheriff, he said genially, "I think Mr. Garret will find these very interesting." He threw a five-dollar gold piece on the desk.

As the portly sheriff jumped to grab for it, Monroe ambled out of the office, already thinking how he would spend his share of Mr. Garret's rustling money.

GARRET ALMOST danced a jig when he saw the poster.

Monroe had put the first poster in a safe place and would bring it out only when Bowman was taken care of. He understood exactly what Garret was planning. Get the Bowmans hung, all legal and proper, or better yet, to avoid the potential embarrassment of a trial, lynched by the good people of Travis City. The Widow Bowman would be the owner of all that land with no man to comfort her in her mourning. Garret would marry her, and when he had control of her property, Monroe would bring out the other poster and negotiate a split with him.

It's beautiful, Monroe thought as Garret continued to read and reread and chortle to himself.

Monroe considered what he knew of his boss. Not a man to follow anybody else, it was a safe bet he'd been the leader of the gang described in the posters.

If there was anything decent, law-abiding people hated more than rustlers, it was the men who led them. Monroe was sure Garret would understand.

Meanwhile, Garret seemed blissfully unaware his foreman was not giving him his undivided attention.

"Oh, that Jake, that slick sonovabitch. Thought he was so goldurned smart, sneaking into that woman's house right under my nose. He'll see who's smarter this time. Look at this, Monroe!" he chortled. "This description right here is Jake, to a tee. Over six-foot, big build, dark hair."

And three or four million other guys, Monroe thought.

"And this one here. Six-foot, big, sandy hair. Left-handed draw. I'll be damned if that ain't Sammy-boy."

Monroe was certain Garret knew these two men well. Hell, they probably grew up together.

"I won't miss you this time, Jake!" Garret yelled at the walls. Quickly turning his attention to his foreman, Garret shoved the poster into Monroe's hands. "Get this back to the sheriff and tell him to paste it up all over town. And tell him to hurry. Wake up the goddamned newspaperman, if he needs more copies. I want the whole town talking about this." He looked out the window facing the river and, beyond that, the MacLannon ranch. "We don't have much time. Garcia was over there this morning and they have almost a thousand head ready to drive. Once Jake gets them on the road, we'll have a hard time stopping him. If they get to market, I'll have to wear that woman down another whole year." He turned again to Monroe. "And, Monroe, I'm getting mighty tired of waiting."

Chapter Sixteen

JAKE SAT ON the top step, puffing his morning pipe and watching nine hundred head of Texas longhorn beef wearing the Double-A brand grazing on the range nearest the house. Another three dozen or so, mostly cows with young calves, milled around in the large corral by the barn -- all they would have to start rebuilding. He felt bad he hadn't been able to stop the rustlers from hitting them earlier on. It wasn't like he didn't know what to look for, he thought with a touch of conscience.

All that was behind him, now. He returned his attention to the herd. They looked mighty good to him, strong, well-fed, and ready for the drive. It was a small herd and he and Sam would have no problem getting them to Kansas, providing there was no extra trouble along the way.

That was really his only worry. He wondered again how long it would be before Wil did something. The quiet made him uneasy.

Sam pulled up in front of the house in the chuck wagon.

"This thing sure has seen better days."

Jake nodded. "Molly told me they almost lost it in the Red River after the big rains last year."

"That explains the warped floor boards." Sam wrapped the reins around the brake and stepped down from the driver's seat. "And the drawers that won't close in the chuck box."

This year will be different, honey, Jake promised her silently. To Sam he said, "I'll go see if she wants to go with us."

When Jake walked into the house, he thought he must already be on the trail. A cloud of dust billowed from the library. He peered in. There was Martha perched on a chair, stretching up to the top shelves of the tall bookcase.

"Molly, what are you doing?"

"Spring cleaning, of course. A little late, but," her eyes squinted closed, "ah-choo...." She sniffed and scratched under her nose with the back of her hand. "Better late than not at all." She pointed to the stacks of books on the floor before her. "Darlin', will you hand me up those books? Be careful you don't get them out of order."

Jake laughed and shook his head, but he took off his jacket, stepped up to the books and started handing them up to her.

"Why the whirlwind?"

She blew away the dust mites that tickled her nose.

"I have to clean before Gloria and Jimmy come to stay. They just got married. You remember. I told you, they're going to watch over the place while we're gone."

Jake had been thinking about that. "Molly, about you coming along...."

"Jake, please pay attention. That stack goes last. Here, change places with me and just put them up like I give them to you." She accepted his hand as she stepped from the chair.

"Excuse me, Miss Librarian."

"Don't be smart. Get on up there."

He smirked. "My dear, tiny wife, I don't need the chair." To add to the insult, he patted her on top of her head. She scowled. "Just hand me the books, Little One." He placed the first handful on the shelf. "So, you've arranged it all?"

"Of course. It's a wonderful idea. They get some privacy. We know there are responsible people watching our property."

He turned to get the next bunch.

"You know, Molly, maybe you should stay here, after all. It's a long trip and I'll tell you, honey, if there were any other way to get those cows to Kansas rather than driving 'em, I'd be all for it. I think Sam and I can handle fewer than a thousand head."

She stopped handing books. Uneasiness passed quickly over her face.

"I'm more afraid of being here alone than anything that could happen on the trail." Their eyes locked together and both understood what she meant.

Jake thought about it. She might be right, after all. He wanted her where he could keep an eye on her. If he left her here, he wouldn't be able to keep his mind on driving cows. After all, he reminded himself, she wasn't a typical woman. If any woman could make a cattle drive, it was his Molly.

He helped her move the books from the next bookcase and even dusted the top shelf for her while he considered the situation. He'd hoped Wil would just back off. The fact that they'd heard nothing from him for more than two months could be a good sign, but Jake had never known him to give up on something he really wanted.

She bent over the stacks of books and Jake savored the sight of her nicely rounded bottom. How did he get so lucky to find a woman like this, after all he'd done?

Rustler's Bride 139

"Here," she said, handing up a bunch of books.

Jake took them from her and placed them on the shelf, thinking all the while.

As far as he was concerned, the past could just stay in the past. He was about at the point where he could leave it to God to take care of punishing Wil for his sins. The future was more important, now, his future with Molly and the children they would have. He wanted a bunch -- strong, lusty boys and pretty girls with their mama's spirit and silky, golden hair.

"Molly," he said, as he put the last book on the upper shelf, "we need to go into town to stock up the chuck wagon. Do you want to come along?"

Her face took on a sudden expression of panic, replaced by embarrassment.

"Jake, we don't have any money. That Butler woman won't extend us enough credit to stock the chuck wagon." She suddenly turned pale and dropped down on her sewing chair.

"Molly!" He was immediately on his knee beside her. He yelled, "Mary, bring some water!" He brushed back the loose hair from her face. "Honey, are you all right?"

Martha took his hand in hers and held it to her cheek. When she looked into his eyes, her smile was like sunshine.

"Yes, I'm just fine. I just got a little light-headed." Docile as a lamb, she took the glass of water Mary handed her and slowly sipped most of it.

Jake was confused. First, she was panicked, then weak, then smiling and sweet. But like most men, he ended up putting it down to female peculiarity, which defied a man's understanding. He returned to the original problem.

"Don't worry about money. I have some put by, enough for this." He placed his finger across her lips when she started to protest. "Would you hold back anything from me?" When she shook her head, he took her hand. "Everything I have is yours, too. We'll either get rich together, or we'll go to the poorhouse together."

She simply smiled in agreement, then stroked his face gently, touching the hair at his temple. "Have I told you today that I love you?"

He kissed the smooth, soft back of her hand. "Not in the last couple of hours. So, do you want to go?"

"A shopping trip is just what I need." She waved her hand in front of her face. "Maybe the dust will settle enough to get a clean breath." She kissed his cheek and went to their room to clean up.

WHEN THEY PULLED up in front of the general store, Jake noted the looks of surprise on the faces of the people standing nearby. Always seemed to be a bunch of gawkers hanging around. He jumped down and turned to help Martha, taking his time about it. She took his arm and they started toward the front door of the store.

"Jake, I can handle this, if you'd like to go over and get yourself a beer."

"That is a right fine idea, sweetheart." He turned to his brother. "What d'you say, Sam? Could you use a beer?"

"Reckon I could at that."

Jake turned back to his wife and pulled a cloth bag from his pocket. He took out ten ten-dollar gold pieces and handed them over.

"Whatever's left, you do some shopping with."

She barely hid the surprise he saw in her eyes with a little smile, and deposited the gold into her little handbag.

"Thank you, dear," she said loud enough for the gawkers to hear and pulled him down for a little kiss. Before she let him go she added in a whisper, "We'll talk about this later."

He nodded and smiled suggestively. "Maybe. If we're not too busy doing other things."

She just laughed and shook her head at him. "Bad man."

With that, she turned and went into the store, pausing at the door to cast a backward glance at her husband. Jake pondered his good fortune. Then, slapping his brother on the back, headed down the street to the saloon.

Clarissa was waiting behind the counter. Several women milled about, pretending to examine the quality of the bolts of sprigged muslin displayed on one of the center aisles. Martha nodded and smiled sweetly as she greeted them and the men around the checkerboard by the front window. The women gathered in small groups and soon the building buzzed as though infested with blowflies.

She slipped quietly through the store, eavesdropping shamelessly from behind a ten-foot tall pile of Mr. Levi Strauss' jeans pants.

"Did you see that? She kissed him right on the street in broad daylight!"

"The way he had his hands on her!"

"No decent woman would permit it!"

Martha stepped around the pile of pants and pretended she was checking the seams. "No decent woman would permit what, Esther?"

"Martha! Oh, I was just saying..." the woman sputtered.

She waited for an answer, still fingering the orange stitching of the indigo blue pants.

Esther regained her sense of outrage. "I was saying you really ought to be more discrete, Martha. After all, you're not just anybody."

She looked at the woman, confused.

"You are a member of the Old Three Hundred. You have a standard to maintain." Esther laid her hand on Martha's arm. "We are the only bastion against the complete destruction of our way of life."

Martha almost laughed. It was as important to a Texan to be a member of the Old Three Hundred as it was to a New Englander to be descended from the passenger list of the Mayflower. At least, it was to Esther.

"Esther, I really don't understand how my kissing my husband is going to bring about the destruction of our way of life." She allowed herself a little smile. "As far as I can tell, Texas is going along pretty much the same as it ever did. We're still ranching. You're still minding everybody else's business."

Esther huffed, "Well!"

Martha hadn't meant to be mean and wanted to mollify the woman. "I know how it looks, but he's so," she paused, searching for just exactly the right word, "affectionate. Being such a strong man, he's used to getting what he wants. When Jake wants a kiss, I can't stop him." She laughed. "Don't really want to, either."

She walked away from the slack-jawed Esther and approached the counter to place her order. Before she could open her mouth, the storekeeper's wife put up her hand.

"I'm very sorry, Martha," she said. "I've already told you, we just can't extend you any further credit."

Martha only smiled. "Clarissa, I don't need credit." She held up her little reticule and shook it. The heavy gold pieces jingled. "While I'm in town, I'll settle up my outstanding bill. Will you get it totaled?"

Clarissa's eyes opened as big and round as those ten-dollar gold pieces.

Martha smiled again. "My husband will be back very shortly and he doesn't like to be kept waiting. Do you suppose you could take my order, now?"

She held out the paper on which Jake had listed the necessities for the drive. Clarissa reached out for it, still eyeing the little bag hanging from Martha's arm. Martha didn't release the paper immediately, though.

The look she leveled at the other woman was reminiscent of the

Martha they had come to know.

"Clarissa," she said, very quietly, so no one else could hear, "I have a very good idea of what all this will cost. Don't inflate any prices on me, now." She let go of the paper. "I'll have a few things to add." She turned and started walking along the aisles, really shopping for the first time in a long time.

THE SALOON HAD become very quiet with his arrival, and Jake was certain his continued good health, despite two months of married life with the former Miss MacLannon, was a stunning surprise to the locals.

Sam was ahead of him at the bar. When he had his beer, he staked out a table by the wall on the left side of the saloon. Gazing around the room, Jake saw Wil Garret holding court on the other side of the saloon, a girl draped over his lap, a whiskey bottle within easy reach. His foreman, Monroe, sat beside him and Jake recognized at least ten more of his hired guns.

He turned back to the bar. "Bartender, give me a beer."

A chair scraped across the floor behind him. It had to be one of Wil's entourage. Jake stood his ground, waiting for his beer.

"Well, Bowman," a slightly slurred voice came from behind him, "you still walk like a rooster, even if you did get clipped."

Jake took his beer from the bartender whose eyes begged him not to wreck the place, then turned slowly and found himself face-to-face with one of Wil's men. The week-old growth covering much of the tough's face hid a multitude of sins. The man's breath would have shamed a skunk and his size and shape brought to mind a well-fed boar. But, as Jake pushed the man aside to get by, he noted the absence of the smell of alcohol.

The sound of steel sliding against leather made him stop.

"Turn around, Bowman," the man said, sounding quite a bit more sober.

When Jake didn't turn, the drunk repeated his demand.

"Goddammit! Turn around."

Jake felt Wil's eyes boring into the back of his head. He stopped and turned around very slowly.

"Call him off, Wil."

Wil only sipped his whiskey, a smile playing over his lips.

Real cool, ain't he? Jake thought.

"Mr. Garret, I believe this man works for you. If you want to keep him in working condition, I suggest you call him off."

"Wooo-eee, listen at that," one of the others howled. "Pretty fancy talk."

The tough snickered. "You ain't even got the guts to turn around and face me."

"Wil." Jake's quiet voice carried to everyone in the saloon. The fancy ladies started moving discretely up the stairs. The piano player, if such he could be called, slipped behind his piano. The bartender seemed to suddenly remember needing more whiskey from the storeroom and went out in that direction. Several patrons slipped out the swinging doors.

Garret's man carefully raised the tail of Jake's jacket. The tough peeked under it, as if he expected a rattler to come out at him from the pockets.

"He ain't even wearing a gun, Mr. Garret," he said, releasing his own to slide back into its holster.

"Leave him be, Slim," Wil said.

The man turned in astonishment. "What? He ain't armed. It'll be easy."

"Shut up, Slim, you damned idiot!" Garret shouted as Monroe got to his feet, his hand hovering above the butt of his gun.

Jake calmly drained his beer and then chuckled. "Slim? Did you hear that, Sam? This fella's name is Slim." He turned and leaned against the bar. Looking up and down the man's portly frame, he asked, "How in the world did you get that nickname, fat boy?"

Sam chortled from his seat on the other side of the saloon. Slim reddened in rage.

"What's the matter, Slim, can't take a little funnin'?"

Jake slipped his right arm around Slim's shoulders. At the contact, the man's hand reached down for his gun. Too fast for any reaction on Slim's part, Jake tightened his arm around Slim's thick neck while bringing the beer mug in his other hand down across the edge of the bar. The heavy container smashed and the handle came away attached to a sharp section of glass. Jake brought the clean-cutting edge up on the underside of the man's jowls.

"Now, Slim, how would you like all these folks to get a look at what you look like inside?"

He slid the glass along the fat man's throat. A sound gurgled from Slim's mouth and his eyes widened as he tried to see the glass blade digging into his neck. Jake ignored everyone but the squirming mass he held around the throat.

"Tell me, Slim. Did you know I got myself shot in the back a couple of months ago?" he asked as he dug the glass knife a little deeper. "Wouldn't know anything about that, would you, Slim?"

The glass slid closer to the artery running under the ear. Jake was sure Slim had killed enough men in his time to know how close he was to meeting his Maker.

"I don't know nothin'," he croaked.

"I'll just bet you don't."

The fat man shivered. Jake clucked.

"Dagnabbit, look at that, Slim. You went and made me cut you." He removed the tough's gun and tossed it on the bar. Once the man was disarmed, Jake released him and reached onto the bar for a towel. He lay it around Slim's shoulders and patted the man on the back like an old friend.

"There you go, Hoss. You'd better make sure you get that looked after. Once saw a man die from an infection in a little bitty cut no bigger than that."

Holding the towel tightly over the wound on his neck, Slim skulked over to sit with his buddies.

As though this sort of thing happened every day, Jake stretched up over the bar and looked behind it.

"Where'd that bartender go? I need another beer."

He went around and helped himself, then joined Sam at his table. They both kept their backs to the wall.

The sheriff walked in and looked the situation over. After a nod to Garret, he approached the Bowmans' table.

"How you boys doing today?" he asked, pulling up a chair and taking a seat, uninvited.

"Right well, thank you, Sheriff," Jake replied.

He could almost feel the man sizing him up. Be careful, Jacob, he told himself, he might not be as stupid as he looks.

The quiet in the saloon had brought back the fancy girls and the bartender. The sheriff yelled to one of the women.

"Annie, c'mon honey, don't let me die of thirst!"

A redhead came up a moment later with a whiskey bottle and a glass. Jake sipped his beer and said nothing, waiting for the sheriff to remember why he'd come in, besides getting his liquid nourishment. The portly lawman sat up and directed himself to Jake.

"Never seen you around these parts before, Bowman. Where're you from?" He downed a whiskey and quickly poured himself another.

Jake looked over the sheriff's head and locked eyes with Garret. Wil was sitting there like a big yellow cat that had just eaten Mama's favorite canary. With the herd he'd stolen from Randall, Wil would have had enough money to buy a little piss-ant like this one.

"Well, Sheriff, we're Texans, born and bred. Raised up near Dallas. We were away for a while because of the war. Fact is, we've never much been out of Texas." Jake took a sip of his beer. As though it just occurred to him, he added, "Oh, well, there was that time in the Indian Territory."

Sam stared at him as though he were crazy. Never volunteer any information was his motto.

The sheriff sat up so abruptly he tipped over the bottle of whiskey. Jake only just managed to catch it.

"The Indian Territory, you say? Where, and when were you there?"

Real smooth interrogator, Jake thought, barely hiding a smirk. Only a blind man could have missed the wanted posters nailed to every wall and post in town. It was interesting that there were two descriptions underlined in bold, black pencil: the tall, bearded man, and the left-handed gun.

He let the sheriff sit for a minute as he took a slow drink from his beer.

"When? Oh, when was it, Sam? My daddy took me with him to buy some horses up there, years ago." He sipped again. "Pretty country, but just a little too flat for my taste."

The sheriff sat back, disappointed. But he hadn't given up. "There's paper on some men that sold some rustled beef in Newton." The sheriff eyed them closely. "Ever hear of it?"

"What? Newton or beef?" Jake asked innocently.

"Either one."

"Well, Sheriff, I have heard of Newton. I've been working cattle the better part of my life, when I wasn't killing Yankees." He looked pointedly at the sheriff, who was, indeed, a Yankee. "That was the big market last year. But I hear it's gone busted. Seems everybody's gone on up to Ellsworth or Wichita. As far as the stolen beef goes, though, I'm a rancher and I bet I hate rustlers just as much as Mr. Garret over there does."

"That's your wife's ranch," the sheriff said.

"Indeed it is. However, I'm her husband. What's hers is mine."

"Miss MacLannon might object to her property being claimed by a drifter." The sheriff smirked and poured himself another drink.

"Mrs. Bowman," Jake corrected him. "And, so far, I haven't heard her object to anything."

Laughter rippled across the room.

An older man sitting at the next table leaned over. "You mean you've tamed the shrew, son?" he asked.

Jake laughed. "Molly's no shrew. She is, in fact, the most even-tempered woman I've ever known."

That caused another wave of laughter. Even Sam chuckled.

Their neighbor continued. "I've known Martha for over thirty years, since she was just a little girl. She was a real pretty little thing, too. Seems to me most of the men around your age in this county wanted to court her. Now, not that she didn't have her reasons, what with all her menfolk getting killed off, but, Bowman, I've got to tell you, she's gotten sour as a lemon these last few years."

Jake looked at the man as though they couldn't possibly be talking about the same woman.

"My Molly, sour?" He laughed and turned to look at the man. "I sure haven't seen it."

Sam cleared his throat, but said nothing.

"You saying she hasn't turned her evil tongue on you yet?" another man asked.

Jake stopped his beer halfway to his mouth, and looked at the man as though trying to decide exactly what he meant.

"Oh, you mean yelling and fussing? Sure, we fight, but," he smiled as he took a drink, "we make up, too." He waited for the snickers to die down. "In fact, I bet she is no more a shrew than any of your women are."

He turned to man who'd started this. "Friend, sounds to me like you have read some Shakespeare." At the man's nod, he continued, "So, you're familiar with Petruccio's bet?" The man nodded and smiled. "Well, then, I'm willing to make you fellas a little wager."

"Jake," Sam warned, "she's not gonna like this."

Jake had to hide his smile at the murmurs of interest that swept through the saloon after that remark. Even Garret sat up. Jake couldn't resist the chance to twist the knife a little, so he raised his voice a little so he could be heard through the building.

"I believe I know her just a little bit better than you do, Sam." He turned back to the crowd. "I'm willing to cover any bets that my wife will come to me when I send for her. No excuses, no dillydallying. And," he added more inducement, "when she gets here, she'll be sweet as sugar." He looked around the room for takers.

"Sweet as sugar, huh? I'll take some of that," said a man wearing an eyepatch.

"Me, too," came a voice from over near the piano.

Rustler's Bride 147

Jake looked at the older man who had spoken first.

"All right, Bowman, I'll take ten dollars of your money."

"Jake," Sam whispered loudly, "are you sure about this?"

That brought even more takers. Jake smiled at his brother before he headed for the door, leaving Sam to take the bets. Several young boys were passing by.

"Hey, boy, come here," he called to a handsome towhead of about ten years.

"Yes, sir?"

Jake reached into his pocket and took out a quarter. "What's your name, son?"

"Henry, sir."

Jake put one hand on the boy's shoulder and flipped the quarter in the other. "Well, Henry, would you be willing to run a little errand for me?" The boy's head bobbed like a cork, his eyes locked on the quarter. "You know who my wife is?"

Again Henry nodded. "Oh, yes, sir. Everybody knows Miss Martha!"

"Henry, I want you to go over to the general store and tell her I want her to come down to the saloon. I need to talk to her. Can you do that for me?"

The boy's eyes were as wide as the quarter Jake pressed into his hand. Then he looked up and nodded firmly.

Jake patted the boy between the shoulder blades and sent him off down the walk toward the general store. When he turned around, all eyes were on him.

"She'll come all right, Bowman. But when she gets here, she's going to cut you to pieces!" said one of the men sitting at the table nearest the door. There were laughs of agreement and, it seemed to him, anticipation.

He just smiled and went back to his table. "Sweet as sugar," he said.

Annie brought him another beer. Pausing by the table, she leaned over and whispered.

"If you need some company later on, dearie, just come on up. First door on the right."

"Why do women always move on you first?" Sam asked, scowling into his beer.

"They respect age and experience, kid," Jake answered, "but since I'm spoken for, maybe she'll give you a chance."

"Payback is coming, Jakey," Sam promised with a smile.

The crowd sat in expectant silence as the minutes passed. Every eye in the saloon was focused on him, waiting for any sign of nervousness. He'd covered more than three hundred dollars worth of bets, not only on Molly's compliance, but also on her good nature.

Now he'd see how well he'd come to know his wife.

Chapter Seventeen

MARTHA HEARD a boy's voice calling her name long before Henry grabbed the doorframe to swing himself inside.

"Miss Martha!" he chirped and just missed running into her.

"Whoa, there. Where're you going so fast, Henry?" she asked as she reached to push a stray lock of hair from his forehead. She smiled as his eyes widened at the touch of her hand. Henry was momentarily speechless. With a questioning eyebrow, she asked, "Did you have something to say to me, Henry?"

"Oh, yes, ma'am. Miss Martha," he said, "your husband gave me a quarter to come and tell you he wants you to come over to the saloon. He said he needed to talk to you."

Martha laughed gently. "Did he say what he wanted?"

"No, ma'am, just that he wanted to talk to you."

Clarissa snorted as Martha pulled a taffy out of the jar on the counter and sent Henry on his way with it.

"Well, isn't that just like a man? Thinks he can bid you come and there you go. If he were my husband, I can tell you, he wouldn't dare summon me like that! To the saloon of all places!"

Martha frowned in confusion. "But, Clarissa, weren't you telling me just a couple of months ago I wasn't behaving in a ladylike manner? You mentioned my temper in particular. I assumed you meant I should be more submissive."

Clarissa sighed and shook her head. "I realize your experience with men is limited, my dear, but surely you understand a woman must act submissive to catch a husband. However, once you're married, you simply must not allow him to order you about like this." She leaned across the counter in a confidential manner. "He'll start to think he can get away with all sorts of mischief."

"Oh," Martha said, wishing Jake could hear this. He'd really enjoy the logic.

While Clarissa held forth on the training of husbands, Martha imagined herself trying to train Jake Bowman, then she saw herself being turned over his knee. Or better yet, tossed onto their bed. In spite of herself, she giggled. Clarissa paused her lecture.

"What do you find so amusing, Martha?"

Martha stifled her laughter and returned Clarissa's gaze. She put on as serious a face as she could manage.

"What do you think I ought to do, Clarissa?" She looked sincerely into the older woman's eyes. "You're right about my not having much experience. I certainly don't want him to get the wrong idea."

Clarissa didn't miss a beat.

"You mustn't go." She stopped, then got a thoughtful expression. "Though, perhaps nipping this kind of behavior right in the bud is the best thing. If you go down there and set him straight in front of all his drinking buddies, I guarantee he'll never again send after you like a bond servant."

Martha looked around at the flock surrounding her. Several clucked approvingly at Clarissa's advice.

So, I'm supposed to go down there and tell Jake what he can do with himself.

She nodded. "You're right. This simply won't do. I guess I'd better get on down there."

Turning on her heel, she left the store, followed by at least fifteen women. Feeling like she was at the front of a temperance march, Martha led her band of followers all the way down the rough-hewn boards of the walkway. They were right behind her when she stopped just outside the doors.

"Do you really expect me to come in there?" she shouted over the door. A few chuckles came from inside.

"I wouldn't have sent for you if I didn't want you to come in, Molly."

"All right," she said and without another moment's hesitation, she pushed open the doors and went inside.

Normally, decent women wouldn't set foot in the saloon, but the women who had followed her from the general store found their sense of propriety overcome by curiosity. They pushed in and stopped, blocking the entry, none wanting to get further inside than the doorway.

"I'm over here, honey."

She looked toward the sound of his voice and caught sight of her husband sprawled in a chair tipped against the wall. As she approached him, Jake rose and pulled out a chair for her. Primly placing herself on the very edge of the seat, she waited for him to sit.

"Well? Why did you send for me?" she asked, struggling to keep the smile off her lips. The struggle was lost at the sound of scraping chairs and shuffling feet as the observers tried to get closer and her smile grew broader. His eyes twinkled with that mischief Clarissa was so worried about. He was up to something, so she waited patiently.

Jake took his time. He half-smiled at her and took a long drink from his beer. Finally he said, "I forgot to ask you to pick me up some pipe tobacco. I would have come down myself, but I was right in the middle of my beer."

Clarissa snorted.

"You called me down to this saloon to ask me to get you some tobacco?" Martha let her voice carry just a hint of irritation.

Jake just smiled. "That's right."

A couple of men chuckled and the air fairly pulsed with the anticipation of an explosion of her famous temper.

It was getting harder to keep from laughing out loud.

"Anything else?"

"Nope, that's all."

"All right, some tobacco. I'll be getting the wagon loaded," she said, rising from the chair.

As she started to go, Jake reached out and took her hand. She lifted an eyebrow at his forwardness when he pulled her down to sit on his lap.

"Molly, there is one more thing, come to think of it." He took her hand and played with her fingers. "Why don't you get some more of that sweet smelling rose water you like so much?"

She gave him a very dubious look. "You mean the rose water you like so much, don't you?"

He smiled and shrugged. "Well, yeah."

"Then you'd better let me get up so I can get Clarissa back down there to the store." Impulsively, she put a little kiss on his cheek before setting his hands aside and getting off his lap. "Don't be much longer. We've got an early start tomorrow." She walked toward the saloon's swinging doors, stopping only long enough to glance back at the gaggle of women standing inside.

"My goodness, whatever are you ladies doing inside a saloon!" To the good Mrs. Butler, she added, "Come on, Clarissa. My husband has a hankering to have some of your finest tobacco."

Clarissa hustled to get herself out of the building to the great amusement of the saloon's clientele.

"Okay, boys," Sam said loudly, "pony up."

The man at the next table leaned over and threw his money in front of Jake, then slapped him on the shoulders.

"Boy, that was something! Never thought I'd see that sweet little girl, again!" Jake shook the man's proffered hand.

"She's been there all the time." Jake looked across the room and met the steady gaze of Wilson Garret.

MARTHA SAW HIM striding along the boardwalk, grinning and patting his shirt pocket. When he reached her, he slipped his arm around her waist.

"Jacob, we're on the street in broad daylight."

"You're right."

"I just got a lecture on decorum from one of Travis City's socialites. Don't you think you should be more discrete?" Even though her tone was stern, she was smiling when she turned and slipped her arms around him. "Of course, after that exhibition of yours down at the saloon, I'll never be able to show my face in this town again." She gave him a sly look. "How much did we win?"

He tried to look innocent. She wasn't buying.

"Oh, come on, Jake. I know you took bets that I would come when you sent for me. How much?"

His eyes twinkled. "Three hundred dollars."

She choked. When she regained her voice, she knew she sounded somewhat like the Martha of old.

"Three hundred dollars! What would possess you to do something so stupid? Betting so much money that I would come to you like a lapdog? What if I'd decided not to?"

If her questioning him that loudly, right here on the street, bothered him, he didn't show it.

"It wasn't stupid, Molly. It was a sure thing." He stroked her cheek and smiled. "I knew you'd never let me down."

She shook her head. "Why can't I stay mad at you?" He knew how to deflect her irritation with just the right words, just a touch. He really did know her better than anyone ever had. "I reckon I won't feel too guilty about everything I just bought then."

"I reckon not." He peeked around her into the back of the wagon. "Did you get my tobacco?"

She held out a small burlap bag. He hefted the bag and frowned slightly. Martha laughed.

"Don't worry. There's a great big one in the wagon."

"That's my girl," he said approvingly and he lifted his hand to her face, pushing back an errant strand of her hair.

"Isn't that a touching sight, Mr. Monroe?"

Tension seized Jake's body at the sound of that voice.

"Well, it surely is, Mr. Garret," the foreman answered.

Both men were looking for trouble and she was afraid they had found it. Garret looked her over with his usual insultingly frank appraisal. She almost opened her mouth to tell him what she thought of his attention, but stopped. There was no point in making Jake aware of what was going on behind his back. It was only bound to make him angry and lead to a fight right here on the streets.

She raised her eyes to Jake's, intending to convince him to leave.

It was too late. His eyes were on her face and he'd seen her expression. Now, the look on his face was one she hadn't seen since the day of Garret's last visit to the ranch.

"Go inside the store, Molly."

"No, Jake. Don't."

She tried to hold him, to stop him from turning around to face the two men. But this time, he was not going to let it pass. He flashed her a look warning her against interfering in men's business and gently, but firmly, pulled her arms from around his waist. Something bothered her, something wasn't right.

He wasn't wearing a gun.

Chapter Eighteen

HE'D SURELY BE killed and she was powerless to stop it.

The world went black and spinning. Jake called her name, his voice heavy with fear. Then the blackness wrapped her in its protection....

Oh, Lord, I fainted. Hiding from the mortification of such weakness, Martha kept her eyes closed long after she regained consciousness.

She lay on one of Doc Mitchell's examination tables trying to ignore the vial of smelling salts under her nose. The first thing she heard was Jake's voice.

"Why would she faint like that if there's nothing wrong?" he bellowed.

Martha prayed the doctor hadn't had a chance to examine her. He was too good not to know the truth right away. But the canny old fox was asking Jake just the right questions.

"Calm down, Bowman. I need some information. Now, just how long have you been married?"

"Right at two months."

"Has Martha been acting different lately? Is she ever nauseous, say, in the morning?"

Risking a peek, she saw Doc Mitchell was watching her. She squeezed her eyes shut again.

"She's been tired," Jake said, "but that's because she's been working way too hard. I think she's been sick the last couple of mornings. Why?"

Jake didn't seem to know where the Doc was leading, but Martha sure did. Time to put a stop to this.

"Jake," she whispered, her weak voice sounding just a little bit faked to her own ears. He rushed over to her and picked up her hand in both his own.

"Molly, sweetheart." He raised her hand to his lips and stroked her hair.

He was really afraid, she thought, her guilt making her heartsick. *If he knew the truth, though, he'd worry even more. I swear, Lord, I'll never again keep anything from him.* Her mind, still a bit foggy, cast frantically around for some story, some explanation he would accept.

Somebody had loosened her corset. She gave him what she hoped was an embarrassed smile.

"I think I'm getting a little vain in my old age," she said. "My corset was too tight and with all the running up and down...." She reached up and touched his face. *Oh, how I love you.* "It's your fault, you know. If you hadn't had me trotting down to the saloon and back again for your tobacco, this wouldn't have happened." She smiled, just to let him know she was joking.

Jake looked way down into her eyes. *Don't look away, Martha,* she warned herself.

"That's all?" he asked.

"Well, cowboy," she said, "you decide. Tight corset, Molly faints. Loosened corset, Molly wakes up." She pushed his hands away when he tried to keep her from sitting up. "Jake, for Heaven's sake, please let me get up. The blood is rushing to my head, lying down like that."

The doctor was admiring her performance. He knew. She decided to brazen it out.

"The least you could do, Doc, is put pillows on these things."

"Well, that's better. You've started bossing everyone around, again."

Only Jake didn't seem amused.

"Take her home, Bowman," the doctor ordered. He slapped Jake on the back and pushed him toward the door. "Go get your wagon and come and get her. She shouldn't walk that far for a little while." At the look of concern on Jake's face, the doctor said, "Once her blood is flowing again, she'll be fine."

Jake was still not quite sure. "Just a minute ago, you didn't know what was wrong."

Doc Mitchell laughed. "Now I do. They just never taught me how to diagnose a tight corset." He all but shoved Jake out the door. When Jake was well down the street, he turned his disapproving gaze on Martha.

"All right, young lady. How far along are you?"

She shrugged, a little embarrassed to be discussing this, even with a doctor she'd known all her life. "My flow was due about a week after we got married, but it didn't come. That was two months ago."

"Why the long face, Martha? Seems to me you'd be happy."

"Of course, I'm happy. But there's a long time to go and I don't have to tell you how many things can go wrong, especially at my age. How can I tell Jake? He'll worry all of us to death long before the baby comes."

"I understood you intended to go to Kansas. How will you explain why you aren't going on the drive?"

"I won't have to explain, because I'm going."

Doc dropped his mouth open to protest.

"Before you start, Doc, you won't change my mind, so save your breath."

But Doc Mitchell wasn't deterred. "Martha, you already said it. You're not a young girl, anymore."

"You seem to think I'm like these hothouse flowers here in town you tend for the vapors. I've taken care of myself for some time. I'll be all right and so will my baby."

"We're not talking about housework. A cattle drive is hard even on a strong man. A woman in your condition, at your age," he ignored her grimace, "needs to take special care."

She knew he was right. It wasn't the way she'd like to spend her first pregnancy. But she only thought about it for a minute before she paused and took a deep breath.

"Doc, believe me, I'd much rather take my chances on the trail with Jake."

Doc Mitchell neither argued nor agreed. She patted his arm and kissed his white-whiskered cheek. "Don't worry, Doc. You'll deliver this one, just like you delivered all of us. Keep your appointment book cleared for me in about seven months."

SHE STOOD IN the bedroom in front of the mirror, considering her profile, smoothing the material of her dress over the slight roundness of her belly.

No, she was imagining it. It was way too soon.

Martha wondered how much longer she could keep it from Jake, though. Even before her little fainting spell in town today, he'd been watching her, his eyes following her every move like a hawk watching a field mouse. Her eating habits, especially, seemed to be a matter of concern for him. She had to admit to a bit of eccentricity lately. Sour pickles on pie wasn't exactly usual.

But he had so much else to worry about and there hadn't really been any time that felt right. She was jealous of their privacy and didn't want to waste any of their time with arguments about her not going along on the drive.

She stood there in front of the mirror, not looking at herself, but thinking of her husband, her lover. Then, her eyes were drawn upward to the reflection of the door. There he was in the doorway, an arrogant smirk on his handsome face.

"Thinking about me, Molly?"

"What makes you think I haven't got better things to do than stand in the bedroom thinking about you?"

He closed the door and tossed his hat on the dresser.

"Do you?"

He walked by her to pull down the shades.

"Not right now."

They both laughed as he swept her up. She wrapped her arms around his neck and pulled his lips to hers. His kiss lingered as he carried her to their bed.

He sighed against her mouth. "Sometimes, I wonder how long something this good can last."

"Forever." Martha whispered in return.

Never taking his eyes from hers, Jake lay her on the bed and then knelt down next to her. The touch of his fingers sent a thrill coursing through her as he unbuttoned her bodice and pulled the sleeves down her arms. He loosened her waistband and slipped her skirt down, then very slowly untied her corset, pulling the shoulder straps of her chemise down, baring her to the waist.

"So, so beautiful," he whispered.

The caress of his gaze warmed her through. His fingers followed the path his eyes made over her skin. Her pregnancy made her breasts more sensitive and his touch sent a jolt surging through her entire body. She sat up, reaching for him.

As her fingers worked the buttons on his pants, he leaned over and gently took her hair out of the net in which she had caught it up. He ran his fingers through it and nuzzled the top of her head, breathing her scent like the sweetest flower. His lips grazed her hair and face with light kisses and she gasped as they found that spot just at the juncture of neck and shoulder.

His mouth moved ever so softly up her neck to her jaw, capturing her chin in a wet, sucking kiss. All the while, his hands lifted her up and slipped her clothing to the floor. She wasn't sure how he did it, since his hands never seemed to leave her body, but soon he was as naked as she was.

He stretched her out on the bed and pulled her arms above her head, gently holding her prisoner. His lips ravished her, moving with exquisite torment over her skin. She could feel only his touch, could hear only the rasping of his increasingly heavy breathing.

Martha tried to pull her hands free. She wanted to touch him, pull him closer. But he wouldn't let her go. He tasted her body, kissing her face, neck, one breast, then the other. She writhed beneath his gentle onslaught.

"Ah," she breathed, "Jake."

Releasing her hands, he ran his palms along her sides, stroking her skin and drawing her breath from her in ragged sighs. She threaded her fingers through his hair and pulled his face to hers, kissing him deeply, aggressively, memorizing the taste of him.

He pulled away from her and looked into her eyes. She held nothing back, but let all the love and passion she felt for him show. With a sigh he leaned back down to her.

"Molly." Her name came from his lips on a breath, lingering in the air.

She felt his body tremble. Her own need caused her to cry out.

"Please, Jake." She could say nothing more.

He only groaned in response and moved to take her. In that part of her that only he knew, where only he had ever been, she grasped him, held him, welcomed him again.

Jake whispered her name and called her such sweet, silly things, all the while holding her, loving her.

There was nothing in the whole world for her, nothing except that part of him, now also part of her. They were one, in perfect harmony, perfect union.

It was so sweet, so gentle. He drew from her ecstasy after ecstasy and gave her back even more.

When she could bear no more of even this joy, her body arched under him in total surrender. Her lips formed his name, but she had no breath to carry it.

He collapsed on her. His lips grazed her face, neck, shoulders, before he lay his head on her breast.

She stroked him, held him, pulled him closer to her.

They never did make it to supper that night.

THAT LITTLE episode in Travis City had left his boss very testy, Monroe thought as he sat in Garret's study.

He was pacing again, the curses coming at the same speed as the steps. He would calm down, mutter just audibly, then, to Monroe's great, though carefully hidden, amusement, his pace would pick up again and Bowman, Bowman's mother, and his whole parentage clear back to the beginning of time, would receive thorough treatment. Some of the words Garret used were completely new to him.

Well, it was a privilege to improve one's command of the language, Monroe thought with a smirk. Jesus, it had been funny to see Garret's face, all pinched and pasty, when Martha Bowman had come running down to the saloon at the beck and call of her husband.

Monroe had always thought that one was too much woman for Garret, anyway. You had to hand it to Bowman. He'd shown her who was the boss. She jumped quick enough when he told her what to do. Shame, though, with a man like Bowman around, who apparently took care of the lady in all departments, it wasn't likely she'd look twice at anybody else. That little sister of hers was real pretty, though.

Monroe's attention was suddenly attracted by the lack of motion and profane utterances from his boss.

"Monroe, goddammit! Are you listening to me?"

Monroe raised his eyes to Garret's. "Yes, sir, I'm listening." You whining sonovabitch.

"Have they finished their roundup?"

Monroe chuckled. "Yeah. Their little herd is grazing on the range nearest the house. Just sitting there. Easy pickin's."

"Good. You know what to do, tonight, before they get the chance to get out on the road."

Garret turned. The sight of his boss's face almost caused Monroe to cross himself, though he hadn't been in a church, except to rob one once, in more than thirty years. That face, though, made him believe in the devil, even if he didn't believe in God, anymore. He almost turned away, but the devil was speaking again, so he focused on the words.

"When their herd is taken care of, send somebody into town and tell the sheriff it's time to arrest the Bowman boys for rustling. But not until afternoon. I want them to have a good long time to think about it."

"The sheriff'll need help bringing those two in. That woman ain't very likely to just stand around and let her man be taken to certain hanging."

"Then get the sheriff a posse. Kill the sister if she pulls that shotgun. I don't give a hoot what happens to her." Garret turned, fire in the cold green eyes. "But, Monroe, make damn certain nothing happens to Martha. She is mine."

Monroe finally looked his boss right in the eye. "Bowman won't let you have her."

"Bowman will be dead."

MARTHA RAISED her head from Jake's shoulder and listened. There it was again -- the sound of muffled hooves and the soft, complaining lowing of cattle. Then, she heard Dave barking at the front door, scratching frantically.

"The herd." She jumped, naked, from the bed.

Jake groaned softly as her elbow caught him in the stomach.

"Molly, quit fidgeting...." He stopped as he woke fully and heard Dave barking at the front door and saw Martha at the front window. Then the shots and the yelling started.

"Dadblast it all!" He pulled on his pants and boots and jumped off the bed. Shrugging into his shirt, he grabbed his gunbelt on the way out the door.

"Jake, where are you going? Don't go out there alone! Jake!"

Martha followed him out into the hall. He never stopped, but yelled back at her over his shoulder as he got to the front door.

"Get back in that room and get some clothes on. And stay in the house!" He and Dave left the house with a loud slam of the door. Jake's shouted summons for Sam was unnecessary. He was already on his way at a run toward the barn.

They rode off in just a few minutes. She heard Jake's voice, cursing above the din of the horses, cattle, the dog, and more shots.

Ignoring Jake's order, she ran back into the bedroom and grabbed the bedspread, throwing it around her shoulders as she dashed back toward the front door and out into the yard. She walked across the dry, dusty ground, pulling the bedspread closer around her to ward off the chill creeping along her spine as she started to make out the scene before her eyes.

It was a battlefield. Bodies littered the ground, bodies that this morning would be worth eighteen dollars a head in Kansas. They lay dying or dead, their throats cut, their lifeblood draining out in pools, soaking into the thirsty ground. She walked on, as the bedspread covering her soaked up the red tide beneath her feet.

Her mouth went dry. Her stomach turned, replacing the dryness with a sour wetness. She dropped to her knees in the metallic smelling mud.

Darkness filled her vision and she vomited, retching until she was exhausted. Even with her eyes closed, she could still see the blood, the death, the terrible waste. The stench of the gore filled her nostrils.

Strong arms embraced her and held her until she could take a breath without being sick. In some part of her mind, the part that was still able to function, she knew she was crying, screaming, cursing. Those strong arms were attached to a broad chest she struck again and again in her rage and frustration. He let her release it all on his body.

Once her rage was spent, he picked her up and took her back into the house. He lay her on their bed, then removed his gunbelt and boots and stretched out beside her, taking her into his arms.

Jake held her and let her cry. After she fell into an exhausted sleep, he filled the china basin with water and washed the dust and blood from her feet. She twitched her toes when he scrubbed the soles of her feet and a little chuckle bubbled from her lips.

He smiled at the sound and stroked her foot, just to hear it again. Then he covered her with a clean blanket and started out the door with the basin of bloody water.

"Jake, why?" Her voice was a little hoarse.

"I thought you were asleep."

"Why?" she repeated.

Jake set the basin on the washstand and returned to the bed to sit by her side. He reached for her hand. Martha sat up, giving him her whole body to hold. He wrapped his arms around her, enveloping her, protecting her as best he could. He anchored himself, too.

"You already know, don't you, sweetheart?"

She shook her head. "No. Why the waste? Why didn't they just steal the whole herd?"

"It was a message. A warning."

"What kind of message?" she stopped. "That low bastard. I should have expected him to do something like this." She looked at Jake. "I should have let you kill him."

The look on his bloodthirsty bride's face made him smile.

"What now? Are there any left?"

He shook his head. "They're all gone, even what we were going to build with next year. What they didn't kill, they took."

"But, Jake," she said, suddenly breathless, suddenly hopeful, "we can catch up to them. We can get them back."

"No, honey. They'll have broken up into small groups by now. They'll take the cattle to places where they can alter the brand and then sell them to a dirt farmer for whatever they can get." He paused and halfway laughed at the irony. "It's what I'd do."

"So, it's all over, then?" She stated it more as fact than question. Her voice barely audible. "It's almost a relief."

Jake cupped her face in his hands. "Hold on, Martha Bowman. Don't you go giving up on me."

"But there isn't anything left."

She watched him, waiting for him to give her a reason to keep on.

He wished he had something to offer her, something more than just plain stubbornness. He also considered that he really ought to tell her the whole truth -- about him, about Wil, about how they came to be here. If for no other reason than she was his wife and had a right to know. She might even forgive him, if he told her before she found out some other way.

Martha raised her hand to his face, her fingers feather-light on his lips. He felt her silent question, asking him to tell her what was on his mind. Not yet. First, he had to save this place for her, for their children.

"Molly, do you trust me?"

"Of course. What are we going to do?"

"We will do nothing. I'm not exactly sure what I'm going to do. Don't you worry, honey. We're not done, yet." He pulled her up from the bed and swatted her bare bottom, then stroked the smoothness of her skin. "You get some clothes on like I told you. Then make me some coffee."

He pulled her close and claimed her lips in a kiss that was, all at the same time, gentle, hot, and desperate. Then, he pulled his boots on and left her to carry out his orders, while he got started cleaning up the mess Wil's men had left them.

JAKE WATCHED the butcher's huge wagon head down the road. He fingered the ten-dollar gold piece.

"Quite a come down from eighteen dollars a head, ain't it, Sam?"

His brother snorted at little. It was a laugh, sort of.

"A dollar a head is better than nothing."

"Yeah, I reckon you're right. We still have to get rid of the rest, else the buzzards and coyotes'll take over the ranch." He looked up at the elegantly lazy circles the scavenger birds etched in the sky.

"We'll never be able to bury them all."

"Guess we'll have to burn them, then," Jake answered.

Martha and Mary gathered and piled brush for kindling while the men, the mule and the horses dragged the carcasses and piled them high. They plowed deep trenches around the pyres to keep the fires from getting out of control.

They got the fires going in the early afternoon, then sat on the ground watching the hungry fires consume their herd.

"You know," Sam said, "it don't really smell all that bad. All we need is some beans and we could have one hell of a Texas barbecue."

"Maybe we ought to get one pulled out and cook it right, and we'll all eat beef until we get sick," Jake suggested.

For some reason, nobody seconded.

He sat there all afternoon, even after everybody else had enough. When the sun was about to dip behind the horizon, a gentle hand stroked his shoulder. Another handed him a cup of coffee. He took the steaming mug gratefully. Martha smiled and rubbed a streak of dirt and soot from his cheek.

"It seemed so much worse this morning." She turned toward the pyres of burning cattle, littering the pasture. "How many was it, finally?"

He took a deep breath. "Thirty-seven, including ten calves." He turned to her at her sigh of sadness. "Rosenburg came out and took the calves for his butcher shop." He smiled at her and held out the ten-dollar gold piece. "Got a dollar a head for 'em. Some bargaining, huh?"

Martha sat down beside him and leaned her head on his shoulder. Jake placed a little kiss on her golden hair.

"I'm sorry, darlin'," he whispered.

"So am I. This isn't exactly what you bargained for when you rode up here, was it?"

He slipped his arm around her and pulled her tightly up against him. "Nope. I got a whole lot more," he said, squeezing her. "I wouldn't trade places with any man in the world."

They sat there, together, watching months of work go up in smoke.

Even after the fires were dying down, Jake and Martha sat there in the twilight. Wanting desperately to give him some good news, she almost told him about his baby. But, when she looked at his face, she saw how tired he was. She knew he was thinking of some way to turn this around. It was no time to pile more responsibility on his shoulders. Instead, she sniffed at his sleeve. His clothes were permeated with the smell of burned cowhide and wood, charred meat, sweat, and blood.

"You need a bath and some clean clothes," she said, wrinkling her nose at him.

Jake sniffed and wrinkled his nose in imitation of her. "Only if you get in with me."

"Deal!" She laughed.

He rose and helped her up, then they started toward the house, hand in hand. They had no sooner climbed the three steps to the front porch when the sound of galloping horses reached them. Jake's arm went around her, tightening until she was almost unable to breathe. The sheriff of Travis City was leading what looked a whole lot like a posse right up to their front porch. Martha felt an icy fist close around her heart. She knew with complete certainty they were coming for Jake. She dared a glance at his face.

"Sonovabitch," he whispered.

The sheriff slowed his horse and approached the porch, bleary eyes darting left and right. A few men broke away from the posse and took off toward the bunkhouse.

Martha recognized each and every one of the men riding with the sheriff. "Jake, they're Garret's men."

"I know."

The sheriff and several of the men with him drew their weapons. Dave bounded up toward the sheriff, teeth bared, a terrible growl coming from deep in his chest. The sheriff's eyes widened in fear and the revolver moved to cover the dog.

"Dave. Here," Jake commanded and the dog obeyed instantly. He jumped up on the porch and sat at Jake's side.

The sheriff holstered his gun and rode up to the porch, his horse stomping all over Martha's petunias. He shifted slightly in his saddle and pulled a piece of paper out of his back pocket. The word Wanted, in big black letters blazed across the top. Opening it up, he held it out to Jake, who made no move to take it. After an awkward pause, the sheriff replaced the poster in his pocket.

"Bowman," the sheriff started, clearing his throat, "I'm here to arrest you and take you in for trial."

In the heavy silence that followed the sheriff's announcement, Martha felt Jake summoning the strength to ask the next question.

"What's the charge, Sheriff?"

"Rustling. You coming peaceful?"

Martha's legs gave out under her. Jake held her up. But the shock was gone as quickly as it came. Her backbone returned and she turned on the sheriff.

"You lying weasel! Get off my property."

She was just getting wound up, about to grab the shotgun from inside the front door and fill the sheriff's worthless hide full of buckshot, when she heard the soft voice come through her rage.

"Molly, be quiet." Jake tightened his grip around her even more.

The sheriff took the chance to continue.

"There's paper from the Federal Court that ties you and your brother to a gang that worked from Kansas to Mexico and west into Arizona Territory. Got to give it to you, Bowman, you boys sure did get around." He snickered. "He can't deny it, Miz Bowman, not 'less he's a liar, too."

Though she was afraid to, afraid of what she'd see on his face, Martha turned to him, silently begging Jake to deny the charges. He held her tighter and kept his attention on the sheriff.

"You don't have the authority to arrest me on federal paper, Sheriff."

"I have all the authority I need, right here," the man answered, jerking a thumb toward the guns backing him up.

"Jake, this can't be true." But even as she said the words, she knew the truth.

She struggled from his arm. A rustler? She couldn't even picture it.

Until she thought back and remembered the little things that should have tipped her off. The offhand comments about what the rustlers would do with the stolen herd. His guilty reaction the day he was planting her spring grass -- she recognized it for what it was now -- when she'd declared that he was no thief. His reluctance to talk about his past.

His eyes begged her to understand. Martha knew she wasn't that understanding.

"No," she whispered, "a rustler?"

"Molly, I'm sorry," he said as the sheriff dismounted and approached the porch, backed up by three of his posse.

They jerked Jake around and tied his hands in front of him, so he could ride, then dragged him into the dusty yard. Several of Garret's men came up from the bunkhouse dragging Sam. He was bleeding from cuts around his eyes and his breathing was ragged.

The screen door opened behind her and Mary came out onto the porch.

"What's going on out here? Sam!" Her whisper was full of fear and concern.

Martha was worried, too. It looked like his ribs might have been bruised, or maybe even cracked.

Too much was happening too fast.

"Well, Bowman," a shout came from the middle of the posse, "since it looks like you're gonna swing, maybe we'll just save the county the cost of a trial."

Martha shivered as she remembered Jake saying those words so many weeks ago to the rustlers they'd caught on her property.

Another man pointed toward the tall cottonwood in the front yard.

"How about that one, Sheriff? It's a real good hanging tree."

Jake's drinking buddy, Slim, dismounted and walked around to look up into Jake's face.

"I'd be glad to do the honors. Then maybe," he cast a look at Martha standing on the porch, "we'd have time for a little fun before gettin' back to town." Slim laughed roughly at the look of warning in Jake's eyes. "Don't worry. The boss has put his brand on your woman. Think on that when you swing."

No, Martha thought. There wouldn't be another hanging on her property. Even if this one might deserve it.

She gave in to her impulse and grabbed the shotgun from the house. Walking to the edge of the porch, she carefully pointed the weapon at the sheriff's ample belly.

"Sheriff, my husband and brother-in-law had better make it to Travis City alive, and they'd better stay that way for their trial, or I'm coming after you. And when I'm finished, there won't be enough left to bury."

"Miss Martha," the sheriff started, his eyes never leaving the barrels of the shotgun, "you shouldn't talk to me like that. It shows a lack of respect for the law."

"Why, you drunken, fat, degenerate, son-of-a-bitch! You live in Garret's back pocket and everybody knows it. Lack of respect for the law!" She lifted the shotgun a little higher, both barrels aimed directly at the sheriff's chest.

"Molly, put that damned gun down before you kill somebody." Jake's voice was calm, which only infuriated her more.

"I intend to kill somebody. Maybe I ought to start with you, you liar."

"Molly."

She lowered the gun, but her face hadn't lost its determination. "Remember what I said, Sheriff. No matter what he's done, he deserves a fair trial."

One of the posse came up with the horses. He helped Sam mount. Then he led Jake's pony over to him.

"Let's get moving, Bowman." The sheriff turned and started out of the yard.

Jake mounted up and sat there for a long moment, staring into Martha's eyes. She could feel him memorizing every line of her face, knew he wanted to say something to her. But he just turned his pony toward the road and kicked him to a trot.

Martha stared at his back as he rode away, surrounded by the posse. She watched him until she could no longer see him. Even then, she watched the cloud of dust, barely visible in the pale twilight, that marked their progress toward town.

She sank in a heap to the top step. How could he have fooled her so completely?

"Molly," Mary dropped down beside her, her face anxious. "Are you all right?"

Martha couldn't answer. They were taking him to jail, to hang. Her worst fear used to be that he'd leave her with a child. Well, that one had surely come true. Only now, she'd have to tell her child his father was a rustler who'd met his end at the end of a rope. She'd also have to tell him his mother was a fool who'd been taken in by a pair of beautiful eyes and broad shoulders.

Her eyes went back to the road, straining to see any sign of him.

What was she going to do now?

Chapter Nineteen

"HERE'S YOUR supper, boys."

"Thanks, Annie," Sam said, taking the two tin plates through the small opening in the bars.

The saloon girl stood there, hands on her hips, studying them. "You don't look much like rustlers."

Jake smiled as he took his plate from Sam. "What does a rustler look like?"

"You know what I mean. You're respectable-looking." She swept her wild red hair back from her brow and leaned closer to the bars. "For my money, I'd say some of Garret's men have been on the other side of the law."

"Honey, you know how hard it's been for a man to make an honest living these last few years," Sam said.

Jake turned to his supper. It was beef, and the nauseating feeling that it was some of the same beef he'd sold to Rosenburg the butcher earlier in the day took away any appetite he had. He set the plate on the floor.

"What's the matter, dearie? Ain't you hungry? Big fellers like you need to eat."

"I guess we just don't have much of an appetite tonight, Annie." Sam looked at the mugs on the tray by the door. "Is that coffee?"

"Oh, yeah," Annie said, as she hurried to pass them the hot brew. "It's a shame, really. You boys are way too good-looking to be hung. A real waste."

"Why, Annie," Sam said, "thank you for noticing."

Jake took his cup and stood at the back window of the cell.

Annie glanced toward the door that separated the cells from the main office of the jail. Her tongue flicked out to moisten her lips as she came closer to them.

"They're planning to lynch you, you know. I heard the sheriff and Monroe talking about it."

Jake and Sam exchanged a look, but neither commented on Annie's news.

"Don't you care?" Annie asked.

Sam gave her a crooked smile. "Darlin', we're locked up in here real good. I reckon it don't rightly matter what we care or don't care about."

"Ain't they done yet?" the sheriff yelled as he stuck his snout around the door.

"I'd better go." She retrieved the plates and cast a regretful glance at the prisoners. "Yep, a terrible waste."

Jake turned to look out the pitiful excuse of a window at the back of the cell. Annie's skirts swished as she sashayed through the doorway. The rusty bolt grated as it slid into place. He caught his breath to ward off the panic as the walls started to close in.

Just like the wet, stinking walls of the prison where he'd lost years of his life.

Standing at the window, he wondered what Molly was doing, what she was thinking. He cursed his stupidity for not telling her everything before she found out this way. She must hate him.

Sam jumped up onto the upper bunk and stretched out.

"Well, Jakey, how the hell are we getting out of this one?"

"I don't know. If we make it to breakfast, maybe we'll have thought of something."

HER BACK RAMROD straight, Martha rode in the seat beside Mary. Their bags were packed and loaded in the back of the wagon.

"You know Jake's not going to like this," Mary warned as they rounded the last curve before entering Travis City.

"Right now, I don't give a fig what he likes."

Travis City was quiet this sleepy, late spring morning. The quiet became a hush as the buckboard rolled down the street. Martha kept her eyes looking forward, despite the wave of talk following them as they drove along. Mary pulled up in front of the office that housed both the stage and freight lines.

"You buy the tickets, Mary. I'm going over to the general store to see if I can hear some gossip."

"I'm sure Clarissa will be glad to tell you everything she can," Mary said.

Martha handed Mary enough money, Jake's money, to buy the stage tickets, then got down from the buckboard. A snippet of sadness nagged her as she thought how long it had been since she'd had to get down without Jake's strong hands at her waist. Shrugging off the pain, she turned and headed toward the general store. When she arrived, she stood outside and, with a deep breath, clamped an iron grip on her temper.

Clarissa's face lit up when she saw Martha approach the counter.

"Well, Mrs. Bowman, what a surprise to see you in town today. We're so sorry to hear about your misfortune."

I'll bet, Martha thought. "Thank you for your concern, Clarissa, but you needn't worry about me." She looked at the patent medicines displayed on the front counter.

The woman refused to leave her alone. "I hope you understand, even though we're sorry for you, Martha, the respectable citizens of this town are going to make an example of your man."

Martha stared at her. "What do you mean by that? He'll be taken to Austin for trial, won't he?" A small gaggle of the local women had gathered. "If he's found guilty, the respectable citizens of this county can hang him. That's what a rustler deserves, isn't it?" she asked rhetorically, returning to her examination of the horehound drops.

"Don't you care that your husband is going to die?"

"All I said was, if he's guilty, feel free to hang him. I'm not so sentimental about him that I'll go against justice being done."

"How can you be so calm? And so cold? If it were my husband, I'd be ever so upset." A friend of Mary's stood by Martha's elbow.

Martha turned to the young woman.

"Well, Gloria, he's not your husband. Jimmy is an honest man and certainly wouldn't stoop to stealing from his own wife."

The group of women gasped as one.

With a disgusted roll of her eyes, Martha said, "Yesterday, every cow on my place was killed or stolen, just before my husband was arrested for rustling. Just a bit too convenient, don't you think?" She picked up a bottle of Dr. James's Miracle Cure for psoriasis, parasites, and various mysterious female problems, and opened it, sniffing loudly. "Maybe the whole blasted thing is just a little too convenient."

The women were silent, for once. Only Gloria spoke.

"Martha, why would he bother stealing the cattle? From the time he married you, they were his, too."

"That ranch is mine! He's nothing but a good-for-nothing cattle thief and who knows what else he's done? Thank the Lord I discovered what kind of man he is before it really was too late." She took a calming breath and turned to the shopkeeper. "Clarissa, what do you have for stomach trouble?"

Clarissa was caught off-guard. "I really don't know."

"Give me a bag of peppermints, then. I need something to settle my stomach in the stagecoach." She turned to Mary who'd just walked in the door. "Did you get those tickets, Mary?"

Clarissa perked her ears up just like a good bird dog. "Going somewhere?"

"To Louisiana, back to our mother's people." Martha took the bag of peppermints from the shopkeeper's hand and paid the few cents for them. She popped one into her mouth.

She pulled a key from her bag. "Here, Gloria. If you and Jimmy still want to stay out there, feel free." She laughed, but without humor. "I hope you make better memories than I have."

"What about the ranch?" Gloria asked.

"To blazes with it." A gasp rose from the assembled. "Maybe Garret still wants to buy it. It's been nothing but trouble for years. Guess I should try to get something out of it, though. I'll be in touch with Jimmy to handle the sale. If I never see Texas again, it'll be too soon."

Gloria took the key. "All right, Martha. We'll look after the place, but aren't you staying for the trial?"

"No. We're leaving on the noon stage for Galveston. From there we'll take a boat over to New Orleans. Our mother's people live just up the river. Maybe we'll never even have to see a cow for the rest of our lives." Martha sucked pensively on her peppermint and gazed around, as if taking her leave. "Well, come on, Mary, let's get over and say goodbye to Doc Mitchell."

JAKE COULD JUST see out the front window of the jail and moved from one end of the cell to the other, trying to get another glimpse of Martha.

"What in tarnation is she up to?" She was moving in the direction of the doctor's office now. "She shouldn't be out there all alone. There's nothing to keep Wil from grabbing her off the street."

The door opened and Wil strolled in.

"Speak of the devil," Sam muttered from his bunk.

"Hi-dy, boys. Just dropped by to see if there was anything you needed. Cigars, French postcards?" He looked over the cell and laughed. "What fine accommodations. Not quite what you've become accustomed to, but better than we used to have on the trail, eh, Jake?"

Wil stood back and tipped his head as though really considering the picture.

"You do look natural in there. You, too, Sam. Too bad your stay won't last long. By this time tomorrow, you'll be dead and that woman will be mine, along with her ranch, of course. After I restock it with the cattle we took yesterday..." he smiled, "but I suppose you already knew who did it."

"You were my first choice," Jake said.

"I'll have one of the biggest spreads in Texas." He looked into Jake's eyes, obviously enjoying the anger he saw there. "By the time tomorrow night is over, that little woman is going to know who her new master is. Maybe I'll give her little sister to Monroe. He's been looking at her with real interest."

Sam jumped to his feet.

Garret stepped back, even though the bars were between him and the enraged Sam.

"Oh, so the younger brother has it all hard for the little sister? Ain't that kinda close to incest?" He grinned. "Guess I'll have to find me a lawyer to give me an opinion on that one."

Jake stepped up to the wall of bars.

"Stay away from Molly, Wil, or I'll kill you. Slowly, like you did that girl in the Territory."

"You still worked up over that Indian whore?" Garret shook his head. "You boys can make all the threats you want, but tomorrow morning, you'll be dead." He smiled. "When we slap the horse out from under you, Jake, I want you to think about me on your woman." He got a pensive look. "Tell me, does she like it? I wonder if she'll like it the way I do it to her?"

Jake's eyes locked with Wil's. He was barely able to contain the rage that grew with each passing moment, with every promise Wil made. Wil looked away first.

"Goddammit, Jake," he whispered, "why did it turn out like this? You and me, we're the same blood. We coulda had it all. I would've shared with you."

"You lying bastard," Jake said, his voice a hiss. "You beat and murdered an innocent girl and an old woman. You left me and Sam bleeding to death in that yard, didn't even have the guts to put a bullet in our heads to end it. You crippled my brother. You tried to rape Molly and force her to marry you, so you could take everything she had. Don't you try to turn this whole thing into my fault."

"It is your fault. Here I am trying to build a decent life, I find a woman who's a match for me, and you come in and steal her away."

"You had a decent life, Wil. What did you do with it?"

"I had nothing. I was nothing to my own daddy." Wil's face flushed red. "Do you know how goddamned tired I got of hearing how poor I stacked up next to you? Or how ashamed he was that I didn't sign up to get my ass shot off or starve to death in a prison camp? Well,

I guess I showed you, Jake. You went off to answer the call of the Confederacy and lost everything for your trouble. I'll have a big ranch, a beautiful woman in my bed and, best of all, I'll never have to hear your name again."

"I'd rather be dead than live knowing I'd stayed behind while others died." Jake moved even closer to the bars of the cell. Wil stepped back. "You're a coward, Wil. You've always been a coward. You'll always be a coward. If you had any balls at all, we would be dead now." Jake knew exactly where to twist. "You'd better believe, boy, if it'd been me, I'd have finished the job. Just like I'm going to do this time."

Garret laughed. It was a dry, strained sound.

"How do you plan to do that, Jake? You're locked up tight and you'll hang tomorrow. Just in case you're thinking help might come from your little wife, you should know she bought tickets for the noon stage to Galveston."

Wil's words landed like a punch in the stomach. Jake couldn't say a word. Would she leave without giving him a hearing?

"More than that, she's let it be known all over town she don't care if you live or die." Wil tipped his head as though he were thinking. "No, let me correct that, she thinks you ought to hang. So, Jakey, how do you plan to finish the job?"

He still stood away from the cell, just out of Jake's reach, like a kid taunting a caged animal.

Jake recovered his senses and locked his eyes with Wil's.

"Wilson, have you ever known me to make a promise I couldn't keep?"

Wil's face paled, fear showed in his eyes, and, though he really tried to stop it, he gulped. His hand reached for the gun at his side.

"Come on, Wil. Draw and try to hit me," Jake taunted him.

Wil's hand hovered over the gun.

Jake kept his eyes locked with Wil's, daring him. What's he waiting for? It wasn't like the sheriff was likely to arrest him for discharging a firearm in town. In the course of two days, he'd lost everything that mattered. He'd lost Molly. If she hated him as much as it sounded, a bullet would be a blessing.

Except there would be no one to protect Molly. Until they shoveled dirt onto his face, there was a chance he could still take care of Wil and protect her from that danger, at least. Jake calmed down. No need to be in a hurry to die. "But, maybe you ought to wait for the hanging, since you've gone to all the trouble."

Wil stepped back and relaxed. "You're right. What am I in such a hurry for? Tomorrow'll be soon enough." He tipped his hat. "See you later, boys. Sleep tight. I'm off to find your soon-to-be-widow. Can't let her get on that stage and miss the show." He left, whistling.

Jake watched him pass in front of the jail window. Could it really be true? He peered out between the bars, desperate for a glimpse of her.

"Watch out for him, honey," he whispered.

Twenty minutes or so later, she left the doctor's office and crossed the street, headed straight for the jail.

She was coming to him. His heart beat faster. He'd finally have a chance to try to explain.

He recognized her footsteps when she arrived. The door to the office was open and, by jamming his face against the bars at the corner of the cell nearest the door, he could just could see the sheriff's desk. She strode up to the desk, Mary right behind her. The sheriff looked up, eyes wide with surprise.

"Sheriff, I want to see my husband."

He sat on his flat behind and looked at her.

"Sheriff," Martha said, "right now, if you please."

"Molly, are you sure you want to see him?" Mary asked.

"Yes, I'm sure I want to see the no-good, lowlife." She paused, catching her breath. "Just one last time before he gets his hash settled!"

Jake puffed out a half-laugh, trying to convince himself she wasn't serious.

The sheriff lifted one corner of his mouth in a smile. Then, he lifted himself out of his chair and led the women into the cell area.

"You got a visitor, Bowman," he shouted cheerily to his prisoners.

In spite of what she'd said, Jake started to smile when he saw Martha coming through the door. The smile faded when he saw the set of her chin and the cold blue of her eyes.

Wil was telling the truth. She really does hate me.

At that instant, Jake would have gladly walked to the gallows to escape the accusation he saw in those eyes.

They were separated by only a couple of feet, but with the heavy iron bars between them, it might just as well have been a mile. She didn't come close enough for him to touch her.

He needed to touch her.

Martha turned to the sheriff. Her voice was strained, and she sounded tired. Had she gotten any sleep?

"Sheriff, would you do me a great favor? I would like to speak to my," she turned a raised eyebrow toward Jake, "husband alone, please?

There are some things I would like to say to him, and, well, Sheriff, you know my reputation is already somewhat tarnished in this town." She lowered her lashes and looked at the sheriff from under them. "I wouldn't want it to get around that I was behaving in an unladylike manner."

"Of course, Miz Bowman," the sheriff said.

Jake didn't believe for a second the old rascal had been charmed, but he did turn to leave. He even closed the door behind him, where Mary took up her station.

"How is Sam?" Martha asked.

Jake was irritated her first words were about his brother.

"He'll be fine. Doc Mitchell said he had a couple of bruised ribs and wrapped him up tight."

She nodded. "They're planning on taking the two of you out of here tomorrow morning and hanging you. If they end up having to try you, there's a rancher from the Indian Territory coming down here to testify. He claims some rustlers murdered some folks and he's itching to see somebody hang for it." Her expression was as cold and hard as he'd ever seen her.

"If you'd spied during the War, the South might have stood a better chance. Where did you get all this information?" he asked.

"All over. You're the main topic of conversation."

He weighed his words. "Molly, I need to tell you some things -- things I guess I ought to have told you already."

"Save it," she said brusquely, "I don't have the time."

"Molly, the sheriff's coming," Mary said from the door.

Martha's eyes narrowed and her voice got a bit louder. "I hope they do hang you, you good-for-nothing, cow-stealing, honey-fuggling scoundrel!"

Honey-fuggling? It had to be an act. But her voice grew louder and louder, giving the impression she was just getting wound up.

"If I didn't have travel plans, I'd like to be there when they hang you. I'd sell lemonade and cookies. Then, I'd watch them lead you up those steps, you rotten, shifty, piker...."

He couldn't take her seriously. She wasn't serious.

"I'm not a piker, Molly."

"Shut up! I'd enjoy watching you choke to death. Maybe I'll even see you in hell, so I can make your eternity even more miserable."

He couldn't believe she'd said that.

Martha put her hand to her bosom, as though to still her racing heart. Her next words made his own heart stop.

"Good-bye, Mister Bowman," she said with as much dignity as she muster.

"Molly, please. You've got to give me a chance to explain."

If she would just listen, he knew he could make her understand. But she refused to look at him again. Turning sharply, she started for the door and almost collided with Wilson Garret. Wil looked at her as though she were already his property.

Jake saw the fear in her eyes. His grip on the bars turned his knuckles white. The impotence of being locked behind them was unbearable.

"Mrs. Bowman," Garret said, tipping his hat. "I hope you'll be up to seeing callers after your husband is hung."

"I'll never be up to seeing you." She started to move by him, but Garret blocked her way, one arm across the doorway, his back brushing the bars of the cell. He grabbed her elbow and pulled her against him.

"Let her go, Wil."

He ignored Jake's warning.

Then he and Martha were both pulled against the bars.

Jake had one arm around Wil's neck and was prepared to kill him then and there. He might as well be hanged for a real crime. With his free hand, he pulled Garret's head sideways against the bars, crushing his fancy Texas hat, and repeated in a measured whisper, "Let her go, Wil."

Wil did as he was told. Martha hustled through the door, not even looking back. Only after she was safely out of the jail, did Jake release Garret.

"I ought to kill you." Wil straightened his shirt and slapped his ruined hat against his thigh.

"Wasn't that always the plan?"

Garret suddenly smiled. "You're right, as usual, Jake."

"Mr. Garret," the sheriff called from the door, "Miz Bowman is getting on the stage."

Chapter Twenty

JAKE LOOKED AT the sheriff in disbelief. "What?"

Wil smirked. "Don't you worry, Jake. I've sent some of my men ahead to meet her at the first stop in Bastrop. She'll be here to see you swing. And just remember," he taunted as he left, "I'm going to take her and it can be whatever way she wants it."

Sam stood next to him, silent for a minute after Wil left.

"I'll toss you for him."

Jake didn't say a word. His eyes followed the stage as it passed the front windows of the jail.

MARTHA LOOKED out the window of the stage. One last look.

"Are they coming?" Mary asked, peering over Martha's shoulder.

"Looks like it. Better get ready." They opened their bags and Martha unpacked the very unladylike clothes she did ranch work in. Mary pulled out a widow's weeds. The stage was empty except for the two of them.

"Do you think I can fool them?" Mary asked.

Martha waved away the cloud of powder Mary used to gray her red hair.

"You look just like Aunt Livona with your hair all white like that. Here." She handed Mary a two-shot Derringer and a handful of cartridges which Mary slipped into her pocket. "You do what you have to do. Give me as much time as you can."

Mary nodded and checked the barrels of her shotgun, then slipped it underneath her skirt.

"We're almost there."

Martha banged on the roof of the stage with her rifle. "Max, stop at that grove."

"Right, Miss Martha."

"Molly, maybe I ought to stay. You might need my help."

"No. Make them follow you as far as you can. Hide in Galveston and wait for word. I don't want Garret to have anything he can hold over me."

"Good luck, Molly." Mary wrapped her in a quick hug just as the stage lurched to a stop. Martha jumped out the side door carrying her rifle and a carpetbag. Max had the stage moving again before she hit the ground, running toward the grove. Hiding behind a big maple, she looked down the road toward Travis City.

Garret's foreman led three more men after the stage.

"Why on earth would he send four men after two women? He must think we're mighty dangerous." She had to chuckle at that. After they passed, she went to the place where Mary had left Chief. "Good boy, Chief." She stroked his forehead and thought about what was to come.

JAKE COULDN'T SLEEP. It was truly aggravating that Sam lay on the bunk above him, snoring away, while he couldn't even close his eyes. How could she have just left him like that? She had to know there was an explanation.

For all his big talk, it looked like Wil was going to win. He couldn't even denounce Wil and get him hung, too. Not as long as Molly was all alone out there.

To top it all off, some fool kept throwing rocks in the window.

"Jake, wake up."

At the sound of her voice, he jumped off the bunk and peered out the window. He couldn't see anybody in the dim moonlight. It couldn't have been her voice. She'd left on the noon stage.

"Molly," he whispered, hoping in spite of everything.

"Get ready. I'm coming in."

"Molly. Wait, dammit all! Sam, wake up." He smacked his brother's leg.

"Huh?" Sam sat up, rubbing his eyes.

The key turned in the lock of the oak door.

"She's coming in the front door!"

There she was, big as life, dressed in those damned boy's clothes, again. She had the keys, too.

"What'd you do, honey, kill the sheriff?" He cast a quick glance toward the door.

She smiled as she unlocked the cell.

"The sheriff is taking a little nap. Come on, boys."

They followed her through the main office. Jake stopped when he saw the sheriff slumped over his desk, whiskey bottle all but empty by his arm.

"Molly, you didn't poison him, did you?"

"Of course not. I just had Doc Mitchell put a little something in a bottle and Henry brought it over this afternoon. The sheriff'll be sleeping all night long."

"The doctor helped you drug the sheriff? Molly, that makes him an accessory before the fact to a jailbreak."

"We don't have time to discuss this right now."

"Where's Mary?" Sam looked around.

"She's on her way to Galveston."

"Alone? Martha, are you both crazy?"

"Worried about her, Sam? Be sure to tell her that when she comes back. She'll be happy to hear it." Martha turned all the lights down, locked the front door, and led them to the side door to the alley. She motioned them to follow her. "We're going to the livery. Stay in the shadows."

He admired her cool efficiency. Of course, that was Molly. She had thought the whole thing out and was pulling off her first jailbreak flawlessly. Her surprises hadn't run out, though.

The horses were already saddled. Martha took a carpetbag off her saddle and opened it. Reaching inside, she pulled out their hats and jackets and tossed them over.

"Your guns are on your saddles," she said.

Jake had already found his and strapped it on.

"Let's get the Sam Hill out of here," he said, taking the reins of his pony and making a move to mount.

Martha jerked around, her eyes wide. She set one small fist on her hip. "I suppose you think we ought to tear out of town, running like we've got the devil on our tails?"

He put his foot back on the ground and looked right back. "I think, Mrs. Jesse James, we oughta get outta here, just like I said. Of course, I didn't realize your vast experience in this sort of enterprise. Perhaps you have a better idea?"

"In the first place, Jesse James is a bank robber, not a cattle rustler. Secondly, of course, I have a better idea. If you saw a bunch of people galloping out of town, especially from the area of the sheriff's office at this hour, wouldn't you wonder who they were and why they were in such a hurry?"

He couldn't help it. His big, dumb mouth hung open for a second.

"Martha, I'm not stupid," Jake muttered.

She smiled. "Of course, you're not. But I've got it all figured out. The sheriff is out for the night. If we ride out nice and slow, nobody will notice. It'll be morning before they discover you're gone."

"You ever break anybody out of jail before?"

"Certainly not!"

"Well, lady, you sure do have a flair for it."

"Thank you." She actually smiled.

Jake laid his hand on Sam's shoulder. "Sam, ride ahead to Austin. Maybe we can hole up at Zelda's."

Sam grinned and tipped his head toward Martha. "You sure about that, Jake?"

"Yes, I am," Jake replied. He already had a lot to explain. One more thing wouldn't make that much difference.... He hoped. "We'll give you fifteen minutes, then we'll leave on the south road and meet you in Austin sometime tomorrow."

Sam nodded. "Thanks for breaking us out, Martha." He led his mount down the back street. Jake watched him slowly ride out of town.

He sank in the hay and pulled Martha down with him. They sat in silence for several minutes, waiting, listening. Martha pulled a piece of dry bread from her pocket and nibbled at it.

She looked pale to him.

"Are you all right, honey?" he asked.

"Yes, I'm fine," she answered, too quickly. "Just hungry is all. Want some?"

He shook his head. "No, thanks. I do want an answer to a question, though. What was all that today about wanting to see me hang and making hell more hellacious?"

She wasn't a bit embarrassed. "I wanted people to think I didn't care about you so they wouldn't suspect I might try to break you out." She put her hand to his cheek, combing his beard with her fingers. "You didn't think I'd let them hang you, did you?"

"You had me wondering for a while." He only now admitted to himself how afraid he'd really been. "I couldn't quite believe you'd take off without giving me a chance to explain."

"Is there an explanation, Jake?"

He didn't know how to answer her. There were so many things he wanted to offer in his defense, to make her understand. More than anything he wanted to hold her, to explain everything. But there wasn't enough time.

"Sometimes a man gets caught up in things, Molly," was the best he could do.

She nodded and he believed, somehow, she did understand.

Jake looked around. "Where's Dave?"

"I left him behind. Seemed to me he'd be too conspicuous. Our temporary tenants are still going to stay. Jimmy thinks he's going to arrange the sale of the ranch. They'll look after him."

He nodded. "Do they know what you've done?"

"They still think Mary and I are on our way to New Orleans."

"How did you avoid Garret's men?" He tipped his head toward the street, listening for any sound that the jailbreak had been discovered. "He told me he'd sent men after you."

"I saw them. They passed the stagecoach and went on ahead to Bastrop. They'll be plenty surprised when it pulls in and one old widow lady is the only passenger." She smiled. "When Mary was little, she always wanted to go on the stage. I don't think this was what she had in mind, though."

He laughed and nodded, imagining his sister-in-law's performance for her hapless audience. "What a clever girl you are. You think of everything."

"I try."

They sat silently for a few more minutes before he rose.

"Let's go, sweetheart."

He helped her up and they started walking the horses slowly to the door of the livery. Martha froze in the darkness when she heard men approaching. Navy revolver in his hand, Jake handed her the reins and moved to the door, watching the men for their intentions.

"Garcia, let's go find us some women."

"Slim, don't you ever think of anything except food, women, or liquor?" It sounded like they'd both been drinking.

"Nope, can't say as I do."

Garcia grunted a laugh. "The boss told us to go over and make sure the sheriff is taking real good care of his prisoners."

Martha cast a panicked look at Jake. He warned her with a shake of his head to stay still.

"You suppose Garret will share that woman with us? Or maybe her little sister?"

Martha almost went after Slim for that. Only Jake's hand on her arm stopped her.

"Garret intends to marry the old one and I reckon he ain't the sort to share his wife with anybody."

Jake noticed with amusement the frown shadowing Martha's face as she mouthed the words "old one."

Garcia stepped up onto the porch in front of the jail. "The little sister might be another matter, though."

"That'd be all right. I like that red hair."

The men continued to the front door of the jail. Once they were out of sight, Jake led Martha into the alley and toward the main street of town. He stopped just before stepping out into the street, listening for the two men. After helping her onto her horse, he mounted his own, then led her south, on the short road out of town. This way lay the cemetery and the stockyard and not much else. Garcia shook the front door.

"Locked. How's it look in there?"

Slim peered in the window. "Shit, looka that, will ya? That sombitch is drunker'n a skunk, all slumped over by a whiskey bottle. Come on, you know they're still in there. Ain't nobody escaped from that jail in over thirty years."

Garcia snorted. "At least he remembered to lock the door before he got soused. I reckon we can go over and get us a drink and maybe a woman. We'll need our rest for the job of seeing justice done tomorrow."

Jake looked back in disbelief. Shaking his head, he grinned at Martha and motioned her to go ahead. He followed, protecting her back. When they were out of town, he pulled up next to her.

"As soon as we're out of town, we'll head southeast for a bit, then we'll cross the river and head back toward Austin."

They kicked their mounts to a canter and moved faster down the road.

THEY HAD BEEN following the Colorado just south of Travis City for a couple of hours. Jake looked up ahead at the first pink tinges in the eastern sky, then turned back and scanned the horizon for riders.

None in sight, yet. He hoped that meant they hadn't discovered them missing, but he couldn't count on it. Wil's plans included an early morning hanging. Once a posse started out after them, he wanted to give them a good long trail to follow, while he and Martha doubled back on the other side. With luck, they could be in Austin before morning.

A glance back at Martha killed that idea. She was slumping in the saddle and looked like she was about to fall off. He couldn't push her any harder. Maybe they could just lay low and let the posse go right on by.

"Hold on, honey," he said, "there's a cabin up ahead. We'll stop there for a bit."

"No, we're on his land."

"Good. He'll never think of looking for us here."

"MOLLY, WAKE UP."

Jake gently shook her. She opened her eyes and found herself looking into his. It was like waking from a bad dream. With a smile, she reached for him, but he moved away. It was a moment before she fully realized they were not in their bedroom, but in a rough line shack on Garret's land.

Jake brought her water to wash the sleep from her eyes. "Feel better?"

She nodded. "What time is it?"

"'Bout noon."

While he unpacked the food she'd brought along, she sat in silence, feeling unsure of him for the first time. He'd made her promises. Had he known, then, he might not be able to keep them?

"We have some time if you still want that explanation." He didn't look at her, but kept his eyes on the bread and dried beef he placed on a checkered napkin.

"Do you have an explanation?"

"I ought to have told you weeks ago." He handed her the napkin with her dinner. "It's all true, Molly. I rode with a band of rustlers until July of last year."

She'd known it was true, of course. But hearing him admit the crime, a hanging crime, chilled her.

Still, she couldn't quiet believe it.

"How, Jake?"

He lifted her hand tenderly and grazed her palm with his lips.

"What I told you that first night is the truth, far as it went. The only family we had left were our uncle, Bud Garret, and his son, Wil."

"He's your cousin?" There had to be an end to the bad surprises, somewhere. Now she was related to that coyote?

"Yes, ma'am. Wil and I are of an age, though I'm a little older, somewhat smarter, and much better looking." He took a bite of bread. "When we got back from the war, I must admit to being a bit resentful of Wil. I'd lost everything, including two years out of my life in that Yankee prison. He'd bought his way out of the army and was still living in the house he'd been born in. My daddy died trying to keep the carpetbagger sheriff from coming in." His voice grated. "The bastard shot him like a dog. He was too good a man to die like that, Molly."

Martha put her arms around him. "I'm sorry, darlin'."

He was quiet for a moment. With a deep breath, he went on.

"Sam and I took work on a ranch in the Indian Territory. Wil was much too busy whoring and drinking to do his duty by his daddy, so Sam and I would come down from the Territory to help out every few weeks or so. Uncle Bud finally turned him out. That's when Wil started reclaiming Texans' property from carpetbaggers." Jake laughed roughly. "People talked about him like he was some kind of Robin Hood, robbing from the Yankees to give to the Rebs. But the only Reb who ever got anything from this Robin Hood was Wilson Garret."

"Did you know what he was doing?"

He shook his head. "Not exactly. I should have, though. He had money and no visible legal means of support. But I didn't know he was the 'Rebel Rustler' until later."

"So how did you find out?"

He chuckled. "The hard way. We were headed back up north one night to the Indian Territory. I must've been crazy, 'cause I always wanted to go by the old home place. You know, to see how it was, if anybody was taking care of it. This one night, we saw some men around a branding fire with fifty head right out there in the open. We figured they were ranch hands, so we rode up to see if we knew 'em. We got about thirty yards out before I saw Wil, standing apart like he always did. Didn't want to get the smell of cowhide and burning hair on his fancy clothes, I reckon."

Jake took a drink from the canteen.

"He waved us in, all friendly-like. Many times since that night, I've wished I'd just kept riding right on by. He got us over to the fire and made sure we got a good look. They were altering the brands. He gave us a choice, join up or they'd kill us right there." He made a little shrug. "Didn't seem to be much of a choice to me."

"Would he really have killed you? Could he really kill kin?" she asked, unbelieving.

"He's tried at least twice since then. Three times, if you include planning a lynching." He smiled grimly. "That's really more Wil's style, you know, get somebody else to do his dirty work."

He grinned, this time with true mirth. "You know, Molly, that first time, it didn't seem so bad, stealing those particular cows. They still had my daddy's brand on 'em, at least they did until I changed 'em. Actually, technically, I didn't steal any cattle. I was a fireman. Had a real talent for it, too. I was much more careful with the iron, so my brands turned out real pretty."

"You sound proud of yourself!"

"Listen to you, Miss Jailbreaker."

She felt her face warm with a well-deserved blush.

"A man's always proud of doing something better than anybody else." He grinned. "Anyway, that's how I set out on my life as an outlaw." He put the last bit of dried beef in his mouth, chewing thoughtfully.

She sat silently, hating herself for what she was thinking, for doubting him, even a little bit. But she knew she had to ask him, to get it out in the open, one way or the other.

"Why didn't you just leave? What was holding you there?"

He shrugged. "I don't know." Then he slapped his leg. "Aw, yes, I do. It didn't matter to the law that we'd been forced into it. Once we changed those first brands, we were as guilty as he was. So we rode with them awhile and it seemed all right, somehow, so long as we only stole from Yankees."

Jake stopped and she could tell the next part still hurt him. "Then Wil took us up to the Territory. 'Injuns got no use for ranches,' he said. So, naturally, they had no use for cattle, either. Wil decided to relieve them of the responsibility. He thought it'd be fitting if we hit Randall Tall Tree's place first. Randall was the woman we'd been working for. All the way up there, I tried to think of some way to stop him. But he had his boys watching Sam and me all the time and they wouldn't have thought twice about shooting either one of us. I figured I couldn't do Randall any good if I got myself killed, so I played along, looking for a chance to do...." He shrugged. "Something."

He blew out another deep breath, as though forcing out a memory that was still, even after all this time, too fresh to be borne easily. "Randall must have heard us coming, because she met us out in the front yard with her rifle."

Martha saw the pain and the guilt.

"She saw me and let down her guard. Without so much as a word, Wil drew and killed her. The last thing she did was look me right in the eye. Sometimes I dream about that, how she accused me without ever opening her mouth. She had a daughter, a real pretty girl, named Nancy, who used to follow Sam around like a puppy. He fussed over her, flirting and such. It wasn't anything serious, 'cause she was so young. When the shots were fired, Nancy came running out of the house, crying and carrying on over her mama. Wil and his boys got one look at her...." His pause carried all the meaning his words lacked. "We tried to talk him out of it. We tried fighting them all, but there were six of them. I ended up shot and knocked out cold. When I woke up, Nancy was dead and Sam was about half out of his mind. The bastard had made him watch."

Martha gasped in shock.

He closed his eyes against the memory and sighed. "Just before they left, Wil tried to kill us both. He knew we'd be after him. Thank Jesus, Wil's not a real good shot, but the slug he put in Sam's arm left him too stiff to draw. A neighbor of Randall's found us and tended us. That Indian medicine is some pretty powerful stuff."

Jake shook his head. "As soon as we were able, we started tracking him. We followed him up to Kansas, where he'd taken Randall's herd. We almost had him, too, but before we could get to him, he'd sold the herd, knocked off the rest of his gang in a saloon in Newton, and took off down here."

"That's how you ended up here."

Jake nodded. "I made Sam a promise I'd kill Wil for him." He took a long drink from the canteen and wouldn't meet her eyes. "I'm sorry, honey. I surely didn't mean to come here and ruin your life."

"What are you talking about? You haven't ruined my life." She sat up and put her hands on his cheeks, turning his head up for a sweet, hard kiss. "I was just existing, trying to keep from becoming a beholden spinster cousin in somebody else's household, holding onto a piece of dirt so my daddy's life wasn't in vain, fighting off bad luck and a bad man. Now, I'm married to the handsomest man in Texas." She smiled at his arrogantly raised eyebrow. "I've learned my husband is a wanted cattle rustler. I've planned and executed my first jailbreak. Now, I'm on the run from the law. I think I should start my memoirs. Maybe somebody'll write a dime novel about me."

He threw his head back and his laughter rang through the rickety shack. Martha joined him, her heart filled with joy at the sound. She knew it wasn't her little joke, but her forgiveness, that lifted his spirits.

"I've done my duty, then, bringing adventure and excitement into your life. I just hope I can pull out a happy, romantic ending for you," he said as he wrapped his arm around her, holding her close. They sat in easy silence for a moment before he muttered, "Sure do wish I had my pipe."

Martha pulled his pipe, already packed with tobacco, from her coat pocket.

The lines at the corners of his eyes crinkled with pleasure. "Molly! You are one beautiful woman, you know that?" He covered her mouth with his, plundering her and turning her bones to jelly. "Got a match?" he whispered against her lips.

With a smile, she produced a match from her pocket, struck it, and held it while he puffed.

"You know, sweetheart," he said, "the only thing I know of better than a good pipe is you."

Jake enjoyed his pipe and Martha enjoyed the feel of him holding her. When the tobacco was burned out, he glanced out the window.

"Let's get back on the road. It's only a few more hours."

Chapter Twenty-One

JAKE BOWMAN was a liar.

He'd said it was only a few more hours, but it felt like she'd been riding for days. In fairness to him, they'd had to take to the trees a few times to elude the posse dogging their trail. But she was afraid her backside would permanently assume the shape of the saddle and worse, everything hurt. Her back hurt. Her neck hurt. Her hands hurt. Even her hair hurt.

The churning in her stomach worsened with every step. In spite of the discomfort, she kept nodding off. That's all she needed, to fall asleep and fall off her horse.

Her head rolled forward again just as a strong arm pulled her off her mount. Jake took the reins of her horse and urged his own on a little faster toward the haven in the distance. She breathed deeply, relishing his familiar scent and, nestling against the wonderful feel of his body, gave herself up to sleep.

She knew it was Sam who took her from Jake's arms. Too dead tired to say anything, some part of her was relieved he had arrived here safely. Wherever here was.

Jake took her again and carried her up a couple of steps into a house. She couldn't even open her eyes to take a look around. Soft, whispered voices, too soft to even be discernible as male or female, exchanged greetings. *Jake's friend in Austin. That's where we are.*

He carried her up a flight of stairs and laid her on a very comfortable bed. Her boots, then her stockings, then her jacket, came off. With her last bit of strength, she reached for him and pulled him down. Her lips touched his gently and she managed to open her eyes just enough to look into his. The last thing she saw before she curled up under the blanket on the featherbed and went fast asleep was his smile.

JAKE'S NOSE twitched. The smell of good, strong coffee filled his nostrils and he took a deep breath. He opened his eyes just a crack and saw her sitting there on the edge of the bed. She looked like a cat playing with a mouse.

"Good mornin', honey."

"That's all you have to say to me?" she asked, voice like velvet, smooth and rich. "I think you have a little explaining to do."

He raised an eyebrow, innocently questioning.

"Don't you put on that whatever-do-you-mean face, either. You know exactly what I'm talking about."

"I haven't got any idea. Is that coffee for me?" He reached for the mug, but she held it away from him.

"Why didn't you tell me you were taking me to a lewd house?"

Jake just shrugged and looked around at the fancy, red brocaded wallpaper, the gilt paint, the red tassels hanging from the lampshades, the painting on the ceiling of the reclining nude woman....

"Well, Molly," he said, taking another quick look at the ceiling, "I thought you'd figure it out by yourself."

"I was hoping these folks just had incredibly bad taste."

Jake nodded. "They do."

She laughed and was still smiling when she asked, "Just how friendly are you with the ladies who live here?"

He sat up and leaned back against the brass headboard. Weighing his words very carefully, he said, "Honey, they're real nice women, but a man doesn't remember which whore he's been with."

He wondered if she believed him.

"Well, you'd better tell Sam. He and Sudie are down in the kitchen reminiscing."

Martha handed Jake his coffee and climbed into the bed beside him. He put his free arm around her and pulled her close. She snuggled against him, then started winding her fingers in his chest hair. The light scrape of her fingertips against his skin made him tighten with want.

He took a sip of the coffee.

"Ahh," he sighed, "you made the coffee, didn't you?"

"How could you tell?"

"Zelda could never make a decent cup of coffee and she was always too cheap to hire a cook." He smirked at her. Martha looked as if she'd like to empty the cup over his head.

"As a matter of fact, she has a cook, a nice, Irish girl named Colleen." She grabbed his chin and turned his face toward her. "How did you know I made the coffee?"

"A man can tell his wife's touch."

"Uh-huh," she replied, her voiced dripping sarcasm.

He laughed as he hugged her tightly and she stretched her body to fit his.

"How well do you know Zelda?"

He'd hoped she wouldn't ask. "You really don't want to know

about me and Zelda, sweetheart." He didn't look at her.

"Oh," she whispered. The sound of disappointment in her voice cracked him as hard as a judge's gavel. He felt as guilty as if he'd hit her. But Molly was still Molly and her bout of self-pity was short-lived.

"Wait a minute. She just treated me like I was carrying typhoid down there. She looked down her nose at me like I was a..." her face turned red, but she said it anyway, "like I was a strumpet."

Jake tried to stifle a laugh. Her eyes flashed fire when she turned on him. He frantically wiped hot coffee from his naked belly.

"Molly, be careful!" Hiding his smile, he reached around her and set the cup on the table by the bed.

"I think you'd better be the one to be careful."

"Why, Molly, you're jealous." He dared a grin.

"Of course, I am!" Her narrowed eyes examined him closely. "You've been with that woman, haven't you?"

Jake enjoyed her jealousy. She was a firecracker when she was mad. "Well, yeah. Zelda is a..." he paused, as though searching for the right word, "an old friend of mine."

One of her fine eyebrows arched. "An old friend. How old a friend is she?"

"Now, honey, you'd better not be asking questions like that. It doesn't matter anyway. You're the one I love."

"Don't try to change the subject," she said as she moved his hands. "I think it's despicable that you'd bring your wife to a place like this, where one of your paramours is plying her trade!"

"Paramours?" He couldn't stand it anymore, breaking out in laughter as he caught her hands and pulled her down on him. "Now, Molly, don't you start with me. I got better things on my mind than fighting with you." He looked at her closely. "We might start with a fight, though."

"So, you don't want to talk about it, huh? What's the matter, Jake, are you ashamed of yourself?"

Jake lifted her up to look into her eyes.

"No. I'm ashamed of a lot of the things I've done in my life. But, I'm not ashamed of being with Zelda." He smiled. "C'mon, Molly, you didn't think you were my first woman. And nice women don't mess around with men they're not married to. That sort of limits a single man's choice for a paramour."

"I knew I wasn't the first. But I never counted on running into any of the others. Did you love her?"

He smiled and kissed her forehead. "No, I love you. Zelda's my friend. If she's mad it's 'cause she knows I won't sleep with her, anymore, now that I'm married."

His arrogant remark hit the target. She slapped at him playfully and laughed.

"She has dozens of men!"

"I don't know, Molly. Zel doesn't take care of customers. She inherited the house from her mother. Anything she does is strictly for pleasure, not business."

"So you think she's been waiting around for you to show up and give her a good time?"

He laughed. "No, I never thought she pined away for me. Zelda likes men way too much for that. But she was always available whenever I was around, so I just figured she liked me better than most." He tightened his arms around her and pulled her up so he could claim her mouth. "Now," he whispered into her slightly parted lips, "I really don't want to talk about Zelda, do you?"

THE SUN'S LIGHT poured through the window. Still hazy and warm from his lovemaking, she reached across the bed. Jake was gone. Rubbing the sleep from her eyes, she looked around the room. The decor was no more tasteful than it had been earlier, but she was getting used to it.

Her outlaw husband was having a very bad influence on her. Pretty soon, she'd be shopping for tassels for her lamps and red brocade wallpaper.

She dressed and went down to the kitchen. Jake sat at the table, reading the newspaper.

"Good morning, sweetheart. Come have a seat." He reached over to get a clean cup and the pot off the stove and poured her some coffee.

"My, my, such service. You never poured my coffee, Jake."

Zelda stood by the door to the front hall. Tall and proud, she wore a very respectable cotton dress, very flattering to her excellent figure, but not as revealing as that usually worn by women in her profession. Martha corrected herself. Jake said she wasn't a whore -- she was a madam. She was just loose, Martha thought, grabbing onto any reason to dislike her.

"Zelda," Jake warned. He turned back to Martha. "I have some business to see to. I might be all day. Now, I know this is awkward for you, honey, but I want you to stay here, where you'll be safe."

"With her?"

Jake glanced at Zelda. "She's a friend, Molly, and she's taking quite a chance letting us stay here."

Martha was sorry she'd let her jealousy get so out of hand. "All right. You go on and do whatever it is you need to do. I'll be good."

"Thanks, honey." He kissed her lightly on top of the head. It didn't escape her that Zelda had turned away. "I'll be back as soon as I can." He stopped at the door. "Zel, I really do appreciate this."

The madam smiled. "For old times' sake."

He smiled and nodded.

They were left alone in the kitchen, Martha and a woman who'd known Jake longer and, perhaps, better. The tension between them was thicker than the smell of French perfume that filled the room and she hated it.

Zelda came to the table and sat across from Martha.

"Look, I'm sorry about this morning. Jake told me what you thought about how I treated you."

Martha was horrified that he would do that. Zelda saw her discomfort.

"No, no. He was right to tell me. He knows me pretty well and he knew I wasn't looking down on you." She tried to smile. "The truth is, I'm a bit uncomfortable having you here."

Martha raised both eyebrows at that. It didn't seem possible such a beautiful, confident, independent woman could be uncomfortable.

"Why?"

"Because I know you don't approve of me or my business, for one thing. But mostly, because you have him. You don't have to worry about me and Jake, Martha." Zelda's manicured fingers caressed the china cup Jake had used, tracing the delicate design. "He made it very clear last night how he feels about you," she paused and took a pained breath, "and that it was over between us." Her pride asserted itself and she straightened up. "I never make a fool of myself for any man. Not even Jake Bowman."

Martha felt terrible, as strange as that seemed, to be the cause of so much hurt.

"I'm sorry if our being here is painful for you. I had no idea we were coming...." She stopped, suddenly self-conscious.

Zelda just smiled. "To a whorehouse? Of course, that's what you meant. Don't be embarrassed about it. It's not much of a defense, but we do honest business, here. It's the only thing some of these girls know how to do." She gave Molly a crooked smile. "Besides, I'd rather be an honest whore than a woman who sells her body to a man for security and calls him husband."

That was so close to what she'd said more than once to Garret, she had to smile.

"You've got me there, Zelda."

Zelda looked up from her coffee. "Jake's meant a lot to me." She put her hand over Martha's. "Now don't feel sorry for me. There was no way he'd ever have married me. It's not because I run a whorehouse, either. You know Jake better than that, I bet. All we had was a good time. I always knew if he ever married, he'd be faithful to his wife. That's just the kind of man he is." Her gray eyes again sought and held Martha's. "As long as you treat him right, I'll always be your friend, if you're willing to have a brothel keeper for a friend."

"I'll take a friend anywhere I can find one, Zelda."

"That makes you a lot more Christian than most people."

They sat in surprising ease and enjoyed their coffee.

"You know, Martha, I was getting worried about him. He hasn't been here in almost a year. He used to come into town with his brother on business."

"Business? What kind of business would rustlers have in Austin?" Martha eyes shot up to meet Zelda's, shocked she'd let it slip out. Jake hadn't mentioned whether or not Zelda knew about their legal problems.

Zelda waved away Martha's concern.

"Don't worry about him being tied up with Wil and that bunch. I knew all about that. I'm talking about before the war, when he was practicing law." She sipped her coffee. "He often had business before the state court. He used to tell me...." Her brow furrowed with concern. "Martha, are you all right?"

Martha stared, her jaw hanging open like a fool. "Law? He's a lawyer?"

Chapter Twenty-Two

JAKE AND SAM strolled, bold as brass, into the office of the clerk of the county court. It was nearly noon, quitting time on Saturdays. A seedy little man sat alone in the office, shuffling papers from one side of his desk to the other.

"Excuse me," Jake said smoothly, "are you the county clerk?"

The little man peered at Jake over the tops of his half-moon reading glasses.

"The office is closed. Please come back on Monday." He returned his attention to his work.

Jake leaned over the desk and gently laid a small burlap bag on the papers, right under the man's nose. His nose twitched at the smell of gold, fifty dollars' worth, wafting its way up from the confines of the bag.

"I have a small problem, Mister," he looked at the nameplate on the front of the desk, "Smith, is it?"

Smith took the bag and laid it in the middle drawer of his desk.

"What can I do for you?" the clerk asked.

Jake sat in the cane back chair in front of the clerk's desk.

"My name is MacLannon. I'm Jacob Bowman's lawyer. Frankly, Mr. Smith, I need information, specifically which judge will be hearing the Bowman trial. With the charges being what they are, well, I'm concerned." He leaned forward, just a bit. "You, as an officer of the court, are aware the right judge can make all the difference."

"Yes, that certainly is true." The clerk was flattered to be included in the legal circle. "However, your client is a fugitive. He's likely to be shot on sight. If I were you, I'd see about placing a lien against Bowman's estate for your fee." Smith laughed.

Jake smiled at the weak lawyer joke.

"Yes, of course. However, if I'm able to reassure Mr. Bowman he'll receive justice, I may be able to persuade him to surrender to the sheriff."

Smith shuffled a bunch of papers and moved the pile, from one side of his desk to the other, then back again. Jake exchanged a look of amusement with Sam.

"Ah, here it is," Smith said, lifting the first page off a stack he'd rifled through at least three times and squinting at the loopy handwriting. "Judge Winstead will be hearing that case Monday morning. Providing the defendants are located before then."

Jake sat up, hardly believing his luck.

"Justin Winstead? I thought he'd retired years ago."

"No, indeed, Judge Winstead is quite vigorous."

Sam smiled. "Couldn't ask for a better man."

"Certainly not. The Judge is a man of unimpeachable character and loyalty to the Union. I believe he was a staunch supporter of Sam Houston's efforts to keep Texas from seceding." The clerk sniffed. "Not at all like the usual riffraff Confederate trash one sees around here."

He was starting to get on Jake's nerves.

"Is there any information on evidence, witnesses?"

Mr. Smith flipped through the pile of papers again.

"No, I'm afraid we don't have that. You'll have to go to the county prosecutor. That would be Mr. Cook. His office is just down the hall."

Mr. Cook was a bit more helpful. He wasn't in. So, Jake helped himself to the contents of the man's desk.

"Dang."

"What?" Sam asked from the doorway.

"Here's a check, drawn on the Travis City bank, for five hundred dollars." Jake held it up. "Signed by Wilson Garret."

"Dang," Sam repeated. "So, he's bought himself a sheriff and a prosecutor."

Jake turned back to the desk while Sam went back to the door. "Where would a county prosecutor put a case folder?"

"Why're you asking me?" Sam said.

"Thought you might have an idea," Jake laughed as he swivelled the cheap desk chair around to the filing cabinets behind him. "Aha, here it is. Under B."

He opened the folder and started leafing through the few pieces of paper in the file. Sam came and looked over his shoulder.

"Here are the wanted posters. What's this?" Jake held up a piece of yellow paper bearing a scrawled message. "Telegram from Owen Tucker." He looked up at Sam. "He should be here today. Looks like he'll be staying at the National on Congress Avenue."

Sam reached over and lifted the few scraps of paper.

"Cook ought to be ashamed, if that's all he's got. The Judge'll eat him alive for wasting his time." He slapped his brother on the shoulders. "Nothin' to it, Jake."

Jake laughed. "Yep." He replaced the folder in the cabinet and leaned back in the prosecutor's chair. "Now, all we have to do is get to Owen Tucker, find out exactly what he's going to testify to." He looked up at Sam.

Sam nodded. "Consider it done."

Jake sat up and crossed his arms on the desk. "That friend of yours still work at the bank?" Sam nodded. "Good. Go down there, will you, Sam? Make sure Molly's taken care of in case things go wrong in court. Then we'll see to taking care of Wil."

"Amen to that," Sam said.

SHE WAS WAITING when he came in the back door.

"Hey, honey, been waiting for me, eh?" He pulled her out of her chair and gave her a good kiss. She didn't respond like she usually did when he kissed her good like that. Something in her eyes started warning bells to ringing in his head. "Molly, is something wrong?"

"What could be wrong?" She eased out of his arms and went to pour him a cup of coffee.

Zelda came through the kitchen, buttoning the cuffs of her fancy satin dress.

"Back at last? We were starting to worry, weren't we, Martha?" She looked behind him. "Where's Sam?"

"He had some business at the bank." He turned on his old friend. "What did you say to her, Zel?"

Zelda pushed him back with a finger in the middle of his chest.

"It wasn't what I said, Counselor, it was what you didn't say."

At the word *counselor*, he got a sick feeling in the pit of his stomach and turned to see Martha's expression.

"You told her?" he asked Zelda.

"I didn't know it was a big secret."

Martha smiled, but it didn't reassure him. She set his cup of coffee at the head place of the table.

"Why don't we have a little talk," she said.

Zelda finished her long cuffs.

"I have business of my own to tend to. Make sure you go up the back stairs, Martha. Don't want any of the cowboys getting any wrong ideas." She smiled at Jake's frown. "Good luck, Lawyer Bowman. You're going to need it."

Martha pulled out the chair. "Have a seat."

He felt like a suspect being hauled in for questioning.

She got right to it, too. "Why did you lie to me about how you made your living? How could you not tell me you're a lawyer, of all things?"

"I didn't lie. I always told you the truth, just not all of it. And I don't believe the subject of education or work experience beyond ranching ever came up in conversation."

"Stop talking like a lawyer."

"Molly, I am a lawyer," he said with a laugh that quickly turned sour as he felt the loss like that of a loved one. "I was a lawyer."

She looked pensive and crossed her arms on the table.

"A lot of things make more sense now. Seems, though, there's still a lot I don't know about you. I don't like that. I want to know everything."

Their quiet conversation was interrupted by the slam of the back door.

Jake sucked in a terrified breath when he saw Sam leaning on the jamb, holding his hand on his bloody left leg.

"My God!" Martha whispered and they both jumped up.

"What the devil happened?" Jake put his arm around Sam and helped him to a chair by the table.

"Monroe. He saw me at the bank and followed me down an alley. I thought I had a drop on him, but the sneaky snake slipped." Sam laughed weakly. "Must'a been a Confederate boy. No Yankee ever got by me."

Martha knelt beside him and examined the wound.

"The slug went clear through." She ransacked Zelda's kitchen drawers for something to use as bandages. Tossing three old towels to Jake, she said, "Tear these into strips."

They worked quickly, tying the wound to stop the flow of blood.

"Get him upstairs and into bed, Jake. I'll be along as soon as I've gathered what I need."

"Come on, Sammy." Jake helped him stand, but Sam was out before Jake got him to his feet.

"He's lost a lot of blood," Martha said, her expression telling him more than he wanted to know. He hefted Sam over his shoulder and headed upstairs.

While Martha cleaned the wound and bandaged Sam's leg, he sat by the bed, feeling as powerless as he had the other time he'd sat by, useless, as his brother fought for his life. That had been Wil's fault, too. He thanked the Lord Martha was here to take care of him.

"Molly," he reached out for her hand. "Tell me."

She shook her head.

"I don't know, darlin'. We'll just have to watch him and pray." She joined him in his watch. After a few minutes, she reached over and took his hand, holding it in her lap. "Mind if I ask you something?"

"Course not, honey," he answered.

"What kind of lawyer were you?"

He smiled. "I thought you were going to ask about Zelda and all the thousands of other women I've had in my sordid life. Or how many cows I stole, or how many men I've killed." He tossed her a teasing glance. "Of course, there are many people who put cattle rustlers and whoremongers and murderers a rung or two higher on the respectability ladder than they would a lawyer. I suppose you want a divorce now that you know you've married an attorney?"

Martha squinted at him. "Well, at least rustling has some romance to it. I'm not sure lawyering has any redeeming value. I might just have to think about that divorce."

"Well, ma'am, if I had any business cards, I'd give you one. I'd be proud to represent you."

"My husband wouldn't like it if I tried to get a divorce."

He gazed at her, long and hard. "No, ma'am, I reckon he wouldn't."

They sat there for a long minute, then they both sighed.

"Well? What kind?"

"I mostly did contracts, wills, that kind of thing."

"Did you have a fancy office?"

He laughed. "Why do you ask that?"

"I still don't think I can see you behind a desk."

"It so happens, Mrs. Bowman, I had a nice office in Dallas. Real big desk...." He spread his arms wide, palms down as though he could touch the rich, warm wood again. "A fancy leather chair, imported from Italy. High-backed, with wide, cushioned arms...."

Martha made an impressed face, eyes wide, sweet, tender lips forming an O. "How very elegant," she said. "I trust you performed work worthy of such surroundings?"

"Naturally." He shared a smile with her. "Actually, it was mostly pretty uninteresting to anybody but a lawyer. I took care of things for Daddy and Uncle Bud until the war. Took a few criminal cases, but only the ones I felt I could represent honestly. Sam, there," he motioned toward the bed where his brother lay, "was Dallas county prosecutor." He laughed. "He'd arrest 'em. I'd try to get 'em off. It was a big joke. The Bowman brothers making business for each other."

"Why didn't you go back to it when the war was over?"

"Couldn't." He looked way back into the past. "After the war, Yankee carpetbaggers had control of everything. They were the judges, clerks, prosecutors. Anybody who held an office before or during the war, or served in the Confederate Army was disenfranchised. So, Sam and I hired out and went back to ranching."

"I'm so sorry, Jake." Martha lay her hand on his. "You lost everything, your family, property, profession. I think that last thing bothers you more than you let on." She stroked his face. "I'm sorry for all those nasty comments I made about lawyers."

They chuckled together, sitting there by Sam's bedside, holding hands. Her sweetness and understanding warmed and eased the pain all this remembering had caused. He thought of where he'd be right now if he'd been able to return to the law.

"Well, Molly, I wish it hadn't happened the way it did, but at least there's been some recompense. How would I ever have found you way up there in Dallas?" He kissed the back of her hand. "I just wish Mama and Daddy were still alive. Mama would be relieved to see I finally got a respectable woman to marry me. And I wish they were around to see their first grandchild."

"Grandchild?"

Her tone, the look in her eyes, struck him as panic.

He nodded. "You want to have children, don't you?"

She laughed, in relief, it seemed to him.

"You mean in the future...grandchildren. Oh, yes. I want to have lots of children with you." Moving over to sit on his lap, she kissed him and made him forget all about children.

ZELDA'S WAS jumping. It was Saturday night and though most of the cowboys in Texas were on their way to Kansas, there were still plenty of politicians and state bureaucrats in the capital city to keep Zelda and all her girls busy. The high class of the clientele ensured money flowed like water, procuring liquor, food, and comely female companionship.

While the madam herself was overseeing business in the main house, Jake and Martha slipped out the back door and started off toward Congress Avenue and the National Hotel.

"Jake," she tugged on his sleeve, "is that Senator Biggs?"

He chuckled. "Yep. He's probably coming for a quiet game of cards in the backroom and some good whiskey served by a pretty girl."

They walked quickly along the dark streets of the capital.

"You remember everything I told you?" he asked as he pulled her along faster than she could actually walk.

"Yes, of course. I'm not an imbecile."

"I know, but we won't have much time. If the sheriff has Owen locked up as tight as Sam says, the deputy won't want a strange person in there for very long." He put his hand on her shoulder to stop her in the shadows as a carriage passed by. "Monroe's been snooping around town, looking for us. He's checked in with Wil's pet prosecutor and the sheriff."

"Has he bought the sheriff in Austin, too?"

"I doubt it. Not a more honest man than Aaron Bloom, but it seems Monroe has been deputized by the Travis City sheriff. A badge makes getting into places a little easier, sometimes." He looked down the alley. "Here we are. Are you ready?"

She took a deep breath. "I think so."

He produced one of Zelda's Irish housekeeper's white aprons and a mobcap from his jacket pocket. She put them on as ordered and followed him into the hotel. They eased up the back stairs to the second floor. Jake leaned around the stairway door for a look. It was more than obvious which room was Tucker's. A deputy had his chair tipped against the wall in front of the door. They kept going to the third floor.

Jake looked around as he opened the linen closet and pulled out sheets and a couple of towels which he shoved into her arms. "Here, Molly. Give me a minute or two, then go on down there and get Owen to let me in." He leaned over and kissed her before going down the hall.

She saw him counting doors. When he arrived at the room directly over Owen Tucker's, he stopped, knocked and waited. When no answer came, he turned the knob and grinned at her when the door opened. He disappeared into the room.

He was planning to drop into Tucker's room from the floor above and the window had better be open before he did it.

Better get on with this before I lose my supper. She descended the stairs to the second floor, clutching the linens to her chest.

The deputy noted her approach with real interest.

Flashing a butter-melting smile, she said to him, "Mr. Tucker has asked for some clean towels. Would you let me in, please?"

"Sure thing, honey." He opened the door and let her in, trying to get a pinch of her rear before she closed the door.

"Well, hi-dy, pretty thing." A big man sat in a chair at a writing table.

"Mr. Tucker?" At his nod, she tossed the linens on the bed and headed to the window. "I'm Jake Bowman's wife."

"Jake's got a wife?"

"He does, now." She tried to raise the window only to find it painted shut. "Jake, where are you?" She strained to see if he'd fallen to a splattered demise on the street below.

"What's going on here, Miz Bowman?"

She turned back to the rancher.

"Jake is coming to talk to you."

"He's coming in this way?" The man smiled and pointed at the window.

"That's what he said."

The deputy was banging at the door.

"Come on, sweetheart, come on out. This is a witness under protection of the sheriff."

The doorknob started to turn.

Martha pushed Tucker back into his chair and sat on his lap.

The door opened.

She threw her arms around Tucker and kissed him right on the mouth.

Tucker broke the kiss and turned to the deputy.

"Ain't you got no heart? Finally got me some sympathetic company and you interrupt."

The deputy smiled.

"Oh, sorry, Mr. Tucker. Just let me know when you're done with her," he said as he pulled the door shut.

Tucker smiled at her.

"Jake's not going to shoot me, is he?"

She got up, blushing like a brakeman's lantern.

"I'm sorry. I couldn't think of anything else."

"I'd say that worked fine." He went to the window with his pocket knife, freeing it from the paint, then raised it. "There we go." Leaning backward out the window, he looked up. "Okay, Jake, you can come down, now." Jake's legs came into view, dangling from the upper floor. Owen grabbed hold and pulled him in.

"Thank you, Owen."

"Seems I'm always taking care of your bacon, Bowman."

"You got to kiss my wife. Even?"

"Jake!"

The men laughed as they shook hands.

"Good to see you, Owen."

Tucker nodded. "And you. Where's Sam?"

"Laid up. He got himself shot yesterday."

"That happens to Sam a lot, don't it?"

Jake snorted a chuckle. "He keeps bad company." He pulled a pad and a pencil out of his pocket. "Owen, we don't have a lot of time. I need to ask you some questions."

IN ZELDA'S elegant parlor, Jake sat in a big chair by the fireplace and relit his pipe. He drew deeply and, brow furrowed, glanced over at his brother, sleeping on a delicate settee much too short for him. Martha knew Jake was concerned, but there was nothing to do for Sam except leave him be. For Jake's benefit, though, she went over to her patient and checked his forehead.

"No fever. He just needs to rest and build up his strength."

Jake nodded and reached for her hand. She took his and let him pull her down to sit on his lap.

"Honey, I'm going to turn myself in to the sheriff here in Austin." She turned on him in horror. "Now, Molly, we don't have any choice. Wil is out there and Sam is out of commission."

"What about the law, Jake? You already admitted to rustling cattle." She got an inspiration. "Why not just turn him in? Tell the truth about how you got tangled up in it all."

"I never admitted rustling any cattle. I only said we rode with Wil and altered brands. But that alone is enough to get yourself hanged in Texas. How we got sucked into the whole business won't matter a hoot in a holler to a Texas jury, anyway. If we implicate Wil, we implicate ourselves."

Sam grunted agreement from the settee. "We might as well bring the rope with us."

"So, you are alive," Jake said.

"Sort of," Sam answered.

Martha was furious. "How can you two joke at a time like this?"

"'Cause it's better than the alternative. Look, sweetheart, Wil's already bought the prosecutor. My only hope is to get to court." He smiled that endearingly arrogant smile. "I have the best lawyer in Texas."

"Hah! Maybe second best," Sam snorted.

A knot of fear worked its way up from the pit of her stomach to lodge in her throat.

"I know you're scared, honey. So am I." He smiled at her expression of disbelief. "Yep, sure am. Wil's tried to kill me at least twice, and I worry that three might be the charm." He stroked the line of her jaw. "But I'm more afraid for you. As long as he's alive, you won't be safe."

"I don't care about the land. It's worthless without you," she whispered, barely containing the desperation. "We can go someplace else and start over."

"I'm not talking about the land. I'm talking about what he could do to you." His handsome face was set and his mind made up.

She was ready to shoot him, herself. "I can't understand this. Even if he doesn't get you," she grabbed his arm, "cattle rustling is a hanging crime, Jake."

"I hope to avoid being hung."

She dropped his arm in frustration and shoved herself from his lap, pacing the room. As she walked by him, the brushing of butterfly wings tickled her insides. She placed her hand against her belly. It was too soon to feel life, but there it was, just the same. At this point, she wasn't above using any device to make him listen.

"Jake Bowman, I told you once I wasn't going to let you leave me with a child to raise by myself."

He was silent. His face was blank as the realization dawned, then he smiled.

"Molly, a child? My child?"

"Of course, you idiot! Whose else's would it be?"

"How long have you known?"

She wasn't sure she was going to tell him. "I've suspected for a few weeks. I was sure the day I fainted in town."

The joy of learning about his child turned to anger at being kept in the dark. He stood up, but he didn't move toward her.

"You let me drag you around Austin all night? How could you keep this from me?"

Martha backed up a step. "Don't you yell at me. I did it for you."

"Exactly how do you figure that?"

"Just look at you. If I'd told you sooner, you would've fretted over me and driven me crazy."

"A baby," he repeated as he sat heavily in the chair.

She saw her chance to really work on him. Kneeling by his side, she took his hand between her two. "Jake, I've been so afraid that I'd lose you like I lost Daddy and Mama and my brothers. I would rather die than live without you."

"Don't you ever say that!" Fear flashing in his eyes, Jake grabbed her shoulders and gave her a little shake. "Not ever. You have my baby in you. If something does happen to me, you have to raise my child."

"What'll happen to us if he kills you?"

He pulled her close and whispered into her hair.

"I have to make sure he doesn't."

"How can you do that in jail?" She sighed in exasperation. "Or hung? Now you say you and Sam are planning to just turn yourselves in? It'll be like shooting fish in a barrel."

He sat back in the chair.

"First off. Sam is staying right here, for now. Once he's up and around again, he'll take care of any unfinished business for me." She was ready to defame his intellect again as he placed his finger over her lips. "Hear me out, Molly. I can see a way out of the legal part of this. If we run, I'll never be able to come back to Texas without having to look over my shoulder the whole time."

Martha felt her heart sink. He'd never leave Texas, not if there was any way around it.

"As for our problem with Wil, Sam is my insurance."

She was completely confused and it must have shown on her face.

"As long as Wil thinks he can get me hanged without dirtying his hands, he won't take the chance of messing up his nice, clean life as a respectable rancher. When things go wrong for him in court, though, he's going to be mad, and when Wil's mad he's capable of anything. But he's not stupid. Sam was a sniper in the war. He was able to get into and out of places you'd never believe. The Yankees never caught him, until he tried to break me out of prison. Wil won't mess with you as long as Sam is loose." He tipped her head up to look into his eyes. "You have to trust me, Molly. I know what I'm doing."

"So, what'll happen if you've miscalculated and get yourself hanged?"

"Sam will kill Wil." He turned to his brother. "And no talking or waiting for him to draw. You shoot him in the back, through the head, whatever. He will not get his hands on Molly. Got it?"

Sam nodded agreement. "Understood."

Martha's blood ran cold at the businesslike way this last exchange took place. They were talking murder. But it was clear this was the path Jake had decided on. She sighed in resignation.

"When do we do this? Tomorrow?"

Jake turned her to face him. "There's no we. You're staying here until it's over, one way or the other."

"Oh, no. I'm coming with you."

He shook his head. "Molly, why can't you ever just do what I tell you?"

"You said the sheriff was honest."

"I'd trust Aaron Bloom with my life, but there are a bunch of deputies down there I don't know anything about. Wil could've bought them."

"All the more reason I should come along, at least until you're safely locked up. Who else is there to watch your back with Sam here flat on his?" His lack of an answer was all the answer she needed. "I," she took his hand and laid it on her belly, "we, need you alive, and if you're determined to do this, at least let me stand by you."

Jake looked over at his brother, who only shrugged.

"All right, Molly," Jake said. "According to the court schedule we're up first thing Monday morning. But, you have to promise to do what I tell you from now on."

She nodded. "As long as you don't tell me to do anything stupid."

He didn't look reassured.

Chapter Twenty-Three

"WHERE HAVE YOU been?" Martha followed Jake into Zelda's parlor. "I've been worried out of my mind."

"I'm sorry, honey. I just went out for a walk." He pecked her cheek. "Needed some air. How you doing today, Sammy?"

"I've been better. Get anything?"

Jake smiled. "Sure did. Annabelle told me Wil was in to see Winstead. She didn't know what was said, but Justin tossed him out on his backside."

"Who's Winstead?" Martha asked.

"The judge who's trying the case," Jake answered.

"Who's Annabelle? Another old friend?"

"Relax, Molly. Annabelle is sixty-seven years old. She's been keeping house for the Judge ever since I can remember."

"You know the judge?" She wondered if she would ever know everything about this man.

"Let's say, we're acquainted with His Honor." He sat in the chair by the fireplace and turned back to Sam. "My guess is, Wil tried to buy him."

Sam guffawed. "That would put a fly in Justin's coffee."

"Yep. It's looking better all the time."

Martha was confused. Her usual state lately.

"So you know the Judge? How does that help you?"

"The fact is, honey, the only living witness to the fact that we ever rode with rustlers is Wil. Besides, all this talk of being tried and hanged is just talk. Texas can't hang us or even try us for a crime committed anywhere else. All they can do is hold an extradition hearing. There's a good chance we can get Winstead to throw the whole case out. As long as he keeps control of his courtroom, and he usually does, this'll work."

Martha said nothing more, but she wondered why she'd bothered to break him out in the first place.

An hour later, she was wondering the same thing. She and Jake made their way to the side door of the county jail. A voice, loud and angry, floated out the open window on the warm evening breeze. The side door was just ajar, giving them enough of a view of the scene inside.

"So, why haven't you found them?"

Jake peered in. "He couldn't have gotten to Bloom." It was a denial. She peeked in around his shoulder.

The county sheriff wasn't among the men congregated in his office. The deputy they'd seen guarding Tucker was, though, as was Monroe.

For his part, Wil was fit to be tied, and probably should have been. He stomped around the sheriff's office, kicking chairs and benches over.

"God damn you to hell and back!" he roared at the deputy, who squirmed uneasily behind the desk. "You let her into Tucker's room? If she was there, you can bet Jake was there, too, probably using some of his fancy lawyer tricks on him to get him to change his story. They didn't even have to knock you out or break the lock on the damned door! They just waltzed in, nice as you please." Garret stomped over and kicked the stove.

"And you," Garret turned on Monroe. "First, you can't get a couple of women off a stage! Now, you've lost the whole bunch!"

"I think you got bad information from the stage office. There was only one old widow woman on that stage when it got to Bastrop. She damned near took off my head with her parasol when I tried to get a good look at her. But, that's just the women, anyway. I told you I saw the younger Bowman coming out of the bank and I got a clean shot at him. I hurt him bad. He'll either turn up at a doctor's office or die. All we have to do is wait...."

"I don't have time to wait! The longer Jake's out there, the more likely he is to find a way out of this and I'll lose my chance to finally get rid of him." He paced the floor. "He's the slickest lawyer in Texas and I saw him get out of more tight places than a nearsighted seed bull."

Martha blushed. Jake just grimaced. "Really, Molly," he whispered, "even I'm not that slick."

"Well, I bet I know where he's hiding." Garret turned to his foreman. "There's a whore in town named Zelda. Jake was always at her place when he was here."

"I already checked all the whorehouses, including that one, just like you told me, before. If they'd been there, I'd'a found 'em."

Wil marched over to his foreman and stuck a finger in his face.

"Look, Monroe. I'm the boss here. If I tell you to look up the preacher's wife's skirts for 'em, you'll do it. If I tell you to crawl through every saloon and whorehouse in town, then check the State

House and the Governor's Mansion, you'll do that, too!" He turned and paced around. "And, damn it all, find Martha! She was on that stage when it left Travis City. I want her there when we kill him." He looked sharply at Monroe. "Well, what are you waiting for? Get the hell out of here!"

Monroe shrugged and rose from his seat.

"Garret," he said, "if I run into him, I'm going to kill him. I'm not risking my neck just so you can have the pleasure of rubbing his nose in you getting his woman."

Garret's face turned red with rage and he lit into Monroe again, but the man just stood there, unblinking, unconcerned. His calm was much more frightening than the unbridled fuming of his boss.

Jake whispered beside her. "He's more dangerous than Wil."

A sudden, horrible thought gripped her.

"Jake, he's on his way to Zelda's?"

A smile touched his face. "Sam'll watch out for them. Zel's pretty good with a Derringer, too."

She melted down the side of the building. All this skulking around was making her nervous. It all seemed to be so complicated. What if it blew up in their faces?

The three men in the jail's little office were gone. Jake opened the side door silently, smiling at the deputy's lack of attention to detail in leaving the side open while he carefully locked the front.

"Come on. We'll wait for Bloom to come back." He shook the coffee pot on the rapidly cooling stove and frowned, then tossed in some coal.

Martha sat on a chair by the front door.

"Jake," she asked, "I've been wondering something."

He measured coffee and poured water into the pot. "What about?"

"Where did you get the money you gave me back in Travis City?"

"I told you, I have a little money put by."

"Rustling money? Money you stole from other people?"

He looked defensive. The lawyer in him responded to the charges.

"No, I always made sure I spent all that." He smiled. "Usually lost it at poker. What I gave you is from what my mother left me. She came from old South Carolina money. My grandddaddy left her some property she sold long before the war. She put it away for me and Sam while we were in school back east. We never needed it, so it just sat there."

"But what about when the banks failed?"

"Mama put it in a bank in New York. Granddaddy taught her you couldn't beat a Yankee for handling your money."

"Are you rich?"

"Yep," he smiled boyishly, "we are. Well, rich enough to get by for a good while."

"If it wasn't rustling money, why didn't you tell me?" She hadn't had time to get mad yet, but it was coming. "How could you let me worry like that when we lost the entire herd?"

He frowned and didn't answer her right away. "I don't know, honey. I guess I was afraid to let something slip, so I just didn't tell you anything at all." He knelt before her and took her hand. "The whole truth is, I was afraid you'd turn away from me if you found out I hadn't been completely honest with you."

"I probably would have. We've both had to learn to trust again." She lay her hands on his face and pulled him close, staring hard into his eyes. "Just make sure you don't keep anything from me, again. Understand, Counselor?"

His smile melted her heart as it always did.

He raised her hand and planted a kiss right in the center of her palm, then he took a seat in the sheriff's chair. With a clear view of the door, he removed his Navy Colt from its holster and placed it on the desk.

Martha sat in the chair by the door, her rifle on her lap. Only the gurgling of the coffee pot broke the silence.

Heavy footsteps clumped up the walk. Jake motioned her to stand against the windowless wall behind the front door with her rifle ready.

"Howdy, Aaron," he said cordially as the lawman came in.

Sheriff Bloom stood just inside the door.

"Jake." The man's broad face split in a grin. "Good to see you, though I've got to say, I'm a bit surprised." He came into the room and closed the door slowly behind him. "Get out of my chair."

"Yes, sir." Jake vacated the sheriff's place. "Coffee, Aaron?" He reached for two mugs and poured the brew. He handed one to Martha and the other to Bloom, before getting himself a cup and taking a seat across from the sheriff.

"What're you doin' here, Jake? You know I've got to arrest you."

Jake leaned back in the chair.

"You're probably not going to believe this, but I'm turning myself in."

The sheriff carefully settled himself down. "What's the trick?"

"No trick. I want to go to trial."

"What about your brother?"

"He's holed up, waiting to see what happens to me. If I get hung, he's going to take care of a small bit of business."

Bloom leaned against his desk. "Let me get this straight. You want me to lock you up and just make sure you get to trial tomorrow morning? That's it?"

"That's right."

"Finish your coffee, then. That your wife?" Bloom tilted his head toward Martha, still standing against the front wall. "Pleasure, Mrs. Bowman."

"Mine as well, Sheriff."

Jake stood up and laid his gun on the desk.

"Lock me up, Sheriff. I suppose you'll want to search me."

After Bloom made a cursory search, Jake turned to Martha.

"Aaron, may I have a minute alone with my wife?"

"Sure, Jake." Bloom tipped his hat. "Ma'am." He left them by the side door.

Jake touched her face and tilted her chin up to look into his eyes.

"This is the only way I can think of to be done with this once and for all, Molly. I'm tired of running."

He kissed her tenderly. His embrace was so tight she couldn't breathe, but she wanted him to hold her forever.

"Get out of here. Get back to Zel's and stay out of sight."

"I'm going to be in court tomorrow, Jake." She stated it as fact. Though he started to argue, he held his peace.

"All right, honey. Just be sure nobody catches you by yourself." He released her reluctantly. "Keep that rifle loaded."

Martha nodded, her burdened heart aching.

"Jake," she whispered, throwing herself at him. He caught her in his strong arms and kissed her, hard this time. She clung to his broad shoulders, afraid if she let go, she'd never have him back again.

"Sweetheart," his harsh whisper came to her. He squeezed her then set her down. His lips brushed her forehead. "See you in court. Take care of my baby."

Suddenly, she was outside in the alley and she heard the bolt slide.

"If we live through this, I'm going to kill that man."

THE TRIAL OF the notorious rustler was set to begin in the county courthouse at nine sharp. The crowd of curious onlookers parted like the Red Sea before Moses when Martha walked in, head held high, toward the front row. She heard the whispers, rolling wavelike from one side of the courtroom to the other.

Accepting an offered seat right behind the defendant's table on the left side of the courtroom, Martha sat ramrod straight, her thoughts focused on Jake. She hadn't gone to the jail before coming here. For all his good intentions, Sheriff Bloom wouldn't have been able to keep Garret or one of his hired guns from shooting Jake right through the bars of the cell. If something had happened to him during the night, she wasn't ready to face it.

Movement at the near side door caught her attention. Her heart skipped a beat as Jake was led into the courtroom. He winked at her and gave her a smile. She sighed with relief. So far, so good.

The judge entered and the crowd respectfully rose until he settled himself. Judge Winstead was a native Texan, born a Mexican citizen even before Stephen Austin arrived.

"He was a Union man, you know." Martha heard the comment behind her.

The speaker's neighbor replied, "So was Sam Houston, but a Texan, even a Union man, is better than a Yankee."

The Judge's gavel fell heavily on the well-worn bench.

Chapter Twenty-Four

"THIS COURT IS in session." Again the gavel fell, but it wasn't necessary. Winstead's voice, still strong in spite of his seventy years, had already stilled the crowd. "You all know I don't stand on too much ceremony, but I will not have a court of law turned into a circus. You have your only warning. Frank, read the first case."

As he sat there watching Judge Winstead follow the charges as they were read by the bailiff, Jake was sure he'd be on his way to Mexico if any other man were sitting on that bench. He'd trust Justin Winstead with his life any time.

The instant the old gentleman's eyes found the name of the accused, they left the paper to look over at the defendant's table. He looked for all the world like a schoolmaster waiting for an explanation of inexplicable behavior. And damn him, if Jake didn't feel exactly like a naughty schoolboy sitting under that scrutiny. Winstead's eyes returned to the list of charges. When the reading was completed, the old man turned toward the defendant.

"I was hoping there was another Jacob Matthew Bowman in Texas. It's been a long time. What have you been up to, boy?"

A wave of whispers washed across the room as Jake stood respectfully.

"You have the charges there before you, Your Honor."

The judge raised one bushy white eyebrow and then adjusted his spectacles. He looked at the paper before him.

"Um-hum. Rustling, murder." He raised his eyes to look at Jake again. "What's the matter, boy, practicing law not shifty enough an occupation for you?"

Once the crowd decided that was a joke, they shared a laugh at Jake's expense. Again the Judge's gavel hit his bench. When the courtroom was again relatively quiet, Jake answered.

"Judge, you know why I gave up my practice. A Reb isn't welcome in court unless it's as a defendant."

The crowd murmured in agreement.

The Judge nodded his white head in understanding.

"Well, what about these charges, Jake?" With a wave of his hand, he quieted the prosecutor who was about to vigorously protest this breach of etiquette.

"Judge Winstead, I don't deny my brother and I were in the Indian Territory last year, at the time of this crime, I believe. But we are innocent of these charges." He saw Martha glance nervously heavenward for the bolt of lightning she obviously expected as his due for lying in court. "In fact, defense moves that these charges be dismissed on the grounds that Texas has no jurisdiction whatever in this matter."

"Indeed," Winstead said, turning to the prosecutor. "Mr. Cook, you know better than to try to turn this into a capital case. This is, as of now, a hearing on the question of whether the defendant should be held for extradition to Fort Smith to stand trial in the Federal Court."

"But, Your Honor," the prosecutor croaked. "We always hang rustlers here in Texas."

"Mr. Cook, where did you get your training? Even rusty as he is, Jake knows the Constitution of the United States bars trial in a state other than that where the crime was committed. You bring me a rustler who stole cows in Texas and I'll be glad to hang him for you."

"But, Your Honor!" Cook was near apoplectic.

Winstead impatiently waved his hand.

Jake decided to push his luck a little.

"Your Honor, defense requests to see the Federal warrant."

"Sit down, Jake. We'll consider the issuance of the wanted poster to suffice."

"Judge, you know better, that's not good enough. Any warrant must be specific. There is no name on that poster, Your Honor."

Winstead considered. "No, but somehow, your name has gotten mixed up with this case and we'll see it through to clear this up."

"Judge, the only reason my name is mixed up with this case is that I married a woman another man wanted."

"Congratulations. Now, sit down, Counselor."

Jake sat down as the chuckles faded in the room.

"Frank," he said to his bailiff, "bring in Mr. Tucker and let's get this thing over with before dinnertime."

Every head in the courtroom turned toward the door. Jake gave Martha a look of encouragement and she tried to smile for him. As the bailiff made his way to the doors at the back of the courtroom, the crowd buzzed with murmured speculation about the witness.

"He came all the way from the Indian Territory to testify," one man whispered from two rows back. "I heard from a friend whose sister got it straight from a cousin of one of the deputies that this feller caught the rustlers red-handed and they shot him."

"The way I heard it..." his neighbor started.

The discussion died when Owen Tucker entered.

"Oh, what a fine-looking man," one woman whispered. Several titters of agreement followed.

"I wonder if he's married," another woman wondered, just a bit too loudly.

Owen turned and winked at her. "'Fraid so, pretty lady."

The curious lady promptly transformed into a pool of melting jelly. Owen smiled rakishly.

"Ma'am," he bowed to Martha, then approached the witness stand, took the oath administered by the bailiff, and settled into the chair.

Prosecutor Cook puffed out his chest and stuck his thumbs into the armholes of the brocaded ivory vest of his very tailored black lawyer suit. Strutting forward, he approached the witness stand like a cock sizing up his opponent. Jake had to look away or risk a very unprofessional guffaw when Cook tipped his head, ever so slightly, and his overdone hairdo tipped, ever so slightly, just like the comb of the fighting rooster he so resembled. After a dramatic pause, Cook initiated the interrogation with the usual opening question.

"State your name, place of residence, and occupation, for the record, please."

"My name is Owen Tucker and I am owner of Morning Star Ranch in the Indian Territory."

"Now, Mr. Tucker, will you tell us what happened to your ranch during the summer of last year, 1871?"

Tucker nodded, his face grim. "Last summer, during June and July, I got hit at least five times by a band of rustlers. A bold bunch they were, too. In one raid, they took almost five hundred head during broad daylight, right out from under my foreman's nose."

"Mr. Tucker, did you have occasion to witness any illegal acts, yourself?"

"Sure as shootin' did. Near dawn one morning last July, one of my hands come ridin' in, hell bent for leather, yelling about a shooting over at my neighbor's place. We got mounted up and took off over there." Owen shook his head. "Was a terrible thing. My neighbor, Randall Tall Trees, and her daughter, pretty little Nancy...." He cleared his throat. "Well, they were dead and her two hired men had been shot up. Then we heard this ruckus and here come a big mess of cows over the prairie headed north. There were three riders driving them." With a shrug of his big shoulders, Owen added, "Right then, I knew they were rustlers, probably the same ones who hit my place. I sent some men after them...."

Tucker slowed to take a breath. Cook jumped right into the breach, ready to pop his killer question.

"Mr. Tucker, do you recognize the defendant, Jacob Bowman?" Cook pointed in the direction of the defendant's table.

"Yeah."

The prosecutor smirked at the audience and looked at Jake, so pleased with his working of this witness, he almost missed the rest of the answer.

"Sure, I know Jake."

Cook wasn't the only one caught by surprise. Judge Winstead glanced over at Jake, then sat up. Winstead wouldn't miss a single syllable of Tucker's testimony.

Jake relaxed. He sat back, crossed his legs, and tipped his chair against the rail. Serves the little peacock right for putting a witness on the stand without interviewing him first, he thought, keeping his smile hidden. A first year law student knew better than that. He wondered if Cook had gotten his degree by mail-order.

"Quiet in here." The gavel crashed onto the bench again. The crowd obediently fell as silent as that many people could be.

The prosecutor was shaken, no doubt about it, Jake thought, watching the man shift from foot to foot. Wil wouldn't be happy with what his five hundred dollars had bought. He waited, ready for the next question.

"Isn't he one of the rustlers?"

Jake stood. "Objection. Your Honor, prosecution is leading the witness."

"Sustained."

Cook, completely off-stride, simply asked, "Mr. Tucker, how do you know Jacob Bowman?"

"Jake and his brother had worked for Randall for a few years. They were the men who were shot." When Cook didn't ask another question, Tucker went on. "The way I figured it, these rustler boys rode up to Randall's to lift her cows, shot Randall and Jake and Sam when they tried to stop it, then they savaged that poor little girl." Owen bit his lip and drew in a shaky breath.

Jake knew exactly how he felt. He was glad Sam wasn't here, glad he didn't have to relive the whole thing, again. He dragged his attention back to Owen's testimony.

"But, Mr. Tucker," Cook hadn't given up yet. "Didn't you suspect the Bowmans had something to do with this travesty?"

"Hell, no. Jake and Sam wouldn't be mixed up in nothin' like that. They sure wouldn't hit Randall's place. Stealin' from a woman!" Owen puffed a disgusted breath.

The guilt nearly choking him, Jake struggled to maintain an expressionless face.

"Like I was saying, them boys took off with the cows and I sent some men after them. Them boys had some fast horses and a head start and my men couldn't catch up. But we got Jake and Sam to my place and me and my missus patched 'em up."

"So, you didn't see the rustlers?"

"Not their faces, but I'd know the leader if I saw him or his mount again."

"What do you mean?"

"That bold rascal stole Jake's horse, a tall palomino. The devil is fast as Pegasus, and wild as a fury. He did good to sit the saddle on that animal." Owen sat forward. "Mr. Prosecutor, you want to find the man who killed Randall and Nancy and shot up Jake and Sam, you just look for a tall, blond man who rides a big palomino that ain't quite broke to saddle."

A gasp rose in the courtroom. Those who were citizens of Travis City knew someone who fit that description.

Tucker sat back and chuckled. "Sure would like to see if he's been able to break that devil, yet."

"Your Honor, this is hearsay," Cook croaked, sweat popping like blisters on his forehead.

"Son, you don't generally object to your own witness."

"But...." Cook began.

"Mr. Tucker," the Judge said, "would you recognize the man who shot Jake and Sam Bowman?"

"You bet your gavel, Judge," said the plain-spoken man. "Especially if I saw him on that horse."

Jake turned at the sound of the door opening. God was indeed smiling on him. He couldn't have timed Wil's entrance better himself. Wil swaggered up to sit in the front row right behind the prosecutor.

"How's it going, Malcolm?" he asked, uncaring that he was interrupting the proceeding. "I brought the rope. We ready to string him up, yet?"

"I'll be damned!" Tucker said. "That's him!"

"What?" asked Judge Winstead.

"What?" the prosecutor echoed.

Tucker pointed. "That's the yellow-haired, murdering weasel!"

Jake just sat back and waited.

Wil looked around him, attempting to determine whom the witness was indicating. It dawned somewhat slowly on him that he was the yellow-haired, murdering weasel.

"That's crazy!" he said, glaring at Jake. "You did get to him. You bought him off, didn't you?"

The crowd broke out in total pandemonium. This time, the Judge's gavel couldn't be heard about the noise. He was barely able to get the attention of the bailiff.

"Frank, get that man."

"I'll kill you, myself," Wil started toward Jake and reached down for his gun. He drew and leveled the weapon at Jake's belly, causing the spectators to scream and stampede.

"What is that man doing with a gun in my courtroom?" The Judge pulled out his own weapon.

The din of screams, shouts, stamping feet, scraping chairs, echoed in Jake's ears.

"Wil, put it down," Jake shouted, trying to get to him. He didn't want anybody else getting shot. Frank, the bailiff, grabbed him by the arm. "Not me, you fool! He's the one with the gun."

Jake jerked his arm free. His blood froze when he saw Martha step toward Garret.

"Molly, no!"

She dashed in front of Wil, pushing the gun down toward the floor just as the shot went off.

The crowd ducked, some fell on their faces on the floor. The bailiff threw himself in front of the Judge. Wil wrapped his arm around Martha's waist and dragged her backward toward the open window.

"Wil, no," Jake said. "Let her go. I'll go with you."

"You'll come with me, anyway, won't you, Jake?" Wil swung his gun from right to left, holding everyone at bay.

Martha kept her mouth shut. She moved along with Wil, but didn't make it easy for him. Jake prayed she'd stay quiet and watch him, ready for a signal to drop. He looked around. There wasn't anybody else with a gun besides Wil, the bailiff, and the Judge.

He had her by the open window.

"Don't, Wil," Jake whispered.

"Come and get her, Jake." Wil sat down on the window sill and pulled Martha onto his lap. Jake's heart stopped when Wil tipped backward, falling out the window and taking Martha with him.

A wall of people materialized between him and the window.

"Stop him!" the Judge yelled.

The bailiff sailed out the open window before Jake was able to squeeze his way through the human barrier. A shot cracked through the air.

"Get out of my way!" Jake got to the window just in time to see the bailiff slump onto the ground, the back of his head blown off. A yellow blur passed the front of the courthouse, Wil perched in the saddle, Martha thrown over his lap.

"God," Jake prayed as he leapt from the window.

"Not so fast, son. You and me have some talking to do!" the Judge yelled as Jake ran toward the fallen bailiff's body. "You're still in custody and you ain't going anywhere until I'm satisfied about this mess."

Jake turned and saw the Judge wave his gun, but Jake knew it was just show.

"Sorry, Judge," he called back. "That was my wife and child he took off with. I'll be back if he doesn't kill me." He snatched the gunbelt from the bailiff and ran to the nearest hitching post. "Tell whoever this horse belongs to, I'll get it back to him."

He vaulted into the saddle and took off after his family.

Chapter Twenty-Five

THEY FLEW ALONG on the road toward Travis City. Martha raised her face from Garret's dusty leg and gasped for air, only to be pushed back down.

"Better not move around too much, Martha. I might just drop you." He clamped one of his big hands down on her bustle.

"Stop squeezing me, you yellow, sneaking...." Her words were shut off as the big palomino hit a dip and stumbled, bouncing her and forcing all the air from her lungs. The curses she leveled at him burned her mind, though, and she hoped, somehow, he could feel them.

He only laughed and squeezed tighter.

She feared and prayed for her child as she tried to get her hands onto something that would keep her from falling off. Every time Beau's hooves hit the ground, she felt the pounding all the way through her belly to her backbone.

If anything happens to my baby or to Jake, I'll kill this bastard, myself.

JAKE HAD AN easy time following them. Wil was headed toward his ranch, possibly to set up an ambush, maybe to get another horse.

Already sick from all the things going through his mind, Jake thought of her face as she went backwards out that window. The fall was enough to make her lose the baby. He didn't know much about that sort of thing, but it seemed the mother often didn't survive, either.

He kicked his mount, trying to get Beau's speed out of him. Foam flecked the horse's mouth and breast and he stumbled. Jake slowed the horse down when he realized he was killing the poor plug.

"Slow down, boy," Jake said, more to himself than the horse. "I'll not get there sooner afoot."

He was sure Wil would wait for him.

Jake tried to calm down and get his wits about him. Composure under fire had never been one of Wil's virtues, and it might be his only advantage. In a fair fight, Wil was dead, but Wil wasn't partial to fair fights.

If something happened to Molly because of this, Wil would die hard, no quick bullet for him. And it would be a pleasure to do it.

BOUNCING IN time to Beau's stride, Martha's teeth clacked together and her mouth filled with the sharp flavor of blood as she bit the inside of her cheek. The pain kept her focused on holding on when Garret jerked the reins to bring Beau to a slamming stop. She kept flying, off Garret's lap and onto the horse's thick neck. Beau objected to the unaccustomed weight and tossed his head, flinging her to the ground in a dusty heap.

Pushing with shaky hands against the dry earth, she sat up to get her bearings. She couldn't tell how far they had ridden from Austin and was surprised when she recognized Garret's ranch house, a hundred-year-old, single-story mud adobe structure, nestled under a pair of spreading pecan tree.

"What are we doing here?" she asked.

Garret dismounted and tied Beau to the post in front of the house. He paced around, yanking off his hat and running his hand through his heavily pomaded hair.

"Shut up! I'm trying to think."

As he prowled the front yard, muttering and cursing and squinting at the road from Austin, Martha looked around. There were no other people here. No one who might be able to help her.

Was Jake coming? As soon as the question occurred to her, she knew the answer. Whatever was between Jake and his cousin would be enough to make him come, to finish it once and for all. But there was also the child sleeping inside her.

He'd come.

Garret froze by the hitching post and stared in the distance. Then he nodded, as though he'd come to some decision.

"Come on," he said. "We're going to get you a horse."

A shiver of dread skittered up her spine, tickling her neck and raising the hair at the base of her skull. "Why don't you just leave me here? I'll only slow you down."

He shook his head and dismounted. "Oh, no, Mrs. Bowman. Your husband might not follow me if I don't have you."

"That's what I'm hoping."

"Sorry to disappoint you. Now, get up."

She tried to rise, but everything went black all around her. She clutched her abdomen and cried out at the pain that knifed through her. "Oh, no. Lord, please." She sat down hard in the dust.

"What's wrong? Come on. We don't have a lot of time. I don't want to meet him here."

"Please, just let me sit for a minute. I...." The pain knifed again and she doubled over. "Please, Lord," she whispered, "don't take my baby."

"Baby? Martha, are you in the family way? My congratulations. Sorry your husband won't be around to see it."

She slowly raised her eyes to look into his face, horrified that she'd spoken aloud. Now that Garret knew, her child was at the mercy of this man, a monster known for having no mercy to spare.

He jerked her to her feet and forced her to look into his eyes.

"Are you afraid of me, Martha? You're absolutely right to be afraid. Jake Bowman has been a thorn in my side all my life and it's time I paid him back. But before he dies, he'll know I killed his brat and I had his woman." His laugh was a poor imitation a real one. "Unfortunately, I'm afraid I can no longer offer you the life of a gentleman rancher's wife."

Blood pounded in Martha's ears and her eyes saw nothing. Her hands moved to cover her belly in a useless attempt to protect her child.

The feather light touch of his fingertip on the underside of her jaw sent fear crawling down her spine.

"In fact, I may do it the way the savages do. Yes, I think I will. What do you think? Stake you out and when I'm done, I'll just deliver Jake's baby a little early."

A knife, honed to a razor thin edge, appeared before her eyes. He moved it along her skin, the blade following the same path his finger had taken.

Martha stood, numb, unable to move or speak. Garret's words came alive before her eyes. She felt the cold edge of the blade tearing at her. Her child being ripped from her body. She smelled the blood, even while she struggled to rein in her racing imagination. She had nothing left with which to feel the cruel yank on her arm to get it behind her, or the bite of the leather strap he used to bind her. He pushed her along toward the barn.

"Why don't you have a seat for a minute while I get your horse, m'lady?"

He tossed her onto the hay and went to saddle a horse. In the peace and quiet, she regained a sense of control.

"Where are all your men?"

"Most went on the drive." He smiled. "You'll remember, I was a rancher until this morning. Monroe is still in Austin, I expect. Maybe he'll find your sister. He'll show her an interesting time."

"She'll kill him."

"I 'spect she might try." He led the horse out. "Don't see any sign of Jake, yet. Maybe he won't bother. We can have us a little fun."

"You know him almost as well as I do." She forced herself to look into his eyes. She let the anger grow and used it to push the fear down. "He'll come. And when he gets here, he'll kill you."

"We'll see about that." He grabbed her arm and lifted her to her feet. "Now, Martha, let me help you onto your horse. We're going to let Jake follow us to a place of my choosing."

With her hands tied behind her, she was just able to get her foot in the stirrup, but couldn't give herself the lift to mount. Garret spread his hand across her bottom and lifted her up. Her heart ached as she thought of the times Jake had lifted her just this same way, giving her a little squeeze and a pat just before she sat in the saddle.

This hand squeezed, too. Anger replaced heartache.

"You'd better keep your hands off me." Her voice was curiously calm.

"I always liked your spirit, Martha," he said with a chuckle. "I was looking forward to breaking you."

His eyes wandered down along her legs. Her dress didn't cover her anywhere near decently.

"Nice," he said, caressing her leg. His finger skirted the top of her boot. "Boots, Martha? With a dress?"

"Keep your fashion critique to yourself. I had to leave home in a bit of a hurry, if you remember." She kicked at his hand as he tried for another touch.

He laughed, then his eyes turned serious. "I would have made you a queen here. But, you had to go and marry Jake. Now, I have another reason to kill him."

It was said without any trace of hostility, only resignation. He lowered his eyes to the shank of her boot and stroked it once, very gently, before mounting Beau. "If you try to run away, or give me any other trouble, I'll shoot you."

He grabbed the reins of her horse and they rode hard toward her property. As they forded the Colorado and crossed over onto the Double-A, her mind whirled through one idea after another. She devised and discarded a dozen tactics to give Jake time to catch up and even considered fainting, but it probably wouldn't work twice. Then she got an image of Jake being led away by the posse when he was first arrested.

With his hands tied in front so he could ride.

"Garret, please. Wait a minute."

He pulled Beau to halt. He didn't say anything, just looked at her with his cold green eyes and waited.

"Could you tie my hands in front? I'm having trouble holding on."

"I heard you could ride bareback and throw ropes with both hands," he said.

"I can," she threw back, "when I'm riding my saddle horse, and when I'm not pregnant."

His wicked knife reappeared from somewhere on his right side and he leaned toward her, blade out. She instinctively pulled back.

"Do you want me to tie your hands in front of you or not?"

Martha leaned toward him, eyeing him all the while, and turned to give him access to the leather strip binding her wrists. She let her arms fall to her sides.

"Oh, ow," she moaned, stretching and shaking her arms. "My circulation got cut off. I'll be all right in a minute." She rubbed both arms, stalling for as long as she could.

"Come on, give me your hands." He retied her, then raised his eyes to the horizon. A dark smile spread across his face. "Here he comes, Martha," he said calmly.

Martha looked in the direction of Garret's gaze and saw Jake riding hellbent for them. He'd never looked so good to her as he did now.

Garret grabbed the reins of her mount and headed off as fast as the smaller horse could follow.

"Why don't you just let me go? Your horse can easily outrun him," she shouted to his back.

"But, if I run off, when will I have my reunion with my cousin? No, sweetheart, I want him to catch up. You are the bait in my trap."

The true extent of Wil's obsession hit her. He would give up the chance to escape, just for the chance to kill Jake. Because Wil had her, Jake would follow, riding right into whatever trap Wil set.

If she'd ever felt guiltier in her life, she couldn't think of when it might have been.

They rode into a thick stand of oak by a little stream. Garret dismounted and tied their horses to a thick, low-hanging branch. Grabbing Martha by the neckline of her bodice front, he yanked her off the horse and dragged her up to the narrow opening in the trees. From behind their woody curtain, they watched Jake coming closer.

"I'd better make sure you don't interrupt my meeting with Jake."

Still dragging her by her clothing, he got a rope off his saddle.

Selecting a suitable tree, he tossed her on the ground, tying her to the trunk with several loops of the rope around her body.

"Sit right here, now. I'll be back."

Garret had given her a good seat for the show. She was afraid she'd see everything. He pulled a rifle off his saddle and went back to his spot at the opening in the trees. They both watched Jake pull up and dismount a couple of hundred yards away.

Jake stood by his horse, just out of range, looking toward the grove where Garret held his prisoner. Garret fidgeted and muttered curses.

"What's he waitin' for? Come and get it, Jake."

Martha sent a silent prayer above, begging God to keep them safe. She even offered to do something herself, if the Almighty would let her know what that something was.

A glint of metal caught her attention. Garret's knife reflected the afternoon sun like a mirror.

If only I had my knife, I could cut this rope and do something.

"My knife." It couldn't be that easy, she thought, even as she bent her leg close enough that she could get her fingertips inside the top of her boot. When her fingers closed around the hilt, she gave thanks for the hint from the Lord, and that she'd had no other footwear handy this morning.

Martha kept a wary watch on her captor, but she needn't have bothered. Garret's eyes were riveted on Jake. She started to saw on the leather thong binding her hands.

"Wil?" Jake's voice was so strong and unwavering, it gave her confidence. "Let her go."

"What's that you pettifoggers say? Possession is nine-tenths of the law?" Garret laughed. "Looks like she's mine, Jake."

"Wil, you deceitful, woman-killing bastard! If anything happens to my wife, you'll wish you were never born when I'm through with you."

"I'm willing to make you an offer. Come in here and face me. I'll let her go."

"You must think I'm as stupid as you are. I won't trust you as far as I can throw your, I mean, my horse."

"A lawyer talking about trusting somebody, that's a laugh." Wil stepped out further. "Well, believe me or not. I'll kill her for sure if you don't come in here."

"Don't, Jake," she whispered, starting on the last coil. "Stay out there."

Wil waited for his answer. "I don't have all day. There's bound to be a posse coming after me soon."

"You gonna let me get in there alive?"

"Sure," Garret shouted, "it's about time we settled things between us face to face. Come on in."

Jake remounted and started the horse moving at a maddeningly slow pace.

"Dammit, Jake, come on!" Garret's voice was just this side of shrill. His brow was beaded with sweat.

Martha watched Jake ride nearer. Her heart jumped into her throat when Garret raised his rifle. She sawed faster with her little knife, silently berating herself for not keeping it sharper.

"Jake, stop. Go back!" Her voice carried to him. He stopped, sat up. Then, he leaned close over his horse's neck and kicked him to a full gallop.

"That's right, Martha, sound good and scared, just like that. Make him ride right on up here."

Garret smiled as he watched Jake come closer. He raised his rifle and took aim. The first shot was high. Jake only lost his hat as he crouched lower and kept coming.

Garret's second shot rang out immediately. Jake was only about twenty yards away when his horse screamed. Man and beast went down.

Jake lay beside his mount. He wasn't moving.

"Jake!" Martha screamed. "No!"

"Let's finish it once and for all." Garret raised his rifle and drew a bead on Jake's still body.

With one more desperate hack, the coils around the tree went slack. She yanked the ropes off her hands and popped to her feet. Dashing forward, her hands were outstretched toward Garret and his ready weapon. It seemed to take so long to get to him. She closed her fingers around the rifle barrel and jerked it toward the ground just as he pulled the trigger.

Pain from the heat of the barrel and the concussion of the shot made her jerk her hands away.

"Bitch!" Garret spat. He slammed the back of his hand into her face.

Her head snapped back at the blow and she found herself on the ground with blinding flashes of multicolored lights sparkling on the insides of her closed eyelids. When she could open her eyes, she saw the inert form of the man lying by the dead horse. She felt nothing -- no pain, no grief -- and she wished Garret would shoot her, quickly, before her emotions started working again.

"Look, Martha." Garret leaned over her, his eyes burning with triumph. "I killed him. Now, for you." Dropping his rifle, he grabbed her arm, pulling her to her feet. "No pretty talk or kissing this time." He ripped at her skirts.

Chapter Twenty-Six

A SHOT RANG out and Wil's hat fell at Martha's feet.

"Wil, this is the last time I'm going to tell you to let her go."

Garret still had her arm in a steel grip. He turned to Jake, his face a mask of disbelief.

"I killed you, damn it!"

"When are you going to learn to make sure the men you kill are really dead?" Jake had his gun leveled at Wil, and consequently, also at Martha. "Come on, Wil. Don't make me say it, again. Do you want me to kill you right now?"

"You'll kill her, too," Wil said, pulling Martha in front of him.

Jake appeared unmoved.

"Wilson, you and I both know what you have planned for her. A bullet would be merciful. But, you don't need to worry about my wife. I won't be aiming for her. Unlike you, I always hit my target."

She couldn't see Wil, but could tell when he went for his gun. Then her head shook with the shock of the gun's discharge.

A second shot rang out. Wil's grip loosened and Martha dropped to the ground, curling around her belly, protecting her baby. Wil cursed a streak, holding his shooting hand against his body.

"You shot me, Jake."

Jake snorted. "I didn't shoot you, you sissy. I just knocked the gun out of your hands. If I'd wanted to shoot you, you'd be dead now." Jake signaled his disdain by holstering his gun and he moved to Martha's side. He helped her to her feet, his body shielding her from Garret's burning gaze, then, he pushed her behind him.

"Now, what's this about settling things between us, face to face?"

Wil held up his hand. "You've rendered that agreement meaningless, Cousin. I can't draw."

"You got more nerve than a bum tooth, Wil. You tried to kill me while I was riding up here. We didn't agree to that."

Wil moved slowly toward his gun a few feet away.

"Don't, Wil," Jake warned, but didn't draw his gun.

Garret hit the ground rolling.

"Molly, get down!" Jake drew his revolver. She ran behind one of the trees.

Garret came up on his knees, ready to fire. Jake stood ready, his gun on Wil's gut.

"It would be so easy," Jake whispered.

The gun shook in Garret's hands. His forehead shone with a greasy sheen of sweat.

"You know you can't murder me, Jake. Hell, we're kin." His eyes narrowed and he studied Jake, clearly uncertain how this line would fly.

Jake shook his head. "Wil, you know I have to finish this before the posse gets here."

"My God, Jake, you can't kill him in cold blood," she whispered, even though she knew that was exactly what he had to do, if he wasn't to hang right along with Wil.

A crafty expression settled on Garret's face. "She's right. You don't have the stomach for murder."

"I guess we'll all find out."

"Why haven't you done it, then?" Garret backed around toward the opening in the grove. "How 'bout this, Jake?" he offered. "You and me, draw on three. A fair fight. Winner walks out of here a free man."

"And the loser?" Jake asked.

"Dead."

At Jake's silence, he went on. "I killed that bailiff back in town. I'll hang whether or not they can prove rustling." He looked steadily into Jake's eyes. "I have nothing to lose."

"I have nothing to gain." Jake shook his head. "No deal."

"C'mon, Jake. I'm offering you a chance to kill me, all legal-like. That's real important to you, ain't it? You were always faster than me, a better shot than me. The story of our lives, huh?" He cocked his head at Jake. "I had to put up with my daddy holding you up to me as the perfect son, the perfect man. Well, I just wish he could see how you turned out. Big Dallas lawyer. Now, you're just a cattle-rustling outlaw."

Jake offered no defense, no counter accusation.

Garret straightened and started to back out of the cover of the trees.

"Go on out there," Jake said. "A posse must be on its way by now."

Wil quickly looked behind him. He smiled.

"Guess I'm done for, then. I'm going to draw on you, Jake. You can take advantage of it or not. If I hit anybody else," he jerked his head toward Martha, "I apologize in advance."

"Are you that anxious to die, Wil?" Jake asked. His voice was flat, emotionless.

"I won't mind so much if I can take you with me." Wil's right hand hovered over his gun. He continued backing away from them, stopping just at the opening of the trees, where the glare of the setting sun masked his movements.

Jake blew out a sigh.

"All right. At your convenience." He reholstered his gun to make the fight fair. Just as the end of the barrel of Jake's weapon nosed inside the holster, Garret went for his gun. He got off the first shot a split instant before Jake had cleared his holster.

"Ah," Jake groaned. His face was a mask of pain and he rocked slightly to his right.

Martha screamed as he went down. Garret quickly brought his weapon up to cover her.

"Stay where you are, or he won't be the only one to die today." His gun was aimed at her belly.

In spite of his threat, she started to go to Jake's side.

"I said, stay where you are!" Garret's face was red and shiny with sweat. "I'll kill your brat before you can move."

"Molly, don't move. There's no telling where the bullet will end up. I told you he can't shoot straight." Jake rasped as he tried to sit up. Martha saw the oozing stain in the right shoulder of his jacket. Garret walked cautiously toward him, stopping a good ten paces away.

"I'm good enough I got you in your shooting arm."

"Yeah, Wil, but what were you aiming at?" Jake gasped and shook his head as if to clear away the pain.

Garret ignored the jibe.

"You already got shot in that shoulder, didn't you? Wonder if it would've healed up as well this time?" His voice carried a trace of humor. He considered his target, waving the barrel of his gun over Jake's midsection. "Maybe I'll just shoot your balls off and let you live. How about that, Martha?"

"Think you can hit 'em, Wil? Maybe you ought to get closer." Jake looked up and grinned. "Maybe if you aim for my head this time, you might nick one of 'em."

She wondered if the pain had made him lose his mind.

Jake drew a deep, ragged breath.

"Let me get up. You want to remember that you killed me like a man, don't you?"

Garret stood back and moved his gun back to Martha.

"Okay, Jake. Get up, if you can." Wil moved off about twenty paces.

Jake struggled to his feet. His right hand hung useless at his side.

"Ready to draw on me again, Wil? Got the guts to try and finish me off?" Jake was smiling.

Garret's mouth fell open. "You can't draw!" Then he laughed. "You're just trying to get me to lose my temper, so maybe I won't shoot straight. Is that it, Jake?"

"No, I'm just getting mighty tired of your uselessness. You never could finish anything you started. You should have put a bullet in my head, how many times now? How many chances have you had, Wil? You don't seem to be able to get anything right."

Garret's face turned red. "Shut your mouth!" He raised his gun.

"You're right. I can't draw. But let me get my gun and we'll count three, then fire. Winner walks out. Loser dies. Just like you said." He smiled coldly at his cousin. "Just try to get it right this time, won't you, Wilson?"

"Get your goddamned gun!"

Jake reached down and picked up his gun. He held it in his right hand. His eyes never left Wil's.

"Count, Wil. If you can count to three, that is."

Garret roared in rage and lifted his gun.

Almost before she heard the shots, she watched Garret collapse, like a rag doll, to the ground, a perfectly round hole right between his still-opened eyes.

Jake lowered his smoking revolver and fell to his knees.

She ran to him and threw her arms around his shoulders, ignoring the sticky bloody mess. He groaned and whispered her name against her neck while she sobbed in relief. She stroked his hair, his face, his neck, her lips trailing behind her fingers.

She sat down beside him and leaned on his good shoulder. She took a deep breath through her tears.

"What is wrong with me? I've got to have a look at that shoulder." She got to her knees and pulled at his jacket. "Help me get this off. Why are you even wearing a jacket today, as hot as it is? The shirt, too. I have to use it for bandages. Maybe there's something in the saddle bags I can use." Her temper kept her hysteria at bay. She couldn't deal with everything, now.

He grabbed her hand, holding her still. "Molly, are you and the baby all right?" His voice trembled and she saw the fear in his eyes. "You know, honey, I'm a lawyer, not a doctor, so I don't know anything about this sort of thing, like how much punishment a woman carrying a child can take. That's all I worried about all the way out here. What would I find when I found you?" He raised her hand to his lips and kissed her palm.

She laid her hand on his cheek. There was no reason right now to tell him of the pains she'd had.

"You're still a papa, as far as I can tell. We'll just have to wait and see." She tried to give him a reassuring smile. "Now, give me that shirt."

She helped him get his shirt off and she took the shirttail between her teeth to start the tear for bandages. Grit and the reek of sweat filled her mouth.

"Oh, my goodness, this shirt is disgusting!"

He laughed weakly. "I'm sorry, sweetheart. I've had a rough couple of days."

Martha was still too shaken by the whole day to be amused. "Well, it's the best we've got, so I'll make do." She bandaged him up and helped him slip his jacket back on. "I've got to get you home so I can clean this wound properly and sew you up again." She pointed, but didn't look, at the dead man. "What about him?"

"Leave him here." Jake heaved a heavy sigh. "Just like he left us."

They sat for a long moment.

"Help me up, Molly," he finally said.

She lent him her shoulder and somehow he got to his feet. He walked over to the big palomino.

"Howdy, Beau." He held out his hand. The horse nuzzled and nickered. "Good to see you, too, boy."

He untied the horses and handed the reins of the smaller horse to Molly.

"Oh, no, you're not. That horse is a killer. You can't ride him as weak as you are."

Jake smiled and whistled. Beau came up beside him, nice as a lady's palfrey, ready for a Sunday outing in the country. He snorted and shook his head, seemingly at Martha.

Beau didn't move a muscle as Jake mounted. She had to admit, he looked like he belonged up there.

"Molly, don't look so worried. Beau's as gentle as a baby."

Beau stood still, his large, brown eyes studying her. She reached up to stroke the beautifully muscled neck.

"Hold your hand out, Molly, palm down."

She did as he said and Beau nuzzled her hand, moving his lips on her hand as though kissing her.

"Made me real popular with the ladies," Jake said.

Martha just shook her head and mounted her own horse. Here he was, shot and bleeding all over himself, teasing her about using a horse to flirt.

"You'd better watch out, Jacob Bowman, or I won't take care of you this time."

His smile told her what he thought of her threat. He leaned over and kissed her, branding her, again, as his own.

Epilogue

**Travis County, Texas
June, 1879**

"IT'S DADDY! Daddy's home! Mama, come quick!"

Martha put the sleeping baby in the middle of the bed. She looked out the window and saw Matt, the spitting image of Jake Bowman, running toward the road. Old Dave chased after him as fast as his arthritic legs could go.

Billy, who favored the MacLannon side, with softly golden hair and his mama's lighter blue eyes, followed his brother and the dog. The two-year-old twins, Toni and Elly, looked like perfect little ladies as they played, quietly for once, on a quilt on the front porch. The baby, born just three weeks ago, had yet to be named, since it was Jake's turn. It was the only time he'd missed the birth of one of his children.

"Daddy! Daddy!" both little boys yelled at the tops of their lungs, their voices mingling with Dave's tired bark.

"Oh, my." She felt the same thrill when she saw him. He was still so handsome and strong. Even after five children and seven years, she never grew tired of looking at him, especially when she hadn't seen him in almost two months.

He stopped at the head of the drive and picked Matt up first, and hugged him tight. When Matt was sitting behind him on the big horse, he reached down for Billy. After getting a big, dusty hug, Billy sat in front of his father.

Beau set a gentle pace, protecting his precious cargo. Martha was still a little nervous about her little boys riding Beau, but was ignored by her menfolk.

She watched them ride up, Matt and Billy chattering, asking their father about the drive.

"Was there any stambedes, Daddy?"

"Nope, it was pretty boring this year, Bill."

"Did the Injuns shoot arras acha?"

"Not this time. We gave them ten head of cattle and they let us pass through."

The boys were disappointed by the lack of action.

"Did you see any gunfights?"

"There was one, but I didn't exactly see it."

Finally! The boys' eyes got wide.

"Did somebody get killed?" Matt asked.

"Yes, son."

They were silent for a few seconds, their father's somber answer causing the children some reflection. But it didn't last. By the time Jake dismounted, leaving the boys on the big horse, they were buzzing again.

"Daddy, can I go with you next year?" Matt asked, for the thousandth time since he was old enough to know where his father went every year.

"We'll have to see." At his son's disappointed expression, Jake continued, "I didn't get to go until I was ten."

Jake stood at the edge of the porch and reached for his daughters, wrapping them in his arms and hugging tight.

"Give your daddy a big kiss."

The girls obliged and giggled as their father's beard tickled them. He looked around. "Where's Mama?"

"Mama's right here," Martha said from the door.

His eyes went immediately to her belly, as he put the girls back on their quilt. He took the steps in two strides and stopped at the screen door.

"Molly?" The question carried a weight of concern.

"Come on in. I've got something to show you." She pushed the door open. "Matt, you and Billy be careful."

"Okay, Mama," Matt said.

"Mama, it's Bill."

"Oh. I'm sorry, Bill."

She knew they'd sit there on Beau for hours, and for all her motherly concern, she also knew Beau would just stand there and let them pull on his reins and kick at his sides and pretend to race across the plains until they tired of the sport.

Taking her husband's hand, she led him to their bedroom, where his youngest child lay, wrapped snug in a light blanket. The smile, as ever, started in his eyes before it showed on his face. He lay down beside the little bundle and moved the blanket away so he could see better. His big hand touched the tiny clenched fists with heart melting tenderness.

Martha lay down on the other side of the baby.

"When?" Jake asked.

"Three weeks ago, today. I didn't even try to send a telegram."

He tore his eyes away from his child and set them on Martha.

"Thank you, Molly," he said, kissing her softly.

"Oh, that's not enough," she whispered as he pulled back.

Jake laughed and kissed her again. He looked back at the baby. "What is it?"

"It's a baby." At his frown, she smiled. "I've been waiting seven years to say that."

"You know what I mean, smartie."

"A girl. She doesn't have a name yet. It's your turn."

A boyish grin lit his face. "How 'bout Zelda?"

"Hah! Think of something else."

He pondered and then raised his dark blue eyes to hers. "Martha then. We'll call her Molly."

"Now that's original!" she teased. "Besides, Sam and Mary already have a Molly."

"Then we might as well have a Mary."

She smoothed his hair and caressed his cheek. "Mary she is, then."

MARY ELIZABETH BOWMAN slept in her cradle in the corner of her parents' room. Her Uncle Sam and Aunt Mary had taken their brood and gone home to their ranch across the Colorado River. The older children had finally fallen asleep. Beau was fed and rubbed down. The hands who would stay with them through the rest of the year were in town, celebrating the end of another drive. Everyone else was settled in and taken care of. Now Mr. and Mrs. Bowman lay in each other's arms, their breathing just returning to normal.

His homecoming complete, Jake was content to hold his wife, both of them listening to the sleepy cooing sounds coming from tiny Mary. She would wake soon, expecting to be fed.

"I'm sorry I wasn't here, Molly."

She stroked his arm. "It wasn't your fault. Doc Mitchell says she wasn't early, so I must have miscounted." She playfully twisted the gray hair on his temple. "Just goes to show you, Mr. Bowman, you can't have your way all the time."

"Oh, yeah?" He turned her onto her back, intending to show her how easy it was for him to have his way.

The cry from the corner stopped them.

"Oops, suppertime, again." Martha pulled his head down and kissed the tip of his nose. "She'll be asleep in just a few minutes."

Jake watched her walk to the cradle and enjoyed the view she presented as the moonlight imparted a pearly glow to her beautiful body. Her voice caressed him as she crooned to the baby. When Mary was dry and comfortable again, Martha brought her over to the bed. He sat up and nestled them both in the crook of his arm and watched, smiling, as little Mary's open mouth reached for her mother's breast with unerring accuracy. Jake laughed at the baby's hearty gulps and gasps for air as she greedily suckled.

"Just like her daddy, huh?"

"Jake!" Martha blushed at the picture he conjured.

He feigned innocence. "I was talking about her appetite."

"I know you were."

They lay there, father, mother, and child, content to enjoy the quiet and each other's company. Even after Mary fell asleep, they lay there. It wasn't until he started to snore that Martha realized Jake was sleeping, too. She got up and put Mary into her cradle, made sure she was warm, and then returned to their bed.

"Move, darlin'." She made him lie down and pulled a blanket over his naked body. For a long time she just sat, looking at him, thinking of the day he'd come into her life when she'd been ready to give up.

But the hurt of that time was all gone now. Mama used to say that God worked in mysterious ways. Martha believed He surely must.

"Molly," Jake said, reaching for her.

Once again, Martha thanked God for the wondrous results of His ways before she moved into her husband's arms.

The End